IN THE HOUSE OF SECRET ENEMIES

By George C. Chesbro

The Mongo novels

THE LANGUAGE OF CANNIBALS
SECOND HORSEMAN OUT OF EDEN
THE COLD SMELL OF SACRED STONE
TWO SONGS THIS ARCHANGEL SINGS
THE BEASTS OF VALHALLA
AN AFFAIR OF SORCERERS
CITY OF WHISPERING STONE
SHADOW OF A BROKEN MAN

Other novels

BONE
JUNGLE OF STEEL AND STONE
THE GOLDEN CHILD
VEIL
TURN LOOSE THE DRAGON
KING'S GAMBIT

Writing as David Cross

CHANT
CHANT: SILENT KILLER
CHANT: CODE OF BLOOD

IN THE HOUSE OF SECRET ENEMIES

SECRET ENEMIES

GEORGE C. CHESBRO

THE MYSTERIOUS PRESS
New York · Tokyo · Sweden · Milan
Published by Warner Books

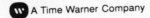 A Time Warner Company

For Dorothy Ehrlich,
Who always understood so much

The stories in this collection were previously printed in the following magazines:

"The Birth of a Series Character," *The Writer*, March 1989.
"The Drop," *Mike Shayne Mystery Magazine*, October 1971.
"High Wire," *Alfred Hitchcock's Mystery Magazine*, March 1972.
"Rage," *Alfred Hitchcock's Mystery Magazine*, February 1973.
"Country for Sale," *Mike Shayne Mystery Magazine*, June 1973.
"Dark Hole on a Silent Planet," *Alfred Hitchcock's Mystery Magazine*, November 1973.
"The Healer," *Alfred Hitchcock's Mystery Magazine*, August 1974.
"Falling Star," *Alfred Hitchcock's Mystery Magazine*, November 1974.
"Book of Shadows," *Mike Shayne Mystery Magazine*, June 1975.
"Tiger in the Snow," *Mike Shayne Mystery Magazine*, March 1976.
"Candala," *An Eye for Justice: The Third Private Eye Writers of America Anthology*. New York: Mysterious Press, 1988.

 Mysterious Press books are published by
Warner Books, Inc., 666 Fifth Avenue, New York, NY 10103

A Time Warner Company

Printed in the United States of America
First Printing: October 1990

10 9 8 7 6 5 4 3 2 1

Library of Congress Cataloging-in-Publication Data

Chesbro, George C.
    In the house of secret enemies / by George C. Chesbro.
      p. cm.
    Stories previously published, 1971–1988.
    ISBN 0–89296–395–6
    I. Title.
PS3553.H359I5   1990
813'.54—dc20

90–33811
CIP

Contents

Not infrequently I am asked how I came up with the idea for a private investigator who is a dwarf. In response to an invitation from Sylvia K. Burack to do a piece for The Writer, *the magazine she edits, I attempted to address that question in the following article.*

The Birth of a
Series Character

For most writers of so-called genre fiction the quest is for a successful series character—a man or woman who, already completely brought to life in the writer's and readers' minds, leaps into action at the drop of a plot to wend his or her perilous way cleverly through the twists and turns of the story to arrive finally, triumphantly, at the solution. Great series characters from mystery and spy fiction immediately spring to mind: Sherlock Holmes, James Bond, Sam Spade, Lew Archer, Miss Marple, et al. These characters may simply step on stage to capture the audience's attention, with no need for the copious program notes of characterization that must usually accompany the debut of a new hero or heroine.

Almost two decades ago, when I was just beginning to enjoy some success in selling my short stories, I sat down one day to begin my search for a series character. Visions of great (and some not-so-great) detectives waltzed through my head; unfortunately, all of these dancers had already been brought to life by other people. The difficulty was compounded by the fact that I didn't want just any old character, some guy with the obligatory two fists and two guns who might end up no more than a

1

two-dimensional plot device, a pedestrian problem solver who was but a pale imitation of the giants who had gone before and who were my inspiration. I wanted a *character*, a detective with modern sensibilities, whom readers might come to care about almost as much as they would the resolution of the mystery itself. Sitting at my desk, surrounded by a multitude of rejection slips, I quickly became not only frustrated, but intimidated. I mean, just who did I think I was?

It was a time when "handicapped" detectives were in vogue on television: Ironside solved cases from his wheelchair and van; another was Longstreet, a blind detective. Meditating on this, I suddenly found a most mischievous notion scratching, as it were, at the back door of my mind. I was a decidedly minor league manager looking to sign a player who might one day compete in the major leagues. What to do? The answer, of course, was obvious: If I couldn't hope to create a detective who could reasonably be expected to vie with the giants, then I would create a detective who was unique—a dwarf.

Believing, as I do, that it's good for the soul as well as the imagination, I always allow myself exactly one perverse notion a day (whether I need it or not). I'd had my perverse notion, and it was time to think on. What would my detective look like? What kind of gun would he carry, how big would it be, and how many bullets would it hold?

Scratch, scratch.

Would his trenchcoat be a London Fog or something bought off a pipe rack? What about women? How many pages would I have to devote in each story to descriptions of his sexual prowess?

Scratch, scratch.

The damn dwarf simply refused to go away, and his scratching was growing increasingly persistent. But what was I going to do with a dwarf private detective? Certainly not sell him, since it seemed to me well nigh impossible to make anybody (including me) believe in his existence. Who could take such a character seriously? Who, even in a time of dire need, would hire a dwarf detective? Where would his cases come from? He would *literally* be struggling to compete in a world of giants.

Scratch, scratch.

No longer able to ignore the noises in my head, I opened the door and let the Perverse Notion into the main parlor where I was trying to work. It seemed there was no way I was going to be able to exorcise this aberration, short of actually trying to write something about him.

Observing him, I saw that he was indeed a dwarf, but fairly large and powerfully built, as dwarfs go. That seemed to me a good sign. If this guy was going to be a private detective, he would have to be more than competent at his work; he would need extra dimensions, possess special talents that would at least partially compensate for his size.

Brains never hurt anyone, so he would have to be very smart. Fine. Indeed, I decided that he was not only very smart, but a veritable genius—a professor with a Ph.D. in Criminology, a psychological and spiritual outcast. His name is Dr. Robert Frederickson. Now, where could he live where people wouldn't be staring at him all the time? New York City, of course.

So far, so good. The exorcism was proceeding apace.

Fictional private eyes are always getting into trouble, and they have to be able to handle themselves physically. What would Dr. Robert Frederickson do when the two- and three-hundred-pound bad guys came at him? He had to be able to fight. So he'd need some kind of special physical talent.

Dwarfs. Circuses. Ah. Dr. Robert Frederickson had spent some time in the circus. (In fact, that was how he had financed his education!) But he hadn't worked in any sideshow; he'd been a star, a headliner, a gymnast, a tumbler with a spectacular, death-defying act. Right. And he had parlayed his natural physical talents into a black belt in karate. If nothing else, he would certainly have the advantage of surprise. During his circus days he had been billed as "Mongo the Magnificent," and his friends still call him Mongo.

Mongo, naturally, tended to overcompensate, to say the least. He had the mind of a titan trapped in the body of a dwarf (I liked that), and that mind was constantly on the prowl, looking for new challenges. Not content with being a dwarf in a circus (albeit a famous one), he became a respected criminology professor; not content with being "just" a professor, he started moonlighting as a private detective.

But I was still left with the problem of where his cases were to

3

come from. I strongly doubted that any dwarf detective was going to get much walk-in business, so all of his cases were going to have to come from his associates, people who knew him and appreciated just how able he was, friends from his circus days, colleagues at the university where he teaches and, for good measure, from the New York Police Department, where his *very* big brother, Garth, is a detective, a lieutenant.

I set about my task, and halfway through the novella that would become "The Drop," hamming it up, I discovered something that brought me up short: Dr. Frederickson was no joke. A major key to his character, to his drive to compete against all odds, was a quest for dignity and respect from others. He insisted on being taken seriously as a human being, and he was constantly willing to risk his life or suffer possible ridicule and humiliation in order to achieve that goal. Dr. Robert Frederickson, a.k.a. Mongo the Magnificent, was one tough cookie, psychologically and physically, and I found that I liked him very much.

And I knew then that, regardless of how he was treated by any incredulous editor, I, at least, would afford this most remarkable man the dignity and respect I felt he so richly deserved. I ended by writing "The Drop" as a straight (well, seriously skewed actually, but serious) detective story.

"The Drop" was rejected. The editor to whom I'd submitted it (he had published many of my other short stories) wrote that sorry, Mongo was just too unbelievable. (Well, of course, he was unbelievable. What the hell did he expect of a dwarf private detective?)

That should have ended my act of exorcism of the Perverse Notion. Fat chance! On the same day "The Drop" was rejected, I sent it right out again to another editor (after all, Mongo would never have given up so easily), who eventually bought it.

The next day I sat down and started Mongo on his second adventure. Mongo was no longer the Perverse Notion; I had created a man who intrigued me enormously, a man I liked and respected, a most complex character about whom I wanted to know more and who fired my imagination.

My Perverse Notion in that second story was to include a bit of dialogue in which Garth tells Mongo, after some particularly spectacular feat, that he's lucky he's not a fictional character, because no one would believe him. "High Wire" sold the first time out—to the first editor, and this time he never mentioned a word again about Mongo's believability. Nine more Mongo novellas followed and were published. In the tenth, "Candala," it seemed I had sent Mongo out too far beyond the borders defining what a proper detective/mystery story should be, into the dank, murky realms of racial discrimination, self-hate and self-degradation. I couldn't place "Candala" anywhere, and it went into the darkness of my trunk.

But Mongo himself remained very much alive. I was still discovering all sorts of things about the Frederickson brothers and the curious psychological and physical worlds they moved in; they needed larger quarters, which could be provided only in a novel.

Six Mongo novels later, Mongo and Garth continue to grow in my mind, and they continue to fire my imagination. In fact, that Perverse Notion proved to be an invaluable source of inspiration. Mongo has, both literally and figuratively, enriched my life, and he and Garth are the primary reasons that I was finally able to realize my own "impossible dream" of making my living as a writer.

"Candala" finally appeared in print, between hardcovers, in an anthology entitled *An Eye for Justice.*

It is always risky business to try to extrapolate one's own feelings or experiences into the cheap currency of advice to others (especially in regard to that most painfully personal of pursuits, writing). However, the thought occurs to me that a belief in, and a respect for, even the most improbable of your characters in their delicate period of gestation is called for. That Perverse Notion you don't want to let in, because you fear you will waste time and energy feeding and nurturing it for no reward, may be the most important and helpful character—series or otherwise—you'll ever meet in your life.

•   •   •

What I wrote is all well and good, and even true, but I might have included my strong suspicion that Mongo's birth was also strongly attended by the fact that I felt so much like a dwarf psychologically in the face of the awesome task of becoming a writer. And so we have the dwarf as metaphor for my own feelings of inadequacy as I tramped

5

around in the puny foothills of what appeared to me to be the mountain of a towering and seemingly unscalable goal.

I can't help but wonder if Mongo does not owe a good part of his success to the fact that he may strike a similar chord in many readers, for it is the rare person who does not occasionally feel like a "dwarf in a world of giants"—giant people who press upon and threaten us in one way or another, giant problems that threaten to crush us. Perhaps Mongo, with his disdain for his "handicap" and his indomitable will to make the most of his talents, holds out to all of us the hope that, with courage, any of us may not only survive but prevail in that very large, occasionally cold and hostile environment that is our lives.

The Drop

He was a big man, filled with a guy-wire tension and animal wariness that even his three-hundred-dollar tailored suit couldn't hide.

He came in the door, stopped and blinked, then walked over to my desk. I rose and took the proffered hand, waiting for the nervous, embarrassed reaction that usually preceded mumbled apologies and a hurried exit. It didn't come.

"Dr. Frederickson?"

Now, there are any number of disadvantages to being a dwarf, all compounded when you've chosen the somewhat unlikely career of a private investigator. I stand four feet eight inches in my socks. I've been told I don't exactly inspire confidence in prospective clients.

"I'm Frederickson," I said. "'Mister' will do."

"But you are the private detective who also teaches at the university?"

You'd be surprised at the number of people who get their jollies from playing practical jokes on dwarfs. For my own protection, I liked to try to size up people fast. He had manners, but I suspected they'd come out of a book and were things that he put on and took off like cuff links; it all depended upon the occasion. His eyes were muddy and the muscles in his face were tense, which meant that he was probably going to hold something back, at least in the beginning.

7

I put his age at around thirty-five, five years older than myself. I'd already decided I didn't like him. Still, there was an air of absorption about the man that suggested to me he hadn't come to play games. I wanted the job, so I decided to give him some information.

"My doctorate is in criminology, and that's what I teach at the university," I said evenly, determined to lay everything out in the open. "It's true that I operate a private practice but, to be perfectly frank with you, I haven't had that much experience, at least not in the field. I don't have a large clientele. Much of my business is specialized lab work that I do on a contract basis for the New York police and an occasional Federal agency.

"I'm not running down my abilities, which I happen to think are formidable. I'm just advising you as to the product you're buying."

I might have added that hidden beneath the brusque patina of those few brief words was the story of years of bitterness and frustration, but, of course, I didn't. I'd decided long ago that when the time came that I couldn't keep my bitterness to myself I'd move permanently to the protective cocoon of the university. That time hadn't come yet.

I waited to see if I'd scared my prospective client away.

"My name is James Barrett," the man said. "I don't need a list of your qualifications because I've already checked them out. Actually, I'd say you're quite modest. As a forensic lab man, you're considered tops in your field. As a teacher, your students are patiently waiting for you to walk on water. It was your work on the Carter case that finally—"

"How can I help you, Mr. Barrett?" I said, a bit curtly. Barrett was being oily, and I didn't like that. Also, he'd touched on the subject of my success, and that was a sore point with me. It's not hard to be a great civil servant if you've got a measured I.Q. of 156, as I have. It *is* hard to achieve in private life if you're a dwarf, as I am. And that was what I craved, private achievement in my chosen profession.

Barrett sensed my displeasure and made an apologetic gesture. I swallowed hard. I was the one who'd been pushing, and it was time to make amends.

"I'm sorry, Barrett," I said. "I'm out of line. You see, I run up against too many people who go out of their way to spare my feelings. You don't see many dwarfs outside the circus, and deformity tends to make people uncomfortable. I like to clear the air first. I can see now that it wasn't necessary with you."

The fact of the matter was that *I* had once been one of the dwarfs people see in the circus; eight years while I was studying for my degree.

"Mongo the Magnificent," which looked better on a marquee than "Robby Frederickson." Mongo the Magnificent, The Dwarf Who Could Out-Tumble the Tumblers. A freak to most people. The memory made my stomach churn.

"Dr. Frederickson, I would like you to go to Europe and look for my brother."

I waited, watching the other man. Barrett wiped his brow with a silk handkerchief. To me, he didn't look like the type to worry about anyone, not even his brother. But if it was an act, it was a convincing one.

"Tommy's a few years younger than myself," Barrett continued. "The other end of a large family. A few months ago he took up with a woman who was, shall I say, a bad influence on him."

"Just a minute, Mr. Barrett. How old is your brother?"

"Twenty-five."

I shrugged, as if that was the only explanation needed.

"I know he's of age, and can't be forced into doing anything. But this problem has nothing to do with age."

"What is the problem, Mr. Barrett?"

"Drugs."

I nodded, suddenly very sober. We'd established instant communications, Barrett and I. That one obscenity, drugs, spoke volumes to me, as it does to anyone who has spent time in a ghetto or on a college campus.

"I'm still not sure I can help, Mr. Barrett," I said quietly. "Addiction's a personal hell, and a man has to find his own road out."

"I realize that. But I'm hoping you'll be able to give him a little more time to find that road. Tommy's an artist, and quite good, I'm told by those who should know. But, like many artists, he lives in a never-never land. Right now he's on the brink of very

9

serious trouble and he must be made to see that. If he does, I'm
betting that it will wake him up."

"I take it the serious trouble you're talking about is in addition
to his habit."

"Yes. You see, Tommy and Elizabeth—"

"Elizabeth?"

"Elizabeth Hotaling, the girl he took up with. In order to
support their habit they started trafficking, smuggling drugs in
and out of Italy, selling them to tourists and students. Nothing
big—they're not Syndicate—but big enough to attract the
attention of Interpol. My sources, which are impeccable, assure
me that he'll be arrested the next time he crosses the border, and
that he'll receive a very stiff sentence."

I wondered who his sources were, and if Barrett knew that my
own brother, Garth, was a New York detective, and a Narco at
that. I didn't ask.

"Mr. Barrett, your brother didn't have to go all the way to Italy
to feed and support a habit. New York's the drug Mecca of the
world."

"Tommy found out that I was considering turning him into
the health authorities here for forced treatment."

"Well, that's not going to work over there. Europe isn't the
United States. The Europeans take a dim view of drug users and
pushers, especially when they're Americans."

"That's why I want you to find him," Barrett said, producing
a thick file folder and placing it on my desk. "I know you can't
force him to come back, but at least you can warn him that
they're on to him. That's all I want you to do—tell him what I've
told you. I'll pay you five thousand dollars, plus expenses."

"You want to pay me five thousand dollars for finding a man
and delivering a message?"

Barrett shrugged. "I have the money, and I feel a responsibility
toward my brother. If you decide to take the job, I think this
dossier may help. It has samples of his paintings, as well as
descriptions of his habits, life-style, and so on."

Something smelled bad, but I'm as corruptible as the next
man. Probably more so. Still, I seemed determined to scare
Barrett off. "You're very thorough, Mr. Barrett. But, why me?"

"Because you have a reputation for being able to establish a rapport with young people. If I sent some tough guy over there, Tommy wouldn't listen. I'm betting that if he'll listen to anyone, it'll be you."

I flushed at the mention of tough guy; Barrett might have been talking about Garth, all six feet two inches of him.

"I'll take the job, Mr. Barrett," I said. "But you'll be charged the normal rates. I get one hundred dollars a day, plus expenses. If I can't find your brother in fifty days, he's not to be found."

"Thank you, Dr. Frederickson," Barrett said. There was just a hint of laughter in the man's voice, and I couldn't tell whether it came from a sense of relief or something else. "There's a round-trip airline ticket inside that folder, along with a check for one thousand dollars. I trust that's a sufficient retainer."

"It is," I said, trying as best I could to keep my own feelings of elation out of my voice. It had been some time since I'd seen that much money all in one place.

"Dr. Frederickson—" Barrett studied the backs of his own hands. "Since time is so very important in this matter, I had hoped that you—well, I'd hoped that you could get on it right away."

"I'll be on the first plane," I said, reaching for the telephone. I allowed myself a smile. "One advantage of being my size is that it doesn't take you long to pack."

●   ●   ●

I landed in Rome, checked in at a hotel near the Vatican, and immediately began making the rounds of the art galleries. An artist, especially a young one, would probably be in either Florence or Venice; a drug user and pusher in Rome. Besides, if Tommy Barrett was as good as his brother said he was, and if he was making it, the chances were that some of his work would be surfacing in the Rome galleries.

I was checking the stuff in the galleries against the art samples in the dossier Barrett had given me. I was looking for work with Tommy Barrett's style or signature, preferably both. If I got no lead on him in Rome, then I could try Florence, Venice, or maybe Verona. Then there were the jails to be checked out; after that the cemeteries.

I made no effort to shake the man who was following me,

mainly because I was curious as to his reasons. He looked young, big, and strong, a professional on his way up. He was good, but not that good.

I decided to lead him around a bit. Following the example of my feet, my mind began to wander.

I was still wondering who Barrett's sources were, and how he had found out about me. I certainly didn't have that many references, not the kind Barrett would know. My light had been hidden under a test tube for most of my short career.

I'd always been interested in criminology, and nature had partially compensated for her small joke by endowing me with a rather impressive I.Q. that put me in the so-called genius category. All of which doesn't make it any easier to reach the groceries on the top shelf of Life's supermarket.

Of course, there isn't a police force in the world that would hire me on a regular basis and, even if there was, I wouldn't want it. Garth was a public servant because he *wanted* to be; me, because I *had* to be. And there was the difference.

It had often occurred to me that I was merely trying to overcompensate for the fact that my brother had been born normal and I had not. But I knew it was more than that. Part of it boiled down to the fact that I had the same needs and shared the same hungers as all men, a yearning for self-respect, for simple human dignity.

All of which tends, at times, to make me a little paranoid. But it wasn't paranoia that had put the man on my tail, and paranoia didn't explain why Barrett had been willing to pay five thousand dollars for the somewhat ephemeral quality of rapport.

On the other hand, I didn't anticipate that much difficulty in tracking down Tommy Barrett. Dead, alive, or imprisoned, I was fairly confident I'd be able to catch up with him. His dossier revealed him to be an artistic, highly sensitive individual, intelligent but lacking the guile necessary to elude the police or me for very long.

Also, Tommy Barrett's life-style and mode of dress limited him in the places he could safely go without immediately attracting attention. Add to that the fact that I speak passable Italian. I figured my chances of finding an expatriate American in Italy were pretty good.

I scored on my fifth stop—Tommy Barrett's work, style and signature, was propped up in the window. The young girl in the store was cooperative; the artist lived in Venice. Fifteen minutes later I was on my way to the train station.

I decided it was time to get rid of my tail and, at the same time, try to get some line on who he was and why he was still following me.

A few years before, I'd almost been killed by a pervert who had a thing for dwarfs. After that, I'd taken steps to make sure it never happened again. I knew every nerve and pressure point in the human body.

The years in the circus had toughened my own muscles, and I had kept them that way. Knowledge of anatomy was my ultimate weapon, and karate had provided me with a delivery system.

I went down a quiet side street, ducked into an alley and immediately flattened myself against the side of the building.

My friend arrived a few moments later. It's doubtful he knew what hit him. I shifted my weight forward, thrusting the stiffened fingers of my right hand deep into the man's solar plexus, just beneath the rib cage. He bounced once on his face, then lay still.

I worked quickly, dumping the contents of his pockets out onto the ground. I found a small, blurred tattoo on the inside, fleshy part of his thumb that I recognized as a Sicilian clan marking. Minor Mafia. His clothes were dusty, as though he had recently walked through a field of grain. There was a small spiral notebook. I slipped it into my pocket and walked hurriedly from the alley.

•　　•　　•

I got off the train in Mestra, a small town a few kilometers from Venice where I had found comfortable lodgings on previous trips to Italy, and which was relatively free from the summer tourist crush.

It was too late to go into Venice that day so I checked into a hotel, rested awhile, then went out for some pasta. Later, I settled down in my room with a brandy to go over the small notebook I had taken from the man I'd decked in the alley.

It didn't take me long to decide there wasn't much in the book that would be of use to me. Most of the pages were filled with crude obscene drawings. There were the names of women, each name accompanied by a sort of sexual rating that I suspected was more wishful thinking than the result of actual research. On the last page was the neatly lettered notation, "823drop10." I put the notebook on my bed stand and went to sleep.

I got up the next morning and took a cab to the outskirts of Venice, then got on a water bus. If Tommy Barrett was in Venice, I had a pretty good idea of where I'd find him, this time of day, in the middle of the tourist season.

I got off at St. Mark's Square, then pushed my way through the crowds to the central *pallazza* itself. I took the elevator to the top of the clock tower and got off on the observation deck. I glanced once more at the dossier photos, then took the binoculars I'd brought with me out of their case.

I didn't need them; even without the glasses I could see Tommy Barrett standing in front of St. Mark's Basilica, directly beneath its famed four horses. Elizabeth Hotaling was with him, shilling his sketches to the shifting knots of people that would gather around him for a few minutes watching him work, then drift on to one of the many other artists at work in the *pallazza*.

Easy cases make me nervous. I descended and attached myself to a group of Barrett's current admirers. Gradually, I worked my way to the front, where I had a clear view of the artist and his girl friend. Elizabeth Hotaling caught my eye and smiled. I smiled back.

The girl in front of me matched the photograph in the dossier, but that was all. The rest of Barrett's description just didn't fit. True, there was a toughness about her, in the way she moved and handled herself. But I was positive that once she'd been tougher, and that most of that quality had been burned out of her; what remained now was only an aura, a lingering memory, like the smell of ozone in the air after a thunderstorm.

She was beautiful, but she had more than that: a confidence, a sense of *presence* that could only have come from a variety of experiences she certainly hadn't gotten in the middle of St. Mark's Square.

Tommy Barrett, from what I could tell by simply looking at him, wasn't in the same league. Not as far as experience was concerned. They contrasted, yet somehow they matched perfectly. I guessed they were happy together.

Of one thing I was certain: Neither one of them used drugs, at least not on a regular basis, and even then not the hard stuff. I can spot most serious heads a block away, if not by needle tracks then by the pupils of the eyes, the pallor of the skin, nervous mannerisms, or any one of a hundred other traits that are apparent to the trained observer.

Whatever the couple's problems, drugs wasn't one of them. And, if Tommy Barrett was a notorious pusher, what was he doing in the middle of St. Mark's Square peddling charcoal sketches to tourists?

And what was *I* doing in Italy?

There was no doubt but that the elder Barrett had lied. But why? It seemed I had inherited a puzzle along with my retainer, and the shape of that puzzle was constantly changing. I decided to try some new pieces.

I stepped forward and touched Elizabeth Hotaling gently on the arm, then leaned toward Tommy Barrett.

"Excuse me," I said quietly. "I'm Robert Frederickson. I wonder if I could talk to you privately? I won't take much of your time."

"I don't bargain on the price of the sketches, mister," Barrett said without looking up. His tone was not hostile, simply businesslike.

"The sketches are two dollars apiece, Mr. Frederickson," the girl said. "That really isn't very much, and it's the best work you'll find around here. If you're interested in oils, we'd love to have you visit our apartment. I make excellent cappuccino."

"I'm sure you do, Miss Hotaling, and I'd like to see Mr. Barrett's work, but first I'd like to talk to you."

I waited for the reaction that came; the man and woman exchanged quick glances. I followed up my lead. "You're Elizabeth Hotaling and you're Tommy Barrett," I said, indicating the two of them. "I'm here to deliver a message from Tommy's brother."

Barrett suddenly paused in the middle of a stroke, then carefully placed the piece of charcoal he'd been working with into the chalk tray of his easel. He slowly turned on his stool, away from the crowd. I walked around to the front of him, the girl trailing a few steps behind.

"Who are you?" Barrett said softly, his eyes searching my face.

"I gave you my name. I'm a private detective from New York. As I said, your brother sent me here to deliver a message."

"Mister, I don't have a brother."

I can't say I was surprised. That was the way the case had been going. Now the trick was to discover who the man in my office had been, and what game he was playing. I decided to go slow with Barrett and the girl; reactions were proving more reliable than words.

"I'm sure you must know this man," I said carefully, watching Barrett. "He's big, over six feet. Snappy dresser. He talks good, but you can tell—"

The description was meager but it had an immediate effect on the young painter and his girl friend. Elizabeth Hotaling let out a strangled sob and struck at my back with her fists. The blows didn't hurt but they did distract me long enough to enable Tommy Barrett to bounce one of his wooden easel frames off the side of my head, knocking me to my knees. Barrett grabbed the girl's hand, dragging her after him into the crowd.

The blow had dazed me. Still, I would have been up and after them if it had not been for the man kneeling over me, his knee digging into the muscles of my arm.

Even in this rather untenable situation, pain shrieking through every nerve end in my body, I couldn't help but admire his technique; it was beautiful. To the crowd it must have seemed as though he was trying to help me; only I could see the ugly black sapper he pulled from beneath his sport coat, or the short, hard stroke that slammed into the base of my skull.

•　　•　　•

The smell of rotting fish finally woke me up. I was dangling over the edge of a walkway between two buildings, my face about four inches above the surface of a particularly foul-smelling, stagnant stretch of backwater from one of the canals.

I had no idea how the man had gotten me here. Probably, he'd simply picked me up and carried me off. After all, in this day and age, who asks questions just because you're carrying around a dwarf?

One thing was certain: The man knew his trade, and if he'd wanted me dead I'd be at the bottom of the canal instead of just smelling it.

There had been no need to find Tommy Barrett because Tommy Barrett hadn't been hiding. Anyone could have done what I had done so far, but I had been chosen to do it, which meant that I was, if not the star of the opera, at least first tenor. Why?

I was sure I'd never seen the man in my office in my life and I hadn't been busy enough to make *that* kind of enemy. I tried to make some connection with my work at the university but couldn't. I doubted any parent would go to these lengths because I'd failed a student.

I was hurting. I managed to drag myself out through the labyrinth of alleys to the main square, then got on a water bus. It was late. There wasn't a cab in sight back at the main terminal, and the buses had stopped running. Despite my disheveled appearance, I managed to hitch a ride back to Mestra.

It was time to call Garth. As much as I hated to admit it, Big Brother's help was needed. Actually, what I needed was information, and that information, if it existed, would most likely be found on a police blotter. But it could wait. Figuring the time differential, Garth would be just getting out of bed, and there wasn't much he could do for me there. Besides, I needed sleep myself if I hoped to make any sense over the phone.

I stumbled into my room and immediately knew something was wrong; the empty space on the night stand where I had placed the notebook caught and held my attention like a gun bore aimed at my belly.

Grimacing against the pain in my head, I made a quick check of the room. It didn't take me long to discover that the lock on my suitcase had been sprung. Nothing was missing. My clothes were a bit rumpled, but it almost seemed as if the searcher had made a conscious effort to leave everything as he had found it, despite the fact that I would certainly know he had been there because of the missing notebook. *That* produced a discordant note inside my head, but things up there were already so out of tune that I didn't give it much thought; I hurt too much.

I went into the bathroom and filled the sink with cold water, then plunged my head in and gingerly scrubbed at the caked blood where the blackjack had bounced off. I blew bubbles beneath the water to take my mind off the pain. I owed somebody, I thought; I certainly did owe somebody.

The two policemen were waiting for me when I came out.

They looked like Abbott and Costello. Both men had their guns drawn and pointed at me. Costello was down on one knee, his arm extended straight out in front of him as though he was preparing to defend against the Charge of the Light Brigade. I almost laughed; instead, I muttered a long string of carefully selected obscenities.

Neither man said anything. Abbott jiggled his gun and Costello rose and went to my suitcase. The fat man groped around inside the lining for a few moments, then smiled. Mad genius that I am, it suddenly occurred to me whoever had taken the notebook wasn't entirely dishonest.

Like a pack rat, the man had felt compelled to leave something behind to soothe my ruffled feelings. Like the plastic bag filled with heroin that Costello was now holding in his hand.

"You're making a mistake," I said. The words blurred on my tongue. "Do you think I'd be stupid enough to leave a bag of heroin laying around in an empty suitcase? Look at the lock; it's been jimmied."

"The condition of your luggage is no concern of ours, *signor*," Abbott said evenly. His tone belied his comical appearance. He was a serious man, and he hated me. It was obvious that somewhere along the line he'd picked up more than a passing interest in people he suspected of pushing drugs.

"My name is Frederickson; Dr. Robert Frederickson. I'm a private detective. I didn't put those drugs there. I've never seen that plastic bag before in my life."

"We'll have plenty of time to work these details out, *signor*. In the meantime, you should know that the boy you sold drugs to this afternoon is dead."

"What boy?" I whispered.

"The artist. We found his body in an alley. He had died from

18

an overdose of the heroin you sold him. Fortunately, we have many informants. It was not difficult to find a man of your—"

He hesitated, embarrassed. I rushed to fill in the silence. "What about the girl that was with him?"

"Venice has many alleys, *signor*."

Little tumblers were clicking in my brain, tapping out a combination that spelled a prison cell. Or death. I was glad I hadn't eaten. As it was, I was fighting off a bad case of the dry heaves. I was sure that whoever was framing me wouldn't stop here, and I wasn't anxious to wait around to see what other surprises were in store for me.

"*Signor*, you are under arrest for possession of heroin and for the murder of Thomas Barrett."

Costello came for me and I reacted instinctively, trying to imagine myself back in the center ring, where the punishment for bad timing might be a broken bone or the mocking laughter of the crowd, but never a bullet in the brain.

I drove the point of my shoe into Costello's shin, then leapt forward, tucking myself into a ball, rolling, then exploding into the side of Abbott's knees. Abbott crumpled over me, shielding me for a moment with his body from the death in his partner's hand.

I didn't stop. I used the momentum from my first rush to carry me over into another roll, then planted my feet under me and leaped head first for the window, closing my eyes and balling my fists to minimize any injuries from the flying glass. I opened my eyes just in time, reaching out and grabbing the edge of the steel railing on the fire escape outside the window. That saved me from a five-story fall.

I broke my reverse swing by shortening the extension of my arms and using my right hip to absorb the shock of my body falling back against the railing. Glass was showering all around and I could smell the odor of my own blood.

There was the ugly sound of a gunshot, then the whine of steel striking steel. It was still Circus all the way. There was no time to climb down, so I dropped; story by story, breaking my fall at each level by grabbing at the railings.

My left shoulder went on the last level, yanked out of its socket. I hit the sidewalk in free fall, immediately flexing my knees and rolling. After what seemed an hour or two of rolling around like a marble I came to a stop in an upright position against a garbage can that must have been filled with concrete.

Abbott was leaning out the window of my room, peering down into the darkness. My left arm with its dislocated shoulder was useless, and my legs hurt like hell, but I could tell they weren't broken. I allowed myself a small smile of satisfaction.

I wasn't dead, which meant I must have made it. I got up, ducked into an alley, somehow managed to climb a fence and kept going, keeping to the alleys.

A half mile away I sat down to rest and think.

Mongo the Magnificent? Mongo the Village Idiot. I'd been had. And now I was a fugitive. I tried to rationalize why I had run, reminding myself that my frame was being nailed together by a master. That was true enough, but the real reason was pride.

Pride? A foolish thing, perhaps, to risk one's life for. Still, for me, pride *was* my life—or the only thing that made life worth living. Pride was the stuff oiling the gears that kept me going in a giants' world.

Pride made me care. The matter might have been cleared up while I was in custody, but it would have been done by somebody else. I would leave my prison cell a miserable, stupid dwarf who had been used as a pawn, a little man who had been made a messenger of death. I wanted to know who had involved me in Tommy Barrett's death. And why. I wanted to find out for myself.

The fact that I had run would be taken as conclusive evidence of guilt, and I could probably expect to be shot the next time around. Given my rather quaint physical characteristics, I figured I didn't have too many hours of freedom left.

I needed a phone. I knew where there was an American Express office open twenty-four hours a day and I hurried there. I knew it was risky to put myself inside four walls, but I couldn't see where I had any choice, not if I wanted to *do* something with the time I had.

I tried not to think of the surrounding glass or the fact that the office only seemed to have one door as I entered and walked up to the clerk on duty.

I gave him the number I wanted to call. The lines were free and it took him only a few moments to make the connection with New York. He motioned me to one of the booths lining the opposite wall. I went into the booth, closed the door, and squatted down on the floor, bracing my back against the wall.

"Garth?"

"Mongo! What the hell are you doing waking me up in the middle of the night?! And what's the matter with your voice?"

"Listen, big man, you're lucky I can talk at all," I said. I tried to sound nasty so we could continue playing our family game, but I couldn't. His voice sounded too good. "Garth, I'm in trouble. I need your help."

"Go ahead," Garth said. I could tell he was wide awake now. His voice was deadly serious.

"I need information on a man who may or may not be named James Barrett. It's probably an alias, but I want you to check it out for me anyway. Find out if there *is* a James Barrett with a record, and get back to me as soon as you can. I'll give you a number where—"

"I just left one James Barrett about four hours ago," Garth said. He sounded puzzled. "Jimmy Barrett is my partner."

"Describe him."

"About five foot eight, eyes: blue. Hair: none. He's pushing retirement. Part of his left ear lobe is missing—"

I suddenly felt very sick and my arm was beginning to throb.

"And he has a son," I finished. My voice was barely a whisper.

"Yeah," Garth said. "Tommy. Nice boy. Barrett says the kid's an artist, apparently pretty good. The last I heard he was spending the summer in Italy. What does that have to do with you?"

"He's dead," I said too loudly. "What it has to do with me is that I helped kill him."

There was complete silence on the other end of the line. Slowly, my voice stretched thin by pain and fatigue, I filled Garth in on where I was and what had happened. My own words seemed alien to me, a shrieking whine emanating from some broken tape recorder inside my soul. The words hurt, and I used that pain to lash myself for my own gullibility and incompetence, for not smelling the set-up earlier and maybe preventing the death—or deaths—that had occurred. Finally it was over and

21

Garth's voice came at me, soft but laced with rage, punctuated with heavy breathing.

"All right, Mongo, I know who the man is from your description. His name is Pernod, Vincent Pernod, and he's one of the biggest drug men around, a contractor for the Mafia. You've just had a taste of Pernod's sense of humor and style of revenge."

"Why Barrett, and why me? And what's the connection with the girl?"

"Jimmy and I have spent the last eighteen months trying to run Pernod down, which means building a case. The pressure was building on him to the point where New York, his most lucrative market, was being taken away, and it was only a matter of time before we nailed him.

"Pernod doesn't take kindly to that kind of treatment and obviously he decided to do something about it. Killing Tommy Barrett was his way of getting at my partner; destroying you in the process was his way of getting at me. Add to that the fact that Elizabeth Hotaling is, or was, Pernod's ex-mistress and you begin to get a picture of how dirty the water is that you've been swimming in."

My knuckles were white where I had gripped the receiver. Pernod had had me pegged perfectly. He'd been sure I wouldn't contact Garth until it was too late, and he'd been right.

"Tommy met the girl down at the precinct station. He'd come to see his father about something and Elizabeth Hotaling was waiting while we grilled her boyfriend. You saw the results."

My brain was beginning to play tricks on me. I was having acid-flashes of memory; Pernod in my office, the man and woman in the *pallazza*, the sapper bouncing off my skull. My rage was growing, exploding hot splinters of hatred.

"He has Italian help," I said, thinking of the two men I'd run into.

"Sure. He has a farm outside Rome, somewhere near Cine-città," Garth said absently. "There's a small airstrip there, and we think that's how he gets his drops."

"Drops?"

"Drops—drug shipments. They bring the raw stuff in by plane from Lebanon and Turkey, then—"

"I've got it," I said. That explained the grain on the suit of the man who'd been following me.

"Now listen, Mongo," Garth continued evenly. "You haven't killed anyone, except maybe yourself if you keep running around loose. I have contacts there, and I know the department will put me on the first plane out of here. When the Italian authorities find out you've been messing with Pernod they'll more than likely give you a medal. I don't want them to give it to you posthumously, which means you turn yourself in now. Do I make sense?"

He made sense. I told him so and hung up. I was dialing the local police when I happened to glance in the direction of the clerk. I hung up and stepped out of the booth.

"Excuse me," I said, pointing to the calendar on the wall, "what's today's date?"

The clerk glanced up at the calendar, then ripped off the previous day's sheet.

"August twenty-third, *signor*. I forgot to change it."

I mumbled my thanks and headed out the door. The clerk yelled after me, asking something about my arm. I ignored him. August 23rd: 8-23. Now I knew why they'd wanted the notebook back. *823drop10*. Pernod was expecting a drop this day, either at ten in the morning or ten in the evening.

I planned to do some dropping myself.

· · ·

I found a DKW I could drive, crossed the wires, and was off, heading for the open country southeast of Rome. It would take some fast driving over rough terrain, but I figured I could make it if I didn't slow down for the towns.

I was well beyond any limitations imposed by pain, hunger or exhaustion. My mind and senses were very clear, and I was running on the most efficient fuel of all: high-octane, one-hundred-proof hate. That hate made it a personal thing, a demand that *I* be the one to put Pernod away. Pernod had used me to kill another human being, and that act required a special kind of payment that only I could collect.

Garth's unintentional directions were right on the money. It was 8:30 when I finally spotted Pernod's ranch from a bend in the road at the top of a hill, about twenty minutes outside Cinecittà. It was a spread of about one hundred acres or so, and the air strip ran right up to the rear of the wood and brick farmhouse. The fields of grain glowed golden in the morning sun. It would have made an idyllic scene were it not for the electrified wire surrounding the whole, and an armed guard at the only gate.

I drove the rest of the way down the hill, past the gate. I waved to the stony-faced guard, who stared right through me. I drove around another bend, pulled the car off to the side of the road and sat down in the grass to think.

If there was a drop coming in, I was sure Pernod would be in the house waiting for it. The problem was getting to him without getting myself killed. The fence was about seven feet high, with an additional foot of barbed wire crowning the top. With two good arms I might have tried to fashion a pole and vault it. In my present condition there was no way. I would have to meet the guard head on.

The area in back of me was wooded. Using my belt, I strapped my useless left arm in close to my body, then stepped back into the trees and made my way back toward the guard. I stopped when I was about twenty yards away, picked up a stone and hurled it at the fence. The wire greeted the stone with a shower of electric sparks and a high-pitched, deadly whine. The guard came running down the road.

He was carrying a sub-machine gun, Russian made, which meant it had probably come from somewhere in the Middle East along with a shipment of drugs. It also meant to me that I was right about the drop that morning. Nothing else would justify the risk of arming a roadside guard with such a weapon; a man standing by a gate with a sub-machine gun would be sure to arouse suspicion, and could blow whatever cover Pernod maintained. No, something—something very big—was coming in, and I suspected it could be Pernod's retirement nest egg.

I had to get close to the man, and the gun in his hand meant I had very little margin of error. I doubted that another ruse would work; any sound from me and he'd simply spray the trees with machine gun fire. I would have to go to him.

I waited until he was about fifteen yards beyond me, then took a deep breath and exploded from the line of trees. Suddenly, the scene seemed to shift to slow motion inside my brain. I was running low, my right arm pumping wildly, my eyes fixed on the spot at the base of the man's skull I knew I must hit if I was to get him before he got me. But he'd heard me, and his finger was already pressed against the trigger of his weapon as he began to make his turn.

The muzzle of the gun described an arc, bucking, firing a shower of bullets that kicked into the trees, the circle of death coming closer and closer. The muzzle finally zeroed in on me and I left my feet, arching my back and thrusting up my arm in a desperate effort for height. An angry swarm of steel whirred by beneath me, and then I was at his head. There was no time to do anything but aim for the kill.

I twisted my body to the side, tucked in my left leg, then lashed out, catching the point of his jaw with my heel. The man's head kicked to one side and I could hear a dull click. He fell as I fell.

I landed on my left side and was almost swallowed up by a white hot flash of pain that must have ascended all the way from hell. Somehow I managed to get to my feet, crouched and ready to move in case I had missed. I hadn't.

The hot barrel of the gun had fallen across the man's arm and was scorching his skin, but he didn't move. The click I had heard had been the sound of the man's neck breaking.

I turned and glanced in the direction of the farmhouse. Two figures were running toward the road. Both carried machine guns. I grabbed the dead man's weapon and sprinted back to the shelter of the trees.

They wasted no time examining the body of their dead comrade. The moment they saw him they dropped to the ground on their bellies, their guns pointed into the woods. My mind told me they couldn't possibly hear me breathing; my fear insisted I take no chances. I held my breath. It was like Old Home Week; one man was the one who'd been tailing me in Rome, the other the one who'd slugged me in Venice.

They were patient. It was ten minutes before the older man finally signaled the younger to move out. Both rose to a crouch and began moving off in opposite directions, still keeping their guns trained into the woods on the left and right of me. I crawled forward on my belly up to a large oak at the very edge of the road, then straightened up and flattened myself against the trunk.

I was not at all sure I could even fire the gun with one arm, at least not with the accuracy I would need. Add to that the fact that any move I made would require exquisite timing and you come up with a situation that was not exactly favorable. Still, my adrenaline was running low and I had no desire to simply pass out at their feet. Besides, I hadn't come this far to fight a defensive action.

Now the men were about twenty-five yards apart, on opposite sides of the tree, and still moving. In going for an attacking position, I had crawled into a cul-de-sac; sooner or later the angle would be reduced to the point where one of the men would spot me. It was time to make my move.

I knew if I swung on one man the tree would protect me from the other, at least for a few seconds. I decided to go after the older, more experienced man first. He was the most dangerous. I braced the gun on my hip and swung to my right.

"Freeze! Both of you! Freeze, or this man dies!"

Of course, they were going to hear none of it. Bullets beat an obscene tattoo on the trunk behind me while the man in front of me tried to drop to one side.

I had anticipated it. I cut loose with a quick burst and the older man's body danced in the air like a bloody rag doll.

Immediately I pressed back against the tree, counted to three, and rolled around the back to the opposite side. The other man had done exactly what I had expected, running down the road to the other side of the tree. I stepped out on my side and pressed the trigger, catching him in the belly, blowing him backwards.

He was dead before he hit the fence but that didn't soothe my sensibilities. I shielded my eyes from the twitching figure stuck with electric glue to the deadly wire mesh.

It occurred to me that I had killed my first man—plus two others for good measure—in the space of the last ten minutes. Oddly enough, I felt strangely unaffected by the blood and death around me; I kept thinking of a young man struggling for life while a man plunged a needleful of eternity into his veins.

I figured the odds were better than even that one of the men

I had killed had held that needle; the other two had probably held Tommy Barrett down.

But the man responsible for it all was still alive and free. I glanced in the direction of the farmhouse; it was perfectly quiet. I looked at my watch and found it had been shattered. I figured the time at around 9:30, which meant I had only a half hour before the plane landed. I had to get to Pernod before help arrived.

I reloaded one of the guns from ammunition I found in the older man's pocket, then went through the gate. I knew it would be safer to work my way down through the grain fields, but I figured I couldn't afford the time.

Keeping low, trying to ignore the pain in my left arm, I zigzagged down the rutted road to the house. I expected to hear—or feel—a volley of shots at any moment, but none came; there was only the lazy singing of crickets. I reached the house and came up hard against the side, just beneath a window. I rested a few moments, sucking air into my lungs, trying to right the landscape around me, which had a maddening tendency to spin.

I suspected a bullet between my eyes might be the reward for looking in that particular window so I resisted the impulse and crept around to the other side of the house.

There was another window. I counted slowly to one hundred, then looked in.

Elizabeth Hotaling was tied to a chair, a gag in her mouth. Her face was very pale, her eyes wide and red. Pernod was standing over her, a knife pressed against her throat. It looked as if the arsenal had been depleted.

"I'm here now, Pernod," I said quietly. "I just killed off your zoo." I kept the gun out of sight. I was curious to see if Pernod would move away from the girl. He didn't.

"Get in here, Frederickson," Pernod said tightly. "I want to see the rest of you. If I don't, I kill the girl."

"You're an idiot, Pernod," I said evenly, allowing myself a short laugh for effect. I cut it off quickly as I felt it building to hysteria. I didn't look at the girl. "That girl is the only reason you're alive right now. Besides, she's your girl friend, not mine.

27

Chop her head off if you want. In any case, the second her blood spills, you're dead."

Pernod smiled uncertainly. For a moment I thought he was going to drop the knife. I was wrong. Pernod pressed the point into the soft flesh of the girl's throat and blood blossomed. I groaned inwardly.

"I don't believe you, professor. I don't believe you'd let a young girl die if you could prevent it. But we'll compromise. If I can't see you, I want to see the gun I know you're carrying. I want to see it *now!*"

The knife point dug deeper, fractions of an inch away from the girl's jugular. I pressed the loading lever on the side of the gun and the magazine dropped to the ground. I tossed the rest of the weapon through the window. Pernod reacted as I'd hoped, leaping at the gun, picking it up and aiming it at the window.

It was a few seconds before he realized there was no magazine. By then I was over the ledge and into the room, standing in front of the girl. Once again, my left arm had come loose from its impromptu sling. I let it dangle.

Pernod laughed. Apparently he thought he was in charge of the situation. He glanced once at the knife he still held as if to reassure himself.

"All right, dwarf," Pernod said without a trace of the manners I remembered, "stick that good arm behind your back and lay down on the floor."

"If you put the knife down I won't kill you, Pernod," I breathed. I straightened up and smiled.

Pernod blinked in disbelief before rage gorged his eyes and he came at me. I ducked under the knife and kicked out at his knees. It was a glancing blow, not enough to cripple him. Pernod stumbled and sat down heavily on the floor, a stunned expression on his face. He stared at me stupidly.

"Stay down, Pernod," I said, fighting down my own blood lust. "Stay down."

I didn't really want him to, and he didn't. Switching the knife to his other hand, Pernod rose and lurched toward me. This time I let him get close, feeling the blade of the knife cutting through my shirt and slicing across the skin over my ribs.

But I had the shot I wanted. I brought the side of my hand

28

down hard on the bridge of his nose, breaking it cleanly. In the same motion, my hand described a lightning arc and drove those shattering fragments of bone up behind Pernod's eyes and into his brain.

It was almost over, and *almost* was the key word. I couldn't let up now, not even for a moment. If I did, I would be finished but the job wouldn't. I quickly took the gag out of Elizabeth Hotaling's mouth and untied her.

"You—you're the man. He called you—"

"Mongo," I said. "Just Mongo."

She was in shock, which was just as well, because I had nothing to say to her. I felt completely empty, devoid of anything I could put into words. I covered her with a blanket and headed for the door, stopping just once to look back and meet her gaze. The look in her eyes stunned me, and I wondered, now, if that was how other people would also look at me.

A dwarf? Yes. But also a killer, a dangerous man. Never mind the circumstances. Never fool with Mongo. Once I had thought that look was what I wanted. Now I wasn't sure at all, and I wondered how much of myself I had paid for the look in the girl's eyes. And whether it was worth the price.

Clouds had eaten at the sun while I'd been in the house and it looked as if it would rain. I thought I heard the wail of sirens in the distance but I couldn't be sure. It was almost time. I crouched down in the morning to wait for the plane.

The reluctant editor mentioned in the introductory article was Ernest M. Hutter, a friend and early mentor who was among the first to begin actually buying *my short stories and offering encouragement. But he wasn't about to buy "The Drop." If he ever understood that a certain bit of dialogue between Mongo and Garth in the following story was inspired, as it were, by him, he never let on. The important thing to me was that he sent a check.*

High Wire

I'd been lecturing on Suzuki's technique of identifying individuals through lip prints and was turning to a chart I'd drawn on the blackboard when I caught a glimpse of the man standing just outside the door to my classroom. I stopped in mid-sentence, momentarily disoriented, suspended in that spiritual never-never land that appears when widely disparate worlds of the mind collide. It had been a few years since I'd seen Bruno Jessum.

I dismissed my graduate seminar and motioned for Bruno to come in. The students filed out slowly, casting furtive glances at the huge tattooed man who stood shyly to one side. I half smiled; my students were just getting used to the fact that their professor was a genuine, card-carrying, four-foot-eight-inch dwarf, and now their classroom had been invaded by a man who looked for all the world as if he'd just stepped out of a circus. Which, of course, he had.

The smile was ephemeral; I was happy to see Bruno, but he jogged memories I'd just as soon have forgotten. I extended my hand and he shook it, staring down at me with the same soft, gentle eyes that had always seemed misplaced in the giant body.

"It's good to see you, Mongo," Bruno said uneasily.

I motioned for him to sit down and I sat beside him. "Circus in town, Bruno?" I was trying to put him at ease. I always knew when the circus was in town, although I avoided it as one always avoids something that causes pain. Old habits die hard.

"Yeah. Been in ten days. Foldin' up tomorrow."

Bruno obviously had something on his mind, but it looked as if it was going to take him a while to get around to it.

"I have a friend who keeps a bottle in his desk, Bruno. Would you like a drink?"

Bruno shook his head, which seemed to have the effect of loosening his tongue. "Gee, Mongo, you look funny here. I mean, Mongo the Magnificent teachin' a bunch of college kids. Know what I mean?"

"Yes," I said evenly. I knew what he meant.

"I heard you was some kind of a doctor."

"Ph.D. It's just a degree. I'm a criminologist. I was going to school during the years I worked for the circus. You could say Mongo the Magnificent was supporting Dr. Robert Frederickson."

"I heard you was a private detective, too. I went to your office and your secretary said you was up here teachin'." Bruno's eyes shifted away from mine. "I thought I'd come up and say hello."

It was more than that, but I figured Bruno would tell me in his own good time. Actually, I didn't regret the delay. I was having trouble concentrating. Bruno had brought with him the smell of animals, sawdust and greasepaint. It was like a drug, focusing the blurry edges of my life.

I'd been born with a small body and a big mind, statistically speaking. After a childhood devoted primarily to consuming vast quantities of food, I had discovered there wasn't much I could do about the small body, but having a measured I.Q. of 156 made it difficult to accept any of the roles society usually metes out to people like myself. True, I'd ended up with the Statler Brothers Circus, but Nature had smiled, endowing me with improbable but prodigious tumbling skills. It made me a star attraction, but I wanted more and I'd worked for it. I'd always been interested

31

in the criminal mind and, as I explained to Bruno, I'd used my circus earnings to finance my education, eventually earning my doctorate and an assistant professorship on the faculty of the New York City college where I teach.

Not bad for a dwarf, but pride does funny things. I was—and am—a good teacher, but that still left me on the public payroll, so to speak. Some men—my brother, Garth, for example, a cop on the New York police force—are there because they choose to be. I'd longed for the bloodletting of the marketplace and had managed to obtain a license as a private investigator. Clients weren't exactly forcing the city to repave the sidewalk outside my office, but I was reasonably happy, and that's not to be discounted.

"I haven't changed that much, Bruno," I said quietly. "I'm still your friend. You used to be able to talk to me."

Bruno cleared his throat. "I saw your picture in the paper a few months ago. You were in Italy. Said you helped break up some drug ring. I thought maybe you could help me."

"I can't help you, Bruno, unless you tell me what the trouble is."

"It's hard," Bruno said in a voice so low I could hardly hear him. "It's about Bethel."

Bethel Jessum, Bruno's wife, was petite, beautiful, but with the mind of a child—a mean child.

"She's been running around on me, Mongo," he continued, "and I don't know what to do about it. It's driving me crazy."

I studied the other man's face. Pain was etched there, and I thought I saw him blink back tears. I felt as if Bruno had put me in a box and was closing the lid. I don't normally handle divorce cases, not because I can't use the money but because they don't interest me. The fact that I knew Bethel as well as I knew Bruno only served to complicate matters. Of course, I had just finished reminding Bruno that he was my friend; now I had to remind myself.

"You want to know who she's seeing?"

Bruno shook his massive head. "I know who she's seein'. Half the time they meet right in front of me."

I winced. "It's not as hard as it used to be to get a divorce, Bruno. At least not in this state. All you have to do is establish

32

some kind of residence, then state your grounds. You don't have to prove adultery. I have a friend who's a lawyer—"

"You don't understand," Bruno said sharply. "I don't want a divorce. I love Bethel, and I want us to stay together."

"You know who she's seeing, and you don't want a divorce. Why do you want a private detective?"

It might have been a hint of impatience in my voice, or simply what Bruno considered my stupidity. In any case, he nailed me with his eyes in that way only an intensely gentle man can manage. "I didn't say I wanted a private detective, Mongo. I said I thought maybe *you* could help me. As a friend."

"I'm sorry," I said softly. "Go ahead."

"Last winter in camp we picked up this guy who calls himself Count Anagori. Real good. Works the high wire. Statler saw him at a tryout and signed him on the spot. He's headlinin' now."

"What's his real name?"

"Don't know. Guess a guy who walks the wire like he does don't need no other name. Ain't unusual. I never knew your real name until I saw it under that picture."

It figured. Circus people are an insulated group, held together like electrons in an atom by strange, powerful bonds; a man's name wasn't one of them.

"Anyway," Bruno continued, "Bethel and this count guy hit it off real well together, like I told you. He's a good-lookin' man, sure, with lots of manners. But he's no good for her. Havin' a fancy European accent doesn't make you good for a woman. He's gonna hurt her sooner or later, and I want her to see that. I want her to see what a mistake she's makin'."

"I still don't understand what you want me to do, Bruno," I said gently.

"You got an education. You know all the words. I thought maybe you could talk to her, make her see she's makin' a mistake." The tears in Bruno's eyes were now a reality, and he made no effort to wipe them away. "Would you do that for me, Mongo?"

Knowing Bethel, words weren't going to do much good, but I couldn't tell that to Bruno. Instead, I told him I'd talk to his wife after the show that evening.

33

Bruno's face brightened. "I'll leave a ticket for you at the stage door. Best seat in the house."

"Then I'll see you up on the swings?" I wanted to sustain the mood. When I knew him, Bruno had been one of the best catchers around. His smiled faded.

"Don't work the trapeze anymore. Got scared. Happened all of a sudden. One day I just couldn't go up there anymore. Statler hired me as a clown."

I was sorry I'd asked.

•   •   •

Bruno had been right; it looked as if the count was up in the world in more ways than one. His name was on every circus poster in town. It seemed odd to me that a talent like that should have been discovered in a winter tryout camp, but I didn't give it much thought; the fact that Count Anagori might be a late bloomer didn't seem to be part of the problem.

I walked around to the side of Madison Square Garden and went in the stage door; it was like stepping back through time. Charlie Ruler was in a straight-backed chair, riding herd. Charlie was ageless, like an old prop the circus packed away at the end of a run and carried on to the next town. His pale eyes were watery and now almost colorless, but his grip was still strong.

"Mongo! Bruno said you'd be here but I didn't believe it! How's the one and only superdwarf?"

I grinned and slapped Charlie gently on the back. We talked for a few minutes, and I could hear the house band starting. Charlie got on the phone and a few seconds later Bruno came hurrying down the corridor leading from the arena floor. He was dressed, but the wide grin beneath the paint was real. For a moment I thought he was going to pick me up and whirl me around. He didn't act like a man whose wife was cheating. He reached for me and I backed away good-naturedly.

"Easy, Bruno. You have to remember that I'm basically undernourished."

"It's all right, Mongo!" Bruno was practically breathless. "Everything's all right! Goin' to see you was the smartest thing I ever did in my life!"

"I'm flattered, but I haven't got the slightest idea what you're talking about."

"Bethel!" Bruno absentmindedly put his hand to his mouth. His fingers came away blood red.

"Take it easy, Bruno. Slow down and tell me what you want to say."

"Funny, the way it worked out," he said, taking a deep breath and slowly letting it out. His joy was like that of a small boy who has won a reprieve from the woodshed. I was beginning to suspect that his shift from catcher to clown might have involved more than a bad case of nerves; heights, over a long period of time, can do funny things to a man's head, even the best of them. "Right after I talked to you I told Bethel you were comin' to see her. That's when she said everything was going to be better."

"Just like that."

"Well, not exactly. At first she laughed, made fun of both of us. Then she went off to see Anagori."

"How do you know that?"

Bruno flushed. "She always went to meet him that time of day. Anyway, about half an hour later she comes back and tells me she's sorry. Asks me to *forgive* her! Can you imagine Bethel asking anybody to forgive her for *anything*?"

I couldn't, but the question was obviously rhetorical. I also couldn't imagine her having such a rapid change of heart. "What did she look like?"

"Real pale. Shakin' like a leaf. Guess it hit her all of a sudden. I'm sorry if I put you to any trouble."

"No trouble, Bruno. It's always good to see an old friend. I'd still like to see Bethel."

Bruno looked up sharply. "Why?" His voice was sharp, suspicious, as though the mere suggestion threatened to upset some delicate balance he had made in his mind.

"Just for old time's sake," I said easily. "She was my friend, too."

The music was playing louder, and I knew Bruno was supposed to be out on the Garden floor. Bruno knew it, too.

"Uh, can't we make it some other time?"

"You're folding tomorrow.

Bruno avoided my eyes and shuffled his feet. The sharpness

was gone from his voice, and now he was just a man asking me to understand something he couldn't understand himself.

"I'll spell it out for you, Mongo. Bethel doesn't want to see you, at least not tonight, not here. I guess maybe she's ashamed of the circus, now that you're a college professor and all."

"Is that what she said?"

Bruno shook his head. "I'm just guessin'. I only know she made me promise to tell you not to try to see her tonight. Maybe tomorrow, when she's not so upset. We'll both come see you and maybe have a drink together. Okay, Mongo?"

"Sure."

"Mongo, I really feel bad about all—"

"Forget it," I said, smiling. "You'd better get in there before Statler has you selling peanuts."

I felt like the mouse who'd just removed the thorn from the lion's foot. Bruno grinned, mumbled something about seeing me again real soon and ran back down the access tunnel to the arena floor. I absentmindedly took my ticket from Charlie, who was discreetly standing back in the shadows, and headed for the seats.

It was an odd sensation, reentering that world, even as a spectator. People stared at me, as though the circus was the last place they would expect to find a dwarf as one of them. I found the seat Bruno had reserved for me and sat down, cloaking myself in the shadows as the last of the paraders exited and the lights dimmed.

The first two acts weren't much by professional standards, and it suddenly occurred to me that perhaps the circus was an outmoded institution in an age of nuclear terror, guerrilla warfare in the streets and mass refugee camps that no one could seem to find a way to eliminate. Yet the circus staggered on, and apparently there were enough throwbacks, enough men of skill, to keep it on its feet a little longer. From what I'd heard, the count was one of them. I was anxious to see him perform. His connection with the Jessums only sharpened my anticipation.

Now the spotlight swung up to the ceiling, glinting off the thin wire strung here, then sweeping back and forth to reveal the platforms to which it was anchored. A balance pole, heavily taped in the middle, was in place, waiting for its master to take it and step out into the air.

"Ladies and gentlemen! Before we bring on the great Count Anagori, let me introduce another great performer, one of the finest circus acrobats of all time, a man who is our guest here tonight. Ladies and gentlemen, let's have a round of applause for . . . MONGO THE MAGNIFICENT!"

The light struck at me like a snake, blinding me. I immediately experienced two conflicting emotions: disgust and elation. Together, they made a heady brew. I slowly stood up and acknowledged the applause, which was surprisingly hearty considering the fact that Mongo the Magnificent is not exactly Richard Burton. For just a moment I experienced yet another emotion that I thought had been purged from my system forever—the desire, the *need*, to perform, to please, to *entertain*. I quickly sat down.

The light swam away, flowing swiftly over the heads of the people in front of me and coming to rest on the quivering base of a rope ladder leading up into the darkness.

"Ladies and gentlemen! Statler Brothers Circus takes great pride in presenting the incomparable . . . COUNT ANAGORI!"

I leaned forward as the band struck up a lively march. Nothing happened. The musicians went through the short piece, then started again. Still nothing happened; the ladder hung limp in an otherwise empty pool of light. Halfway through the third coda the music died, along with the light. For a few seconds there was utter darkness, etched only by a few electronic screeches as someone fumbled with the microphone.

"Ladies and gentlemen! We give you the peerless . . . PAULA!"

Music and light, and a very young and attractive Paula came bounding out and immediately went into an exciting mix of adagio and acrobatics. She was good, but my mind turned from events in the center ring as I pondered the question of just what had happened to the count. No performer, and especially a headliner, ever pulls a no-show unless there's a very good reason. I couldn't help but wonder whether the count's reason might have had something to do with Bruno and Bethel Jessum.

I rose and started down the concrete ramp toward the access tunnel leading to the dressing areas, but slowed down as I neared the entrance. After all, where did I think I was going, and why? Bruno wasn't even a client; and even if he were, his last message to me had been friendly but unmistakably clear: Butt out. The fact that the count hadn't shown up for his evening stroll didn't give me the right to poke my nose into that business. Pushy, I'm not.

There was a popcorn butcher with a full tray of wares dogging it near the tunnel entrance. He'd been staring at me, and I dislike people staring at me almost as much as I dislike moral dilemmas; the two taken together can make me quite insufferable. I walked up to him, gave him a quick and nasty critique of his parentage and manners and stalked back to my seat.

Paula was followed by a dancing elephant. I decided there was no comparison and went back to brooding over the mystery that seemed to exist nowhere but in my own mind, searching for some connection between Bruno's mercurial shift in moods, a performer who didn't perform, and adultery that supposedly stopped at the mere mention of my name.

I might have thought some more if it hadn't been for the two pistol shots. I was up and racing out of the stands while most of the crowd was still trying to blame the ugly sounds on the whip hanging in the elephant trainer's hand.

There was already a crowd clustered around the door to the Jessums' dressing room; they stood and stared as though there were a performance going on inside. I pushed my way through to the front and gagged. Bethel was sprawled across a small, scarred dressing table, her blood-soaked chest thrust forward. Somebody had shot her in the heart. Somehow Bruno looked even more the clown, sitting upright in a ratty armchair with his painted smile and most of the left half of his skull splattered on the ceiling. There was the smell of burnt powder in the air, emanating from the barrel of the gun trapped in Bruno's lifeless fingers. I had seen quite enough.

•   •   •

"You still don't buy suicide, do you?"

The cold professionalism in Garth's voice grated on my nerves. I glanced up at the figure of my brother sitting next to me on the concrete apron of the center ring in the deserted arena. My eyes still hurt from the exploding flashbulbs of the police photographers, and the night smelled of blood.

"I told you what happened earlier."

Garth shrugged his shoulders, and I suddenly realized that the only reason Garth had stayed behind was to soothe what he assumed was my hurt at losing a friend. The realization generated a dual reaction of gratitude and resentment.

"She was stringing him along," Garth said, "Playing games with his head. Some women are like that. I'll bet she was snuggling up with the count five minutes after she gave her husband this bit about 'forgiving her.' This time she got more than she bargained for. She pushed and he flipped. Simple as that. You saw the gun in his hand."

"Somebody could have put it there."

"Who? The count? You already checked him out."

It was true; the first thing I'd done after recovering from the initial shock was to go after Anagori. It hadn't taken long to find him, or at least find out where he was—in the hospital. It turned out he'd twisted his ankle just before he was scheduled to go on and had insisted on going for X rays. It was understandable; the count's ankles were his bread and butter. However, that eliminated the prime suspect. The accident had occurred a half hour before the double killing.

"Because Anagori didn't kill them doesn't mean that someone else didn't."

"Or that they did."

"Okay," I said tightly, rising to my feet.

"Hey! It's your turn to buy coffee!"

"I'm going to do some checking. Statler still stay at the same place?"

Garth came over to where I was standing. His eyes gleamed with the cold light of a policeman's curiosity. "Yeah," he said. "He's in the Plaza, uptown. At least that's the address he gave me. What do you want with Statler?"

"I want the show's stop list. I want to know where the circus has been and where it's going."

"What the hell for?"

I wished he hadn't asked. I had no answer.

"You're fishing, Mongo," Garth continued, "looking for something that isn't there." He paused, and when he continued his voice was softer. "You're blaming yourself for what happened.

There's no way, brother. No way that works out. First Jessum tells you he wants you to talk to his wife, then he tells you to stay away. You were the one who said he seemed unstable. It's not your fault if he suddenly decided to kill the old lady and blow his own head off."

"Yeah," I said, turning away and heading for the exit. "You've got a rain check on that coffee."

Garth was right, of course. I *was* blaming myself for what happened, primarily because I kept remembering how close I had come to going *all* the way down the access tunnel. I might have prevented it.

Garth was also right when he said it looked like a clear-cut case of murder and suicide. Still, I had an itch down deep in my soul. Asking Statler for the show's stop list and combing those cities for a man with a motive for killing the Jessums might be like chasing a rainbow, but at the moment I felt I needed the exercise.

I went out the stage door, turned right on the empty street.

Somebody else was looking for exercise; the man behind me was coming up fast, almost at a trot. I don't like people coming up fast behind me. I stepped to one side to let the man pass and almost blacked out with pain as the knife skewered me, it's point slicing white hot into the flesh of my side, scraping along my ribs like fingernails on a blackboard and emerging four inches from the point of entry. I twisted with the force of the blow, taking the knife with me. At the same time I reacted instinctively, smashing the side of my stiffened left hand into my attacker's kidney. The man grunted and went to one knee. He seemed surprised, but that was about all. He slowly rose and stared at me, his pale green eyes absolutely expressionless.

I happen to have a black belt, second Dan, in karate, and usually when I hit a man in the kidney he stays down. This man was no mugger. He knew how to absorb pain; a professional, with skills at least the equal of mine. There was no doubt but that the man intended to kill me, and the knife in my side having effectively neutralized my usual bag of tricks, it didn't seem beyond the realm of possibility that he was going to succeed.

Blood was squeezing past the sharp metal plug in my side, my shirt and jacket were soaked, and I could feel the sticky warmth

40

spreading. Dwarfs not having that much blood to begin with, I as beginning to feel dizzy—and cold, very cold.

However, the man had no intention of allowing me the simple dignity of bleeding to death. I watched, fascinated, as he slowly reached into his jacket and pulled out a pistol. Carefully, deliberately, he began to screw on a silencer. His pale eyes never left mine. He moved as if he had all the time in the world, which was understandable since the street was empty and it was obvious that I wasn't going anyplace. Despite the blank screen of his face, I knew the man was enjoying himself; all of the best are endowed with generous streaks of sadism, and this one had to be at the top of his profession. It was my time that was running out, not his, and he liked that. Vaguely, I wondered which of my enemies could *afford* this guy.

I couldn't stand to see the man so happy. I decided to give the sand in the hourglass a little kick.

I reached across from the opposite side, grabbed the handle of the knife and yanked the blade from my flesh. For just a moment pain pierced through the pervading numbness of my body. Pain was life and, for the moment, I found that reassuring. I didn't have time to gauge the balance of the knife—I could see the small hole of the gun's bore pointing between my eyes—so I could only hope that one of my lesser-known skills hadn't deteriorated over the years. The man's finger was tightening on the trigger as I reared back and flung the knife out into the darkness that was rolling over me from all sides.

.   .   .

I awoke in a place that smelled more like a hospital than heaven. Nor did Garth bear the slightest resemblance to an angel.

"I assume I'm to live."

"Which is more than can be said for the other guy." Garth was shaking his head. "You got him right in the heart. Not exactly dead *center*, you understand; about two inches into the left auricle. Of course, you're out of practice."

I twisted uncomfortably. My side was stiff and sore and there were two needles hanging out of either arm. I didn't need my brother's sarcasm.

He let out a long, low whistle. "Mongo, you're not to be

41

believed! A criminology professor, gymnast, former circus great, black belt karate expert, and private detective who just happens to be a dwarf knife-throwing expert. Be thankful you're not the product of some guy's imagination; you'd be rejected by every editor in town."

I wasn't amused. "Who was he?"

The smile left Garth's face. "The Compleat Professional. No ID, no mug shots, acid burns on his fingertips. He'd even ripped the labels out of his clothing. We figure he was a big chicken coming home to roost. You've got to admit you've made a few enemies in your short career. Big ones."

"Uh-huh. Where's the circus?"

Garth thought for a moment. "Albany. Don't tell me you think—"

"Feel like going for a ride?"

"Where?"

"Albany."

"You've got to be kidding."

"How serious is this cut?" I knew the answer before I asked the question. I could feel the tape over the stitches in my side; flesh wound, bloody but not disastrous.

"You lost a lot of blood and they think there's still danger of infection. They said about a week."

"With the shortage of hospital beds they're going to keep me here a week?"

"Ah, but there's also a shortage of dwarf black belt—"

"Knock it off, Garth," I said tensely. "I have to see that circus. That's where the key is. I know it. I *feel* it. I want to see it, and I want to see it tonight. If you don't want to take me, I'll walk."

I started to walk, or at least I gave it some thought. I swung one leg over the bed and willed that the rest of my body should follow. For a moment it seemed as if my head would reach the floor before my feet, but then there were Garth's arms reaching for me, all twelve of them.

I got out three days later, thanks largely to my natural dislike for hospitals and the nurses' inability to track me through a labyrinth of hospital wards, laboratories and corridors. Garth threatened to take me to Albany in my hospital gown, but my natural dwarf charm finally won him over. I promised to sit

42

quietly and do nothing but watch, on the condition that he buy the candy apples.

●　　　●　　　●

We parked on State Street and headed for the Washington Armory. Once there, Garth automatically started toward the rear. I grabbed his arm and directed him back to the lines forming at the main entrance.

"You're not going back to say hello to your cronies? You want to stand in line with the *masses?*"

"Right. Maybe I'll go back later. Right now I just want to get lost in the crowd."

"You're getting paranoid."

"Uh-huh. You just run interference."

Garth was humoring me, but I didn't have to remind him that New York's Finest still hadn't come up with the identity of my attacker, or his motive for wanting to kill me. That left the strange series of incidents connected with the circus, including the deaths of Bruno and Bethel Jessum. I was convinced I had somehow been dealt a hand in a game I hadn't even known existed; it was a deadly game, and I was going to lie very low until I learned the rules.

The cashiers and ticket takers were strangers, local people hired for the occasion. Once inside the armory, I pushed Garth's six-feet-plus into a large knot of people and dived in after, flowing along with the crush. It was tight quarters, but it made for anonymity, something I valued very highly at the moment. Ten minutes later I found seats that satisfied me, high up in the darkness. I immediately took out my field glasses and began to scan the arena. After five minutes I put them away and sank down in my seat to wait for the parade.

"See anything?"

"Yeah," I said tightly. "A bunch of people waiting for the circus to begin."

"And what is your conclusion, Sherlock?"

"Hippies are out and the Great Silent Majority is in. What the hell do you expect? I don't even know what I'm looking for. I just know it's here."

I made no attempt to disguise the impatience in my voice. I

could feel hot flashes of fever running up and down my body, sapping my strength; I felt like a pinball machine about to register TILT.

"Easy, Mongo. Easy. If I didn't take your hunches seriously, I wouldn't be here." Garth paused and grunted. "How's your side?"

"It's fine." It hurt like hell. The few days I'd stolen from the hospital were going to cost me, but this had to be done; circuses move on, and personnel change.

The first clean notes of a circus piece cut through the smoky haze of the arena as a team of clowns bounded out into the center ring and immediately went into an overripe slapstick routine. I put the glasses back to my eyes and scanned the opposite side of the hall. This time I found a familiar face. Garth's voice was strained and low.

"You look like hell, Mongo. That white on your face isn't greasepaint, and if I don't get you home into bed it's liable to become permanent."

"Uh-huh." I handed Garth the glasses and pointed to a white-garbed figure moving in the aisles on the opposite side. "Check him out."

Garth put the glasses to his eyes and adjusted the focus. "The popcorn salesman?"

"Right."

"Nice clean-cut fellow out to make a buck. What about him?"

I took the glasses away from Garth's eyes, waiting until I had his full attention. "That same man was pushing popcorn in the Garden."

"Maybe there's good money in it. So?"

"So, concessionaires don't travel with the circus; they're all locals, the same ones that work ball games, carnivals, and so on. There's just no reason why that man should come one hundred fifty miles to sell popcorn. He'd make more on welfare." I hesitated a moment, groping for the connections. "In fact, I ran into him at the entrance to the access tunnel. I'll lay you ten to one he was there to watch out for me, to keep me from going in. Look at him; he's not trying to sell anything—he's using that tray as a prop."

Garth squinted through the glasses. "You're right," he said quietly. "That badge is probably a phony, too."

At last Garth was listening, truly listening. The trouble was that I didn't have too much else to say. I decided to let my tongue go for a walk and see where it would take me.

"Now, pick up on this," I said quickly. "Bruno didn't kill his wife, and he didn't shoot himself. They were killed because . . . because of their connection with *me*. I couldn't tell whether it was the fever or reasonable logic, but a picture was forming in my mind, a very ugly picture.

"Bruno's reasons for coming to me were real. His wife was running around and he didn't want to lose her. His mind was going and he thought maybe I could stop it merely by talking to her. He told this to Bethel and she laughed at him. That is, she laughed until she talked to Anagori. Are you following me?"

Garth said nothing. He was following me.

"When Anagori found out Bethel knew me and that I was coming to see her he blew. Why? Because I might also see *him*, and he couldn't risk that. He put a big scare into Bethel and she went into her act with Bruno, the idea being to head me off. Probably he figured I'd go home again."

"Then Statler gave you the celebrity treatment."

"Right. And Anagori panicked. He faked an injury to stay off the wire. The Jessums had become a liability to him because of their connection with me, so he sent someone to kill them while he was in the hospital."

"Someone like a phony concessionaire?"

"Someone like a phony concessionaire. Then, to tie up any loose ends, he sent a torpedo after me precisely because he was afraid I might not go for the coroner's verdict."

"Why? Who *is* Anagori, what's his operation, and why run it from a circus anyway?" Garth asked.

The questions hung in the air unanswered. "I'll let you know when I see Anagori."

Garth nodded tensely and leaned forward on the edge of his seat. "I'm going to round up some local help."

"Negative," I said quickly. "Sooner or later that other torpedo is going to be around here. Without you I'm naked as a bird. Let's wait until we find out the whole story."

Garth didn't like it, but I was right and he knew it. He leaned to one side, half shielding me.

"Just don't pass out on me."

"Not likely." It was, but there didn't seem any percentage in stressing the point. I took deep breaths, rationing my strength.

I watched Paula perform her act, but the hall had an annoying tendency to slide in and out of focus.

"Ladies and gentlemen! Statler Brothers Circus proudly presents . . . that master of the high wire . . . COUNT ANAGORI!"

The count had the impact and presence of a laser beam as he sprinted from the wings, a long, black silk cape billowing out behind him. He was rewarded with the greatest homage an audience can bestow upon a performer, a breathless gasp of astonishment and anticipation. Anagori paused once in the circle of light, released the cape and was halfway up the rope ladder before the cloth finally settled on the floor. I leaned forward, squinting into the bank of bright lights that followed him, lighting his way to the platform sixty feet above the floor of the armory. The hall suddenly righted itself with a sharp jolt as the adrenaline squirted into my bloodstream, staving off the effects of the fever.

I had hoped for the exhilarating shock of instant recognition. It didn't come. As far as I could tell, the man standing on the platform was a total stranger.

His *élan*, the electricity of his stage personality, made him seem larger than life. I judged his height at around six feet, his weight somewhere around one hundred eighty pounds. Age was more difficult, but I guessed he was in his early thirties, like myself. Every muscle rippled beneath his crimson tights.

"*Who is he?*" Garth's voice was strangled.

I could do nothing but shake my head, uncertainty falling around me, chilling me like a cloak of ice.

"Damn it, Mongo! Who *is* he?"

"I don't know . . . I'm not sure. Not yet."

Extremely confident, eschewing the traditional equipment checks, the count hefted his long balance pole and stepped out onto the thin, metal umbilical cord that was all that remained between life and a rather messy death on the concrete below; the count used no safety net. My hands trembled as I lifted my field glasses to my eyes and adjusted the focus; the figure of the count blurred for a moment, then sprang into focus. I blinked away a few drops of sweat and stared hard.

Anagori was good, incredibly good. He *danced* on the wire, pivoting and swinging back and forth, his face a mask of indifference. He might have been practicing in the middle of a gymnasium.

Yes. His face—dark, intense and brooding for all its indifference—*was* somehow familiar, but who was he, and where had I seen him?"

One thing was certain: Count Anagori had not developed his skills overnight. He had started at a very early age. A man like that isn't discovered in a Florida tryout, not unless he goes that route intentionally. Knowing Statler, the idea of where Anagori came from had been quickly submerged in the sea of dollar signs implicit in the artist's skills.

I left the man's face and concentrated on his style; his smooth, flowing motion and muscular control, his repertoire of moves. Somewhere . . . somewhere I had seen someone else move like that, many years before.

"You still don't know who he is?" Garth's hand was resting on the butt of his gun inside the waistband of his trousers.

"No," I said. Then, as an afterthought: *"Nyet."*

Nyet? Nyet!

Once again I was cold, cold as the brutal wind blowing across the Russian steppes. Suddenly I knew who Count Anagori was and why he was here.

"Vladimir Denosovitch Raskolnikov."

"Who?"

Garth had leaned close, but other things were happening now, emotions bringing on reactions I couldn't control. The name had brought with it images: the mutilated head of Bruno Jessum staring with dead eyes at the equally dead body of Bethel; the pale eyes of the killer who had left his knife in my body.

Two innocent people killed because of an *accident*, a *coincidence*. Two innocent people dead because Vladimir Denosovitch had simply picked the wrong circus in which to work.

Rage gripped me by the neck and shoulders, pulling me up out of my seat. Garth grabbed at me but it was already too late. I had already cupped my hands to my mouth.

"Raskolnikov!"

Raskolnikov froze on the wire, then swayed, his pole bouncing up and down like an antenna in a hurricane. The crowd moaned; somewhere to my right a woman screamed. Raskolnikov regained his balance and headed back toward the platform.

At the same time something whistled past my ear, collided with the steel beam behind my head and sang off into the darkness. Garth's gun exploded in my other ear and I turned in time to see the white-coated man drop his machine pistol and grope at the hole Garth had opened in his belly. Even as I watched, life blinked out in the man's eyes and he toppled forward, his blood soaking into the popcorn he had dropped in the aisle.

I looked back up to the platform; Raskolnikov was gone. The rope ladder was still, which meant he hadn't come down. He was still up there, hiding somewhere in the darkness of the steel latticework supporting the roof of the armory.

People were milling and screaming. Garth struggled to make his way down through the crowd, his gun in one hand and his police shield in the other. I knew he wasn't going to be successful in what he was trying to do. By the time he got reinforcements, Raskolnikov would be gone.

Where? How? I scanned the ceiling. The armory lighting system was old. Even with all the houselights on there were still patches of darkness staining the roof like squares on a checkerboard.

At the far end of the armory, high up in a large field of night, was a long bank of frosted windows left partially open for ventilation. In my mind's eye I could see Raskolnikov walking the girders, zig-zagging back and forth through the patches of darkness, making for those windows. If I remembered correctly, there was a sloping roof outside. Raskolnikov would find a way to get to the ground.

I had no idea how a man dressed in red tights would manage to hide in the streets of Albany, but if Raskolnikov was who and what I suspected, I knew such small details had already been anticipated and planned for. Statler would be out one high-wire walker, and the police one killer; but if I was right, there was a good deal more at stake. I had a strong hunch Raskolnikov's talents ranged far beyond those of a mere circus performer.

High up as we were, the first tier of supporting girders was just behind and above my head. I tried to ignore my light-headedness and the ache in my side as I leaped up and grabbed the lower lip of the first I-beam, swinging myself up and over until I was sitting astride it. The throbbing hurt beneath the thick bandage suddenly exploded into a fireball of scorched nerve endings and I bit into my lower lip to keep from screaming. Still, the wrench to my freshly stitched wound was not entirely unrewarding. I had traded dizziness for searing pain. In view of where I was going, I did not consider it an entirely bad bargain.

I heard Garth yelling at me from somewhere below, but I didn't look down. Frankly, I don't like heights; still, the only thing between a killer and his freedom was a certain four-foot-eight-inch dwarf. I had to cut Raskolnikov off from his escape route. I could only hope that I could bluff the other man long enough for Garth to get some help. I knew a great deal depended on how much Raskolnikov knew—or didn't know—about the seriousness of my knife wound; the Russian wasn't likely to hang around very long for a dwarf that could be blown off his perch by a moderately strong whistle. Ah, well. It was time to find out just how unbelievable I was.

I clung to the currency of my pain, using it to buy my way up the interlocking maze of girders to the very top tier. Occasionally the sounds of the crowd below drifted up but, for the most part, I moved in a sea of silence broken only by the scrape of my shoes on the steel. Sweat poured off me, but it was the special dampness, the thick, warm *wet* in my side, that worried me most.

I headed for the bank of windows as fast as I could, balancing with my arms, taking a straight route. It was reasonable to assume that Raskolnikov had taken his time, moved carefully along his route, and that I was ahead of him. Reasonable? My life depended on it. In a few moments I would find out if he had been as reasonable as my assumption.

I passed into the lake of darkness covering the windows. If Raskolnikov was already there, waiting in my path, I was dead. It would simply be a matter of waiting behind one of the vertical beams, then pushing me as I passed. In my condition, I'd be able to offer no defense.

I stepped quickly through the dark tangle of girders. Raskolnikov wasn't there. I chose a wide girder about seven feet from the windows and sat down hard, bracing my back against a vertical beam.

That was it. I was broke. My physical and emotional bank accounts were empty. I was a hollow shell filled with whispers.

i didn't say i wanted a private detective   i want you as a friend   you were my friend   want you   everything's all right,   mongo   coming to   see you was the smartest thing i ever did   she asked me to forgive her   forgive her   i love her   love her

I could feel laughter bubbling in my throat, frothing on my lips like specks of foam. I swallowed it and tensed, suddenly knowing that I was no longer alone. Raskolnikov was moving somewhere out in the darkness. I also knew that it would be Raskolnikov who would be alone if I didn't find some new source of strength to tap. I was slumping forward, slipping off the girder.

I closed my eyes, gritted my teeth and slapped my side. Strength returned to my legs and I wrapped them securely around the girder.

Raskolnikov was moving laterally, from my right to my left. He had to have spotted me on the way up, and I guessed he was angling for an attack. Talk was the only weapon left in my arsenal. I knew it was not so much *what* I said as *how* I said it that was important. The other man had to come past me to get to the windows, and I had to convince him I was strong enough to stop him.

"You're a long way from home, Vladimir Denosovitch." I listened to the echo of my voice in the empty vault of the ceiling. It was all right, much stronger than I had any right to expect, and Raskolnikov had stopped moving. I imagined I could hear the sound of heavy breathing, but I was not sure whether it was the other man or my fever. "The trip ends here."

Finally his voice came, almost indistinguishable from the whispers in my mind. He'd been trained to the height of perfection; a Russian, he spoke English with just the slightest trace of an accent.

"I have to get out, Frederickson. You know that. I don't want to kill you, but I will if I have to."

"You already tried that once, and your man couldn't handle the job. And you ordered the Jessums killed. Are you telling me you've had a sudden change of heart?"

There was a long silence, and I wondered whether he had detected the weakness in my voice or knew I was simply playing word games.

"I'm a professional, Frederickson. Surely you realize that. I do what I have to do, but I don't kill when there's no reason."

"There wasn't any reason before. You didn't have to kill the Jessums. The chances are I would never have recognized you, not after all these years. I remembered and made the connections because you *forced* me to. You panicked. That was hack work, Vladimir Denosovitch. Second-rate."

"That was a mistake," Raskolnikov said after a long pause. There was an edge to his voice. "Now the situation has changed. It's no longer necessary to kill you; it would serve no purpose. It is necessary that I escape."

"You're that valuable?"

"I am that valuable. What has happened thus far should have convinced you of that."

"Then you're as good an agent as you are a high-wire walker?"

"I leave such judgments to my superiors. I'm coming now, Frederickson. Get out of my way."

"No!" My own voice sounded detached from me. I could only hope it carried the force I'd intended. "You come close enough for me to see you and you'll look like Bruno Jessum."

"You've been investigated. I know you rarely carry a gun."

He was right, and my only chance was that he was as much a professional as he said he was. "Wrong again, Vladimir Denosovitch. Your men couldn't have had more than five or six hours to do their checking, the time between your talk with Bethel and my show at the circus."

"What are you talking about?" For a moment, Raskolnikov sounded almost as confused as I was scared. "We checked you *after* you killed our operative."

51

"Patchwork job, Vladimir Denosovitch." I said lightly. "You probably used local talent. If you want to stake your life on that report, go ahead. Personally, I'd rather keep you alive."

He was thinking about it, exactly what I wanted him to do. But not too much. Talk. I had to talk.

"You know, I remember the first time I saw you, Vladimir Denosovitch. You were good then, but I must admit you're even better now . . ."

My tongue kept going but, in my mind, I was suddenly back in Russia.

There were sounds behind me. Raskolnikov was moving.

"The Moscow Circus is the best in the world, Vladimir Denosovitch," I said quickly. "Too bad you never made it."

The shuffling stopped. I'd hit pay dirt, his pride.

"My country needed me elsewhere."

"As a spymaster setting up and coordinating a nationwide intelligence-gathering net. Beautiful. Everybody's watching everybody else at the U.N. and the embassies while the big boss himself is off performing for the kiddies at a Saturday matinee. *Beautiful*, Vladimir Denosovitch! Was that your idea?"

"You're guessing," Raskolnikov said softly. "Most of this is your imagination." I had a feeling our conversation was rapidly drawing to a close.

Hot flashes: Russia, city after city, command performance after command performance. Then, in the central city of Chelyabinsk, where my guide said: "This one will be great. This one walks the wire."

Afterward, Vladimir Denosovitch Raskolnikov and I had drunk vodka together.

"But I'm right, aren't I, Vladimir Denosovitch? You're big. As big as they come. They trained you, set you up with false residency papers and smuggled you into Florida. Your assignment was to establish an intelligence drop route corresponding to the stop route of whichever circus picked you up. That circus happened to be Statler's."

"You're thinking out loud." His voice seemed much closer to me now, but I couldn't turn even if I wanted to. My head and shoulders seemed part of a single granite block. It was all I could do to keep talking.

52

"You couldn't have begun to put all this together before a few minutes ago," Raskolnikov continued. "Not before you called my name."

Which was why, now, he *did* have to kill me. As long as the secret of the route was safe, it could continue to expand and operate. Raskolnikov would disappear back into the vastness of Russia and somebody else would be sent to take his place. I was the only one left, besides Raskolnikov, with all the pieces to the puzzle.

"You're badly hurt, Frederickson. Very badly hurt."

Time had run out. Out of the corner of my eye I could see Raskolnikov standing beside me, his arms wrapped around the girder on which I was leaning. There was almost a trace of sympathy in the other man's voice—sympathy and chagrin at being held up for so long by a man who couldn't even stand.

He braced himself with his legs and placed his hands on my shoulders, pushing me forward and to the side. My arms and legs were now hanging limp and useless. I could see my blood flowing out onto the girder, dripping down into the darkness.

"My brother knows," I whispered hoarsely. "We've been talking about this for days. He'll make the same connections and backtrack along the circus route. The ring is smashed."

"No," Raskolnikov said. "There was no time. I'm sorry, Frederickson. I truly am. You are a very brave man."

I didn't find the sincerity in his voice any comfort. It was almost over now, and I vaguely wondered whether or not I would faint before I hit the sharp wooden and steel angles of the seats below.

Then Garth's shot caught Raskolnikov in the throat. It was a good shot, considering the fact that Garth had a bad angle leaning into a half-opened window and was firing into the shadows.

Raskolnikov gargled on his way down. There was the ugly sound of a body breaking on the seats, screams, then silence. I could see Garth in front of me, struggling to get his body through the window.

Good show; but considering the fact that I was already most of the way off the girder, I didn't think he was going to get to me in time.

It was the first time I'd been wrong all day.

53

Here's a piece about chemical manipulation of behavior, among other things. Long-suffering Garth may have his problems here, but years later I will really lay this situation on him in the novel The Cold Smell of Sacred Stone.

Rage

Slow day; anathema to a criminology professor moonlighting as a private detective. I had a graduate seminar to teach later in the afternoon, but my lecture was prepared and I was in my downtown office, staring out my second-floor window, hoping for some business to blow in off the street. I had to settle for my brother.

Someone else was driving the unmarked car, but it was Garth—all normal six feet two inches of him—who got out on the passenger's side, then walked stiffly across the sidewalk and into the building. I ran my finger over a water spot on the glass. It wasn't unusual for Garth to drop by for coffee when he was in the neighborhood, but this time there had seemed a tension—an urgency—in the way he moved that was incongruous. I went out by the elevator to meet him.

The elevator doors sighed open—Garth's face was ashen, his eyes two open wounds. He pushed past a young couple, glanced once in my direction, then rushed into my office. I went after him, closing the door behind me. He had already stripped off his jacket, and the black leather straps of his shoulder holster stood out like paint stains on the starched white of his shirt. He took the gun from its holster and slid it across my desk. "Find a drawer for that, will you, brother?" Garth's teeth were clenched tightly together and the voice behind them trembled.

"What's the matter with you?"

"Put it *away!*" Now Garth's voice boomed. His fists slammed down on the plastic surface of the desk top. A stack of books on the corner teetered and fell to the floor.

Angry men and guns make a bad mix. As a cop, Garth knew that better than anyone. I walked quickly around to the other side of the desk, opened a drawer and dropped the gun into it.

Garth sat down hard in a straight-backed wooden chair. He planted his feet flat on the floor and gripped the edges of the seat. Instantly the flesh around his knuckles went white. His head was bent forward and I couldn't see his face, but the flesh of his neck was a fiery red, gorged with blood. I could see his pulse, framed by muscle cords that looked like steel rods implanted just below the skin.

I spoke very quietly. "You want to talk, brother?"

Garth, in some soundproofed prison of rage, couldn't hear me. He suddenly sprang to his feet, grabbed the chair and flung it across the room, snapping a pole lamp in two and mining an ugly hole in the plaster wall. The shattered pieces fell to the floor; instant junk. In the same motion Garth spun around and with one sweep of his hand cleared the top of my desk. A heavy glass ashtray made another hole in the wall about a foot too low to be a perfect match for the other. Considering the fact that my office wasn't that large to begin with, I estimated that a complete renovation was going to take about three more minutes. I walked up to Garth and grabbed his arm. That was a mistake.

Now, I have a black belt, second Dan, in karate, and am reasonably proficient in a number of the other lesser-known martial arts; when you're a four-foot-eight-inch dwarf you develop a predilection for such things. Still, a man my size must rely on anticipation, leverage and angles, factors that don't normally spring to mind when you're merely trying to calm down your brother. Consequently, I found myself standing on my toes, Garth's hands wrapped around my neck. The whites of his eyes were marbled with red, while the dilated pupils opened up and stared at nothing, like black circles painted on canvas by a bad artist.

I knew I had only a few seconds to act. At the least, I could very well end up with a cracked larynx; at worst, there was the very real possibility I was going to end up as one dead dwarf, killed by my own brother. I didn't like the options.

I was floating in an airless void, Garth's features spinning before my eyes. I extended my arms, then drove my thumbs into the small of his back, just above the kidneys. That didn't do much except make him blink. I smashed my stiffened fingers up into the nerve clusters in his armpits. The animal that Garth had become grunted; his grip loosened, but it was nothing to cheer about; I still couldn't breathe. Finally I raised one hand up between his arms and poked at his larynx. Garth gasped and his hands came loose. I collapsed to my knees, my lungs sobbing for air. I managed to reach the shattered chair at the opposite end of the room. I grabbed one of the broken chair legs and spun around, prepared to bounce the splintered wood off my brother's skull. It wasn't necessary. Garth was leaning against my desk, staring uncomprehendingly at his hands. His face had changed color like a traffic light, from a brilliant crimson to a sickly yellow-white. His gaze slowly shifted to where I was poised like a statue, my improvised club raised in the air.

"Mongo . . ." Garth's voice was a muffled whisper of pain.

"I hope you feel better," I said, trying to sound sardonic. It didn't come out that way. It was hard for me to sound sardonic with a bruised voice box that felt as if it had been pushed back somewhere in the vicinity of my spinal column.

Garth's lips moved, but no sound came out. He was across the room in four quick strides, trying to lift me up in his arms. Enough is enough—I pushed him away with the chair leg. I was building up a little anger of my own, but it vanished as the door suddenly opened. The man who stepped into the room was of medium height, with close-cropped, warm-yellow hair that tended to clash with his cold gray eyes. I wondered if he dyed his hair.

Garth glanced at the man, then quickly turned back to me. His face was a pleading exclamation mark as he shook his head. The movement was almost imperceptible, but I thought I'd received the message.

"Who the hell are you?" I said to the man in the doorway.

Oddly enough, my voice sounded quite normal, with just the right seasoning of surprise. It hurt only when I swallowed.

"Name's Boise," the man said, surveying the damage. "I came looking for my partner here. Saw your name on the directory down in the lobby. Didn't know Garth had a brother."

Or that the brother was a dwarf, judging from his expression. I knew that look from scores of experiences with potential but unsuspecting clients. I didn't like it. Boise wasn't exactly getting off on the right foot with me.

"Garth doesn't feel well," I said. "Why don't you tell MacGregor I've taken him home? I'll call in later and let him know how Garth is."

Boise didn't move. "What happened?"

"I'm redecorating."

"Must be expensive," Boise said without smiling.

"Look, Boise," Garth said tightly, turning to face the other man, "my brother's right. I can't cut it the rest of the day. Cover for me, okay? I'll be in tomorrow."

Boise glanced once more at the wreckage of the room, then shrugged and walked out into the corridor. A few moments later I heard the whine of the elevator and Boise was gone.

"Where'd you pick him up?"

"We were assigned as a team for a case I've been working on," Garth said without looking at me. He had begun to tremble. "I don't know why. Look, get me out of here, will you?"

I went to the desk, took out Garth's gun and slipped it into my own pocket. Garth didn't object. He wheeled and walked out to the elevator ahead of me. I glanced at the clock as I closed the door. Less than ten minutes had passed from the time Garth had walked into my office. It struck me that Boise was a very impatient man.

•   •   •

"Where are you taking me?"

"I don't want you to think I'm being touchy," I said, guiding my compact out of the parking garage and into the cacophony of New York's midmorning vehicular insanity. "Still, the fact remains that you did try to kill me back there, and I don't even owe you money." I glanced sideways. Garth's face was stony, his eyes fixed straight ahead. "You knew enough to dump the gun," I said seriously. "That was smart, but a man doesn't do something like that just because he's feeling a little annoyed. I saw you get out of that car. You looked like Lon Chaney Junior running from a full moon. You climbed right out of your tree, and my guess is that it's not the first time something like this has happened. It's happened before, and you've done nothing about it. That's not so smart. It doesn't take a master detective like myself to figure out that you need a vacation—a long one—and some medical attention. I know a good shrink who teaches up at the—"

"Pull over a minute, will you?"

I debated with myself for a few moments, decided there was no sense in possibly provoking another attack, and pulled over to double-park beside a No Standing sign.

"You're right," Garth said, still staring straight ahead of him. "It has happened before—four times in the past three weeks. Each time it gets worse. I can't think of any words to tell you how sorry I am about what happened back in your office, so I'm not even going to try. But I am telling you I can't go to a hospital or see a shrink. Not yet."

"Like hell!"

Garth shook his head. Still, he remained calm. There was no sign of the terrible rage that had wracked him just a few short minutes before, but my neck still hurt. "Look," Garth said quietly, "you yourself said I knew what was happening. I know I need rest, and I'm going to take it. You can take me to anyone you want, and I'll cooperate fully, but just give me four days."

"What happens in four days?"

"I have to testify before the grand jury—with Boise. I have to be there. It's very important."

I grunted and slammed the car into gear. Garth reached out and touched my arm. I tensed, ready to drop him, but his touch was very gentle. "Just listen, Mongo." I put the gears in neutral but left the engine running. "Have you ever heard of anethombolin?"

I'd seen the word somewhere but couldn't place it. I said so.

"Anethombolin is a hormone produced naturally in the body under certain conditions," Garth continued. "Recently it was synthesized. Among other things, anethombolin may provide a

RAGE

cure for asthma, male infertility, high blood pressure and a host of other ailments. It also induces spontaneous abortions, and that's what makes it potentially worth millions. I say 'potentially' because, so far, nobody has come up with a way to control certain very unpleasant side effects. A New York laboratory named Whalen Research Associates has spent a lot of money trying to find ways to neutralize those side effects, and they've developed a lot of patents along the way. With the liberalized abortion laws, you can see what a drug like this would mean to some people here in this country, not to mention its value to the governments of underdeveloped, overpopulated nations like India. Because a lot of the work was government-financed, agreements were made that would provide for controlled, low-cost distribution. Those agreements go out the window if some *other* company comes up with the same thing, and that's exactly what may have happened.

"A few months ago an outfit calling itself Zwayle Labs announced that it was on the verge of developing synthetic anethombolin fit for human consumption. Whalen claimed that Zwayle couldn't possibly have done the work without violating one or more of the patents Whalen holds—in other words, industrial espionage. A secret investigation was ordered, the results to be presented to a grand jury. I pulled the case, and Boise was assigned as my partner because he'd worked on similar cases before. We started the preliminary undercover work and discovered possible leaks on Whalen's staff. The nature of the business makes it all very tentative, but we did find prima facie evidence of industrial espionage and patent violation. What's needed now is a full-blown investigation, but first our evidence must be presented to the grand jury. If it isn't, a lot of time will have been wasted, not to mention the fact that an injustice will have occurred."

That would have sounded naive—even funny—coming from a lot of cops I know; coming from Garth it didn't.

"Patent law. That sounds like a job for the feds."

"It is, but some aspects of the case come under our jurisdiction. Besides, we were asked to cooperate. We did the groundwork."

"Why can't Boise testify?"

"He can and will, but it's a very sticky deal, and the grand jury is going to want to hear corroborative testimony from either one of us. In other words, Boise needs me and I need Boise if we're going to make a case. Do you understand?"

"No. It sounds like a hell of a way to run an investigation."

"Industrial espionage and patent violations are very difficult things to prove—you'll just have to take my word for that. In any case, I must be at that hearing, and my testimony isn't going to mean much if they have to wheel me in from the psycho ward."

"I don't buy it, Garth. I *saw* you back there. You're not going to do anybody any good if you're dead—or if you're responsible for making somebody else dead."

"That's not going to happen, brother." Garth's voice was harder now, determined. "Four days. That's all I need. After that, a long rest. Agreed?"

Actually, there was nothing on which to agree. I couldn't make Garth enter the hospital and he knew it. He was asking for my cooperation—in effect, my approval, my belief that he could control the strange fires in him long enough for him to complete a task he had set for himself.

"Most of the work is done?" I asked.

"Right. Now it's mostly just a matter of waiting around for the hearing."

"Full checkup when it's finished?"

"Full checkup."

I didn't like it, but I made no move to stop him when he opened the car door and stepped out into the street.

"I'll need my gun, Mongo," Garth said quietly.

It was true. If Garth would have a tough time testifying from a psychiatrist's couch, he'd have an even tougher time explaining how and why his dwarf brother took his gun and wouldn't give it back. I took the gun out of my jacket pocket and gave it to him.

·   ·   ·

I hate hospitals. I'd spent too much time in them as a child while doctors struggled to cope with the results of a recessive gene eight generations removed. The hospitals ran through my childhood like trains through a station. I stayed the same.

Now it was my brother, strapped to a bed in a psychiatric ward, too doped up even to recognize me.

I made arrangements to have him transferred to a private room and took a cab down to Garth's precinct station house. MacGregor, Chief of Detectives, was floundering around behind a desk strewn with stacks of coffee-stained papers. He was wearing his usual harried expression.

"What the hell is my brother doing up in Bellevue?"

"Easy, Mongo," MacGregor said. "I was the one who called you, remember? How is he?"

"Drugged right up to his eyeballs. I asked you what happened."

"I'm not sure. We're still trying to sort everything out. Garth called in sick yesterday. He came in this morning to go over some paperwork with Boise. You knew he's been working on a big case?" I nodded. "Your brother and Boise were having coffee," MacGregor continued. "A few minutes later Garth comes out and gets into an argument with Lancey over some little thing. Anyway, your brother wouldn't let it go; he broke Lancey's jaw for him, then he tries to pistol-whip Q.J. Took four guys to get him down. We called the hospital, and then I called you. We're just as anxious to know what happened as you are." MacGregor leaned forward confidentially. "He really wigged out, Mongo. You had to be here really to appreciate what he was like. Boise says he's been acting funny for some time now."

"Is that right? What about the case Garth was working on? The grand jury is supposed to hear it day after tomorrow. What happens now?"

"Nothing. They won't be hearing anything from this department."

"Why can't the hearing be postponed until Garth is better?"

"Because it wouldn't make any difference. Boise says we don't have a case."

"Now why would Boise say a thing like that?"

"Ask him."

.   .   .

I did.

"You know about that?" Boise asked.

"Garth mentioned it to me."

Boise carefully stirred the coffee in front of him. The sound of

61

the spoon bouncing off the sides of the cup grated on my nerves. "There was never a case to begin with," he said evenly. He punctuated the sentence by dropping the spoon on his saucer. "I hate to be the one to have to tell you this, but this whole affair was a result of paranoia on your brother's part, and that's all."

"Uh-uh. He wasn't the one who asked to initiate the investigation."

"No. We were asked to investigate—we did, and found nothing. Everything Zwayle Labs had done was on the up-and-up. They just worked faster and cheaper than the Whalen people. Certainly we found nothing to present to a grand jury. Some circumstantial evidence, a little hearsay, most of which was sour grapes from staff members who hadn't been able to handle the competition within their own departments. Nothing concrete. The evidence just wasn't there."

"Garth said it was tricky, and you'd have to corroborate each other's testimony."

Boise had finished his coffee and was signaling for another. "What can I tell you? Somewhere along the way your brother took a real strong dislike toward the guy who runs Zwayle Labs, a man by the name of Hans Mueller. Don't know why, but that's the way it happened. Guess whatever it was that finally put him away was working on him even then. He swore he'd get Mueller, and he started inventing evidence in his mind to do it."

The second cup of coffee was served and Boise started clanking around in it with his spoon.

I suddenly felt sick to my stomach. "Why didn't you tell MacGregor all this before?"

"Because I didn't want what happened to Lancey and Q.J. to happen to me. With me it could have been worse; I was alone with him all day. Besides, Garth's a brother officer. I wasn't about to tell him—or anybody else—that he was crazy. I was hoping he might straighten up after the grand jury shot us down."

"What's going to happen to him now?"

"They'll probably give him an extended leave of absence."

"It's more likely he'll lose his shield."

"Probably," Boise said, averting his eyes to his coffee. He didn't have to tell me that the camaraderie between police officers did not extend to asking taxpayers to keep a psycho cop on the payroll.

I didn't like it; all of the pieces seemed to fit, but the finished puzzle was ugly, misshapen.

"You mind if I look at the files?"

That stopped the stirring. "I think I would," Boise said after a pause, "and I think MacGregor will back me up. First of all, you're close to calling me a liar. Second, it's not the policy of the New York Police Department to let private citizens—especially private investigators—examine its files."

I bit off my next remark, rose and turned to go. I was stopped at the door by one of those inspirations I usually know enough to keep to myself. I walked slowly back to the table wearing my innocent, concerned-brother face. It hurt like a mask of nails.

"Mueller. That's a kraut name, isn't it?"

Boise's eyebrows flicked upward. His eyes followed. "How's that?"

"Mueller," I said. "Isn't that a German name?"

"Yeah, I guess so. Why?"

I shook my head. "Nothing, really. I was just trying to figure why Garth would flip out like this. Now I think I know the reason."

"Which is?"

"Germans," I said easily. "Garth hates Germans, It's a real thing with him. He's been that way ever since he was a kid. Too many cheap comic books and war movies. I guess. Anyway, when he was fifteen he almost killed a German classmate. That cost him six months in an institution. I guess it would've been better if they'd kept him a little longer."

•   •   •

I knew I had heard of anethombolin, so I canceled my evening class and went to the university library to find out where. By closing time I'd found what I'd been looking for in the scientific journals. I photocopied the appropriate articles and stuck them into my pocket. Then I went to an twenty-four-hour diner and ate a full meal. It was going to be a long night.

I was about to try my hand at reconstructing a sequence of events, a sequence that, for the moment, existed only in my mind: a play—a drama in which at least one of the players would be an unwilling participant. To make matters more difficult, that player would also be the most critical of audiences. One act—or even one line—out of place and the curtain would come crashing down. If I was right—if there was more fact than fiction in the scenario I was about to produce—my brother's sanity could hinge on the success of my improvisation; his sanity and possibly his life.

At the moment Garth was drowning in a black sea of madness, and his flailing hurt people. Now he was no more than a dangerous animal. Of course, it would not be the first time a good man had gone mad; a psychiatrist would have a field day expounding on the probable causes of Garth's breakdown. Still, I knew something the psychiatrists didn't; I knew my brother. If he was lost in a drowning pool of the mind, and all evidence suggested that he'd jumped in by himself, I still suspected he'd been pushed.

It was dawn by the time I finished. I slept for an hour, rose and ate breakfast, then sat down at the telephone. I tried unsuccessfully to control the trembling of my hands as I dialed the number of Zwayle Labs, but I did better with my voice. It was Mueller who sounded tense as he agreed to meet me in an hour.

Act One appeared to have been well received.

●　　　●　　　●

Zwayle Labs stood in the middle of a lower West Side block like a chrome and glass box tied together with ribbons of plastic. I paused outside on the sidewalk, activated the miniature tape recorder and microphone in my jacket pocket, then went in. The recorder was compact, and sensitive enough to pick up a normal speaking voice thirty feet away. The only problem was that, even running at low speed, there was only about twenty minutes' worth of tape on the tiny reel. I was going to have to do my talking in a hurry.

Mueller did a double take on me in the hall. I brushed past him and walked into his office.

"Ten thousand dollars," I said as Mueller was in the process of nervously offering me a chair. "That's how much I'll take not to blow this whole deal wide open. Considering the stakes you're playing for, that's peanuts. But then I like peanuts."

Mueller's pale Teutonic features were suddenly mottled with patches of red, but I couldn't tell whether they were caused by anger or fear. Thin and professorial-looking, smelling of greed, Mueller wasn't exactly an imposing figure. Still, looks can be deceiving; at least, in my own case, I liked to think so. I was sitting in on the biggest poker game of my life, against a man I didn't know, and I was bluffing blind. I didn't know of any other way to do what I had to do. There just wasn't time.

"My time is valuable, Mr. Frederickson," Mueller said quickly, avoiding my gaze. "Please come to the point."

"You knew my point when you heard what I had to say over the phone." I watched him carefully, very conscious of the time limit imposed by the machine in my pocket, fighting the urge to rush my words. "I didn't know the whole story when I was talking to Boise yesterday. Then I went up to Garth's place and looked around. He'd made some notes on this case, private notes that he hadn't shown to anyone else for obvious reasons. Did you know that? Garth is a very conscientious policeman; he likes to have all the facts before he makes any accusations. That cost him this time."

I punctuated my words by slapping down my manila folder in front of Mueller. He opened his mouth to speak. I spilled the photocopies out onto the polished mahogany surface of the desk and ran right through whatever it was he was going to say.

"Remember these? You should. They're reports on research done in this very lab—research done by you. Before this anethombolin fuss you were well known for your work in isolating and synthesizing drugs that were thought to trigger various emotional responses; all very experimental, but you'd had great success—with rats. The thinking was that the drugs might or might not affect men, but that a lot more research would have to be done. You decided to take a shortcut."

"What are you getting at?"

His voice gave him away. The fact that he had agreed to see me at all had been the first indication that I was on the right track. The fact that he hadn't already thrown me out of his office was, to me, conclusive proof. I'd hooked him. Now the problem was to reel him in before the plastic line of the tape in my pocket broke; or before I made a mistake.

"My brother was your first human subject." Which was precisely why my charade was so important; if I was right, I had to obtain samples of whatever it was Mueller had given Garth so that the lab boys could find some way to neutralize it.

Mueller seemed in perfect control. His eyes were like two opaque marbles. "What you are saying has no basis in fact, Mr. Frederickson," he said quietly. "Even if it did, I find it highly unbelievable that you would accept money to remain silent about something which could gravely affect your brother's health."

I laughed harshly. "That's because you're not a dwarf. In case you haven't noticed, my brother's bigger than I am. Bigger, and better able to take care of himself. It's always been that way, and its going to have to stay that way. He's just going to have to take care of himself—that is, if you cough up the money. What's ten thousand dollars when you're anticipating millions from the exclusive rights to anethombolin? In fact, I suggest that you hurry up and complete the deal before my conscience starts to bother me. Or before I up the ante. Maybe I'll ask for twice what you're paying Boise."

Thin, white lines were appearing around the corners of the other man's mouth. "Boise? Isn't that your brother's partner?"

"You know damn well who Boise is. He's the man you bought off. He's the man who's been dumping your drugs into Garth— probably by way of his coffee. Garth's testimony was needed at that grand jury hearing. He couldn't be bribed; it wouldn't take much checking to find that out. Therefore, he had to be put out of commission by a man who *could* be bribed: Boise. Then Boise could do his number about the whole thing being nothing more than paranoia on my brother's part and you'd be home free— with the anethombolin process you stole from Whalen Research Associates. The testimony of a madman wouldn't hold up very well against that of a perfectly sane partner. It will still work, except that now it's going to cost you a little more money. You don't pay, and I take my story to MacGregor, along with Garth's notes."

Then MacGregor would throw me out of *his* office. There were, of course, no notes and, thus far, the tape contained not much more than a not-too-brilliant Mongologue, though Mueller was sweating. I'd pulled the handle on this particular slot machine as far as it would go, and there wasn't much more I could do but stand and watch the cylinders spin. One lemon and it was all over.

Mueller tried to juggle the machine. "You're forgetting one thing," he said breezily. "Your brother has suffered bouts of paranoia before. Our own investigation shows that your brother was institutionalized for a homicidal attack on a German youth. I happen to be German, and my associates and I have suspected all along that your brother's persecution of me had something to do with my national origin."

I turned away quickly so that Mueller couldn't see the flood of emotion in my eyes. The last number had come up and it spelled jackpot. I turned back and allowed myself a weak smile. "You lose, Mueller," I said easily. "I figured Boise would call you with that choice bit of information. The fact of the matter is that my brother has a special fondness for Germans. He should—both our parents are German."

The last resistance went out of him like air whooshing from a crushed lung. He stared at me helplessly. "All right, Frederickson. Perhaps you are due some money. Say, as a 'counseling fee.'"

"You can call it anything you want. Just get the money up front. Now."

"Perhaps we could negotiate the exact—"

"Shut up, Mueller!" Boise's voice came from behind me. I didn't bother to turn; I could feel the barrel eye of a .38 staring at my spine.

It looked as if the game wasn't over yet. I had counted on Boise calling, but I hadn't counted on his actually being here for the meeting. I was out of cards, and someone had unplugged the slot machine.

"You're a fool, Mueller," Boise said calmly. Now the cold barrel was pressed against my temple as Boise's free hand flew expertly over my body until he found what he was looking for. He yanked the tape recorder out of my pocket, dropped it on the floor, then crushed it under his heel. "He doesn't want money. He's as straight as his brother. He just wanted you to talk, which you did beautifully."

Still keeping the gun trained on my head, Boise knelt and fired the scattered tape with his lighter. The room was suddenly filled with an acrid odor that made my eyes water.

"You're burning a hole in my carpet," Mueller said weakly, staring down at the small pyre of burning plastic.

"Get this, Mueller," Boise said, backing up so that both the scientist and myself fell into his range of fire, "I want that hundred thousand dollars you owe me, and I want to be free to spend it. If you don't start wising up, I'm going to burn a hole in your brain."

The tape was destroyed. Boise snuffed out the last glowing embers with the toe of his shoe. I tried to think of some maneuver that would get me closer to Boise, but you don't mess with a man who practices three times a week on a firing range. The gun in Boise's hand was a tight drawstring on any bag of tricks that I might have been tempted to explore.

Boise wasn't taking any chances either. Slowly he came up behind me. I anticipated the blow and managed to move my head enough to avoid having my skull crushed. Still, it was a long way to the bottom of the rainbow-colored well into which he crudely pushed me.

•   •   •

It was also a long way up.

The sides of the well were dotted with faces of my brother. His lips were curled back like an animal's, baring froth-specked teeth. There were large red holes where his eyes should have been. His hands were studded with hundreds of snakelike fingers, and I wept helplessly as they reached for me, curling around my throat, tearing at my eyes.

I floated up and out of the hole and down onto what felt like a hardwood floor. Finally conscious, my body was a raft cast adrift on a vast, eerie sea of total darkness.

I was still crying, not as a man cries when touched by some deep emotion, but as a child cries in the grip of some nameless nighttime terror. I sobbed and wailed, my hiccuping moans swallowed up by the dark. In one part of me I was profoundly embarrassed; in another part of me, weeping seemed the most natural thing in the world for me to be doing.

Gradually I muffled my cries and wiped my tears with the back of my hand. At the same time my muscles seemed to go rigid. I couldn't move or, rather, I *dared* not move. In the surrounding night I could hear the dry rustle of snakes, large snakes moving toward me, large snakes of the variety that lie in wait along the banks of tropical rivers to crush and eat things that are small and warm.

There were other things out there too, and they all crushed and squeezed and bit and hurt. I began to cry again, and pray to the God I had known as a child.

Another part of my mind, a tiny area where the fear had not yet penetrated, began to stir. I listened to it whisper of snakes and other things that crush, big things, a world of giants that laughed and mocked; things that would hurt a dwarf, things that would eat a dwarf.

It suddenly occurred to me that these fears were somehow familiar, like a scarred rocking horse uncovered in a dusty corner of some attic, an attic of the mind. In this case they were old monsters from the mental storage bin of childhood.

Then I understood. I remembered Garth and Mueller and Boise, and I knew what they had done. The terrors *were* from childhood; all those special horrors that had plagued me when I had first learned I was small, so different from other children, had come back to visit. Something had dredged them all up from my subconscious and scattered them in the darkness around me . . .

Something like a drug, something like phobetarsin; that was what the fear-producing drug had been called in the research papers I had read.

At least the drug Mueller had given *me* had a name.

The terrible dread was still there, but now I knew its source. That made all the difference in the world; I had *labeled* the fear—or at least its cause—and that made it, if no less real, at least easier to deal with it. I was sure I *had* been given a drug, probably phobetarsin. The question remained as to why they had bothered. Perhaps it was an attempt to make me more manageable, or perhaps it was merely gratuitous sadism. Whatever the reason, I knew I needed some defense.

I closed my eyes against the fear and slowly moved out across the room, crawling inch by inch on my belly. I finally bumped up against a wall and paused, cradling my head in my arms. My clothes were drenched with sweat and, once again, I was crying.

Still, I had my single psychological weapon; I *knew* what had unleashed the demons around me. Garth had had no such advantage. Whatever they had given him had somehow had the effect of stripping the scabs off his psyche, simultaneously releasing the thousand and one irritations and frustrations that plague a man every day, bringing them all up in one lump to fester in his conscious mind until a flash point was reached.

Somewhere in every man's mind are the fetid odors of rotted dreams, mercifully flushed into the sewers of the subconscious. Mueller had discovered chemicals that somehow interfered with the mechanism of suppression. He'd been playing games with my brother's sanity, not to mention my own. I owed him.

I curled my legs up close to my body and waited in the dark.

Several eternities later the lights came on, harsh and white-hot on the dilated pupils of my eyes. Now I could see the door, lined with rubber flaps to exclude any light, on the other side of the bare room, to my right. It opened. Immediately I cringed, curling my body up into a tight ball. I covered my face with my hands, leaving just enough space between my fingers to see through.

Boise's gun was the first thing into the room, followed by Boise himself, then Mueller. Boise stopped inside the door, nudged Mueller and pointed at me. He was grinning.

"Boo!" Boise said. That was almost funny enough to make me forget the other, real fears that were still buzzing around inside my head.

I moaned and shrunk even closer to the wall. At the same time I dropped my right forearm and planted it in the angle between the wall and the floor. I would get only one shot at Boise and I wanted all the leverage I could get.

"Hey, dwarf!" Boise barked, still grinning. "You want to die, dwarf?" He was enjoying himself, and that was a mistake.

My sick terror was rapidly being displaced by red-cheeked, eminently healthy anger. I moaned a little bit, prompting Mueller to enter the conversation.

"Boise, I don't see why you have to needle him like that."

"You were the one who suggested doping him up."

"Just to make him easier to handle, Boise. I don't see how we can just—"

"I've already figured out what to do with him," Boise said, coming closer and looking for my eyes. His gun was still steady on me.

"Please let me go home," I said in my best whine, at the same time trying not to ham it up too much. "I promise I won't bother you anymore. Please don't hurt me." I considered my next words, then figured, what the hell. The *coup de grace:* "Please let me call my mother."

That broke Boise up—mentally. The room echoed with his loud, hoarse laughter. He reached out with the toe of his shoe to nudge me in the ribs, and that was what I had been waiting for. I broke him up again—physically.

Shifting all my weight onto my right arm, I tensed and kicked out with my instep at the exposed side of his left knee. It popped with a metallic sound of breaking joints and tearing ligaments. Boise dropped like a felled tree, his gaping mouth wrapped around a long, meandering scream. The gun clattered to the floor and bounced in Mueller's direction. Mueller belatedly reached down for it and got me instead. I slapped him across the bridge of the nose. He sat down hard. I stood and placed the end of the gun in his ear. I pulled the hammer back, and Mueller made a retching sound.

"Get up, Mueller, don't throw up," I said evenly. "You do and I'll kill you. Think about that."

Mueller put his hand over his mouth and struggled to his feet. I glanced at Boise, who lay on his side holding his shattered knee. His eyes had the dull sheen of cheap pottery. I turned back to Mueller.

"The drugs," I said. "I want samples of whatever it was you put into Garth and me."

Mueller's head bounced up and down like a wooden block on a string. He led me out of the room, down a narrow corridor, and into a smaller office. He reached up onto a shelf and took down two small vials.

"Which is which?"

"This is what we gave you," he said, pointing to the vial on the

71

left. I took the other vial and dropped it into my pocket; I felt as if I were pocketing Garth's mind, his sanity.

There was something huge creeping up behind me. It was a green, multilegged insect that ate dwarfs. I resisted the impulse to turn and look for it. I knew there would be many such things waiting for me in the void of time ahead, at least until the contents of the other vial could be analyzed and a way found to neutralize its effects. Or perhaps the creatures would go away by themselves. In any case, I decided I wanted company.

"Let's see how fast you can come up with two glasses of water." I waved the gun at him. He was very fast.

I opened the vial in my hand and tapped a few crystals of the drug into each glass, then motioned for Mueller to pick them up. He didn't have to be told what to do next. We marched back to the closed room, and I waited while the cloudy water disappeared down the throats of the men. Then I left them alone—I shut off the lights and closed the door.

I found a phone and dialed Garth's precinct. Then I backed up against the wall and held my gun out in front of me. The nameless forms sharing the room with me stayed hidden. At last MacGregor's welcome voice came on the line.

"Listen to me closely," I said, struggling to keep my voice steady. "I can probably only get it straight once. Garth's insanity is a setup. I think he'll be all right if you do what I say. If you do a urinalysis and blood test soon enough, I think you'll still find traces of a very unusual drug in his system. I know you will in mine, and I can prove where it came from. In the meantime, send a car to pick me up. I'm at Zwayle Labs. I have a surprise package for you."

MacGregor started to pump me for more information. I was in no shape to give it to him, and I cut him off. Boise was starting to scream. Soon, Mueller joined him.

"Please hurry," I said softly, closing my eyes. "I'm afraid."

The travel notes come out again.

Country for Sale

Irolled over in the dark and swatted the button on the alarm clock. Nothing happened. The jangling continued, bouncing around inside my brain like marbles in a tin cup. The hands on the clock read 3:30. I picked up the telephone and the ringing finally stopped. I pulled the receiver down near the vicinity of my mouth and muttered something unintelligible.

"Mongo? Is that you, Mongo?"

I rummaged around inside my mind until I managed to match the voice to a seven-foot giant with a penchant for collecting sea shells. I hadn't seen Roscoe Blanchard in five years, not since I'd left the circus.

"Roscoe?"

"Yeah, it's Roscoe." The voice was strained, nervous. "Sorry if I woke you up. I know it's close to midnight."

I looked at the clock again. It still read 3:30. "Roscoe, I think you need a new watch."

"Huh?"

"Where are you?"

"San Marino."

"California?"

"No. San Marino."

"I got that. But where's San Marino?"

There was a long pause at the other end of the line.

"San Marino's in *San Marino*," Roscoe said at last.

73

I decided to leave the geography lesson for later. "Roscoe, what's the matter?" I asked him.

"We've got trouble here and nobody knows what to do. I remembered Phil mentioning something about you being a private detective now. I got your number out of one of the books in the office."

"Where's Phil?"

"He's disappeared."

That woke me up. Phil was Phil Statler, owner of the Statler Brothers Circus, where I'd spent eight of the most miserable years of my life. But there aren't that many things you can do when you're a dwarf. If you end up a circus performer, there's no better man to work for than Phil Statler.

"How long has he been missing?"

"Four days. And there are some other funny things going on. Just yesterday—" It ended in a bloody gargle and the muffled sound of something very large and heavy falling.

"*Roscoe!*" I was screaming at a dial tone; the line had been disconnected. I tasted blood and realized I had bitten into my lower lip. I lay frozen, my fingers locked around the receiver.

I sat up on the edge of the bed and leaned forward to stop my knees from shaking. Somewhere at the opposite end of thousands of miles of wire a man was dead or dying, and all I had was the name of a place I'd never heard of. I dialed the operator.

It took ten minutes to confirm that the call had come from a place called San Marino, and another ten to find out where it was: San Marino, a full-fledged United Nations member, was a country which occupied the whole of a mountain top—Mount Titano—in Italy. That was all the information I was going to get; I couldn't get through to a police station, or anyone else for that matter, because the San Marinese phone system had suddenly broken down and the phone people couldn't tell me when it would be operational again. I would just have to live with the sound of Roscoe's dying.

I brushed my teeth and packed a bag.

•　　　•　　　•

I met an Italian on the flight to Venice who filled me in on San Marino.

74

San Marino seemed to be doing quite well despite the fact that I'd never heard of it. It was—well, a dwarf, the smallest and oldest republic in the world, sixty square kilometers with 19,000 people, about enough to fill the football stadium in a small college town. It had been around since A.D. 300, when a Christian stonecutter by the name of Marino hid out on Mount Titano to avoid being fed to the Roman lions.

San Marino's geography consisted of nine towns and three castles, which a Hollywood movie company had helped renovate in the '40s. Its economic assets included heavy doses of authentic medieval atmosphere, huge bottles of cheap cognac, postage stamps, and a thriving tourist trade.

It seemed a strange place to take a circus.

I landed in Venice and rented a car. The drive to the coast town of Rimini took a little over an hour. By then it was noon. I was tired from the Atlantic crossing, and hungry. Most of all I was worried, but there didn't seem to be much sense in rushing at this point.

I stopped in a *ristorante* to exercise my Italian and ordered some pasta and wine. Once my raven-haired waitress got over the fact that she had an Italian-speaking dwarf in her establishment, I received excellent attention. The food and wine were superb. I finished, then asked directions to San Marino. She took me over to a window and pointed east.

Mount Titano was barely visible. I could make out San Marino's three castles sitting on the highest points of the mountain, silhouetted against the sky. It looked like something out of a Disney movie.

I turned away from the window and caught the waitress staring at me. She giggled nervously and dropped her eyes.

"I take it you don't get that many dwarfs around here," I said in Italian.

"I didn't mean to stare."

I introduced myself. Her name was Gabriela. I asked if I could use her phone, and she steered me into a back room. I got hold of an operator who informed me that the lines to San Marino were still out. I hung up and went back into the dining room, where Gabriela was waiting with a glass of cognac. I drank it in the name of international relations and thanked her. It tasted terrible.

"San Marinese," Gabriela said. "I thought you might like to taste it. They sell it by the gallon up there."

I disguised a belch with a noncommital grunt.

"Did you reach your party?"

"The phones up there are out of order."

Gabriela absently stroked her hair. "That's odd. Come to think of it, nobody's been down off the mountain in two or three days."

"Who usually comes down?"

"Many San Marinese work in Rimini. They often stop in here for lunch or dinner. I have regulars, but I haven't seen them for three days. I guess there may be something to the rumors."

"What rumors?"

"It is said they have sickness. They are keeping themselves isolated until they find out what it is and how to cure it."

"What kind of a police force do they have up there?"

"Oh, they're all very nice."

"That's great for public relations. How effective are they?"

She gave me a puzzled look. I rephrased the question. "How good are they at catching crooks?"

Gabriela laughed. "There is no crime in San Marino. Perhaps an occasional drunk or a traffic accident, but never anything serious. The San Marinese are very pleasant people. Very friendly. It will be a shame if you can't get in."

Gabriela went back to the window and pointed up the highway. "The road branches off about two kilometers to the south. The right fork will take you to Mount Titano."

I paid my bill, left Gabriela a few hundred lire, and returned to my car.

•　　　•　　　•

There were two guards at the border. One of them stepped out into the middle of the road as I approached. He couldn't have been more than twenty, but the scattergun he held made him seem older. The other one stayed back, watching me through cold, mud-colored eyes. He was tall, swarthy, and looked decidedly unfriendly. I doubted that he'd ever directed traffic.

The boyish one came around to my side of the car and cleared his throat.

"I'm sorry, sir," he said in passable English. "The border is closed."

"I didn't think that ever happened in San Marino."

"There is sickness on the mountain." He dropped his eyes as he said it. "Very bad. We have closed ourselves off to protect others."

"I understand it's only catching if you're a telephone."

He gave me a sharp look, filled with warning.

"I've had all my shots. I'd like to take my chances."

"I'm sorry, sir. Perhaps in a few days."

I backed my car around and drove back down the hill. I parked it at a service station at the foot of the mountain and gave the attendant some money to watch it for a few days. From what I'd seen, San Marino wasn't exactly impregnable; it was time to test its new border fortifications. I found a convenient vineyard and ducked off the road into it.

I took the vineyard route three-quarters of the way up the mountain, past the guards, then turned left and walked until I hit the main highway. That was all it took to get into San Marino. Staying there might prove more difficult, but I'd worry about that when the time came.

I found myself on the outskirts of a town that I recognized from the Italian's description as the country's capital, also named San Marino. The central thoroughfare was a narrow, cobblestone street lined on both sides with souvenir shops. There were also a number of restaurants and hotels, not to mention the famous three castles, each about a half kilometer from where I was standing.

There was no sign of any circus.

I went up the street and stopped in front of one of the souvenir shops. Its windows were filled with the same things the windows of all the other shops were filled with, plastic junk with a medieval theme: plastic helmets, swords and shields, all undoubtedly made in Japan. There were three revolving stands displaying glassine envelopes filled with San Marinese stamps. All of the usual postcards were already stamped, and there was a large wooden mailbox conveniently nailed to the side of each shop.

Benches on each side of the entrance were loaded with glass jugs containing San Marinese cognac.

The San Marinese didn't miss a trick.

On the other hand, it didn't take much of an experienced eye to see that much of San Marino was authentically medieval. There was a church visible down a side street that had to be at least eight hundred years old, probably of great interest to historians. But the San Marinese had learned their lesson early and well; history doesn't make money, plastic souvenirs do.

A woman emerged from behind the tinted glass and stood on the stoop watching me as though I might be a souvenir that had somehow escaped from her shop. She had been beautiful once, before she'd put away too many San Marinese delicacies. Her green eyes were perfectly complemented by almond-colored skin and dark hair.

Finally she smiled and said, "American?" It was as perfect as English can be when laced with a Brooklyn accent.

I extended my hand. "My name is Robert Frederickson."

"I'm Molly Marinello," the woman said, taking my hand in a firm grip. Her eyes glittered with pleasure. "Please wait here a moment, Mr. Frederickson. My husband will want to meet you."

She went back into the shop, and reappeared a few moments later with her husband in tow. He was a big, handsome man with the ruddy complexion and granite presence of a man who has spent most of his life out-of-doors, working with his hands.

"I'm John Marinello," he said, pumping my hand. "Always glad to meet another American."

"Brooklyn?"

"Yeah. Can't say enough about the United States."

"Too much violence," his wife said gently. "Nobody's safe on the streets."

John Marinello shook his head. I felt as if I'd stumbled into an argument that had been going on for years. It was a ritual, and they knew their lines by heart.

"I earned good money there. I was a construction worker. Stonemason. I'd still be there if it wasn't for Molly. Great place, the United States."

"Too much violence," Molly repeated. "Nobody's safe on the streets. Much better here."

Her husband started to shake his head again.

I cut in. "I take it that things are pretty quiet here."

John Marinello's eyes grew big in mock wonder. "*Quiet?!* Let me tell you—"

"*Peaceful,*" Molly said quietly. "Nobody fights here. People here live like human beings."

The man's head was starting to go again.

"I guess we used to be neighbors," I said quickly. "I teach at the university in downtown Manhattan."

Both of them looked surprised. "We thought you were from the circus," Molly said. She paused and flushed. "I'm sorry," she added quickly. "I just took it for granted."

"It's all right. As a matter of fact, I used to work for the circus. The one that's here now. By the way, do you know where they're camped?"

John pointed up the street. "There's a large field up there around the bend, to your right. It's down in a valley." He paused and studied me. "I'm surprised you haven't seen it."

"I just got here."

"I understood we were quarantined. How did you get up here?"

"Do you believe the story about the epidemic?"

John and Molly Marinello exchanged glances. They both seemed incredulous.

"Believe?" John said. "Why shouldn't we believe it? The order came directly from Alberto Vaicona, one of the Regents."

"He's the head of your government?"

"One of the heads. There are two Regents."

"Why are all the phones out of order?"

"It is nothing," Molly assured me. "These things happen. Whatever is wrong will be repaired soon."

"Uh-huh. Are they giving out shots or anything for this epidemic?"

"We've been told it isn't necessary for now," John said. Flecks of light that might have been suspicion suddenly appeared in his eyes. "Why do you ask these questions?"

I swallowed hard, trying to think positive. "There's a rumor that a man from the circus was hurt the other day, maybe killed."

"It's more than a rumor," Molly said. "It's a fact. It was one of the freaks, a giant. Killed by a knife in the throat."

My mouth went dry. Molly's eyebrows went up as though yanked by strings.

"Isn't that terrible? But that was an outsider killed by another outsider. The man was murdered by somebody from the circus."

"Who?"

"A knife thrower called Jandor. They already have him locked up in the jail."

"They have any witnesses?"

"No, but it was Jandor's knife that killed the giant."

I said nothing, but I was sure Jandor hadn't killed anybody. Like most men who earn their living with the tools of violence, he was personally a gentle man, even tender. And he wasn't mentally defective; if Jandor was going to kill somebody, he wasn't likely to walk away and leave his trademark sticking out of his victim's neck.

"Can't say enough about the United States," John said.

"Too much violence," Molly said.

I bought a souvenir, thanked them and left.

•   •   •

From the rim of the valley the circus below looked drab, spent. The aura that almost always surrounds a circus was missing. The colors of the rented tents were all wrong; the whole encampment looked like a balloon that was slowly leaking air. A trio of armed guards posted around the campsite added to the depressing effect.

The men were empty-handed, but the type of men I was looking at always wore guns. They might forget to put their pants on in the morning, but never their guns.

I put my hands in my pockets, mustered up enough spit to do some casual whistling, then merrily tripped off down the slope. Two of the guards glanced at me, then looked away, apparently unconcerned. The man closest to me kept his eyes riveted on my chest. I walked up to him, nodded pleasantly, then started to walk past.

A hand like a pair of wire cutters reached out and grabbed my shoulder, turning me toward him.

80

"Who are you, pal?" he said in slightly accented English. He sounded like he was talking through a mouthful of marshmallows, as though somebody had walked on his tonsils. I gave him a hurt look and pointed toward the tents.

"Don't you recognize me?" I was hoping all dwarfs looked the same to him.

His eyes skittered across my face, up and down my body. Like most stupid men, the thing he feared most was appearing stupid.

"What the hell are you doing out here?! Where's your pass?!"

I groaned apologetically and started rummaging through my pockets. After a few moments of that number Marshmallow Mouth cursed and waved me through.

I walked quickly down the path and ducked behind one of the tents.

It was noontime and most of the circus personnel would be in the lunch trailers. That was fine with me. At least half of the circus would recognize me on sight, and I wanted to get the feel of things before holding any reunions. I needed somebody I could trust.

I slipped along the perimeter of the encampment to the midway, then cut through to the compound where a number of trailers had been set up as living quarters for the performers and hands. I found the name plate I wanted, then knocked softly on the door of the trailer on the outside chance that its occupant would be in.

"Who's there?" The voice was nervous, edgy.

"It's Robert Frederickson, Nell. Let me in, please."

"*Who?*"

"Mongo."

The door suddenly burst open and Big Nell stood before me. Her beard was even longer than I remembered. She sobbed, jumped down to the ground and hugged me. There were tears in her eyes.

"Mongo!" Nell whimpered. "God, it's good to see you!"

The formalities out of the way, I gently pulled myself loose and let the air rush back into my lungs. We went into the trailer and Nell started to brew some coffee. Her shoulders were still shaking. Big Nell was very emotional, Earth Mother to all the circus creatures, human and animal alike. I'd always liked her.

81

Nell finished making the coffee and brought cups for both of us on a tray. She poured cream into mine.

"I'm so glad you're here, Mongo," she said, handing me the cup. "So many things are happening here that I don't understand."

"Roscoe didn't understand them either. I'm here because he called me. The trouble is that I never got a chance to hear what he had to say."

Molly looked up, and her eyes flooded again with tears. "Roscoe's dead, you know."

"Who killed him?"

"The police say Jandor."

"Do you believe that?"

Nell shook her head. "As far as I know, Roscoe and Jandor never exchanged a word in anger. If you want my opinion—"

"I do, Nell," I said gently. "But first I want a few facts. Is anybody in the circus sick?"

Nell thought a few moments. "Just a few colds."

"What's the Statler Brothers Circus doing camped out in rented tents in the middle of San Marino?"

"We were invited by the government. Mr. Statler got a letter from one of their leaders—"

"A Regent?"

"Yeah, I guess that's what they're called. We were touring through Italy anyway, and Mr. Statler thought it might be fun to come to San Marino. He never said anything about selling the circus."

"Selling the circus?"

Nell blinked. "Didn't Roscoe tell you?"

"Roscoe was killed while he was talking to me on the phone. Did Phil say why he sold the circus?"

Nell wiped away a tear with the back of her hand. "Nobody's talked to Mr. Statler at all. He's disappeared. Mr. Fordamp said he's gone off on a vacation."

"Who's this Mr. Fordamp character?"

"He's the man Mr. Statler sold the circus to."

"Can he show papers?"

"He's got papers. I don't know whether they're any good or not."

"If Fordamp claims everything's on the up-and-up, how does he explain the three gorillas outside?"

"Mr. Fordamp says the men are there for our protection, so that no one will steal anything."

I mulled things over in my mind for a few moments; nothing made any sense. The gunmen outside were all hard professionals, which probably made Fordamp the typical Big Man, supercrook, probably Syndicate.

What would a man like Fordamp want with a circus, and why would he blockade a whole country to get it? That was like boarding up a house to catch a fly.

"Nell, why do you suppose the government of San Marino would issue an invitation to the circus?"

"That's easy. Danny Lemongello took care of the arrangements."

The name was new to me and I said so.

"Danny has a balancing act," Nell continued. "He's been with the circus for two years now. It seems he's originally from San Marino. When he heard we were touring through Europe, he got the idea of performing in San Marino. He went to Mr. Statler and Mr. Statler said it would be all right if San Marino would agree to provide facilities. You know Mr. Statler: He collects countries. Anyway, we came and set up. It was wonderful. I think at one time or another every person in San Marino came to see us.

"Then, right after we closed, Mr. Statler disappeared. Mr. Fordamp showed up the next day and told us that he'd bought the circus. He said he'd honor all our contracts and asked us to stay." Nell stroked her beard, adding an afterthought: "I suppose that was real nice of him. Where else would most of us go?"

"What kind of a man is this Mr. Fordamp?"

"Smooth," she said after some hesitation, "but a bossman, if you know what I mean, the kind of man you don't argue with. He dresses strange. He's always wearing this funny kind of vest under his suit. Real bulky. I think he carries something inside it."

"Probably a gun."

"It's too big. It looks more like a walkie-talkie. And he's always got two men with him. They carry guns."

"Assuming Jandor was framed, why do you think they picked him to pin the murder on?"

"Jandor was doing a lot of talking. Same as Roscoe."

"What were they talking about?"

"They were saying that they didn't believe Mr. Statler really sold the circus. They thought the circus was being stolen, and that Mr. Statler had been kidnapped. They went to the police, but nobody would listen."

"Okay, Nell. Right now, you're the only person in the circus who knows I'm here. I want to keep it that way for the time being, with one exception: I want to talk to Danny Lemongello."

"Now?"

"Now. Can you get him here for me?"

Nell stepped forward and placed her hands on my shoulders. "Everything's going to be all right, isn't it?"

In the kind of wars men like Fordamp and his goons fought, prisoners were rarely taken. They rarely kidnapped anybody; it was easier to kill people who got in the way. I didn't want to tell Nell that, so I said nothing. After a few moments Nell turned and walked out of the trailer.

Danny Lemongello had hair the color of a Hawaiian sunset and a look of wonder about him, the fresh-faced aura of a young man who was still in awe of the circus. He stepped inside the tent and stared at me as I got to my feet.

"Mongo the Magnificent!" he cried, rushing forward with one hand outstretched. "Gee, if you only knew how glad I am to meet you! You're like a legend around here!"

He almost made me feel guilty for my thoughts. I shook his hand. It was wet. "We can talk old times later, Danny. Right now I'd like to ask you some questions."

His eyes clouded. "Gee, Mongo, what kind of questions?"

"It looks like somebody's trying to take over my circus," I said.

Lemongello's eyes flickered to the ground, then climbed back up to my face. "You mean 'your circus' because you used to work—?"

"No, Danny," I lied. "I mean my circus because I'm a part owner. Half, to be exact."

"I didn't know that," Danny said after a long pause.

"Is there any reason you should?" I asked evenly.

84

"Well, Phil and I talked some, especially during the past year, and I guess I'm surprised that he never mentioned that he shared ownership with anybody."

I glanced at Nell. She had retreated to a corner of the trailer and was stroking her beard. I glanced back at Lemongello. "You and Phil talked a lot, Danny?"

"Yeah. We're good friends."

"And you were the one who got the circus an invitation to come here?"

"Yes. I'm proud of the circus. Maybe Nell told you; I come from San Marino, and I guess I wanted to show off for the hometown folks, so to speak. I'd already written a letter to Mr. Vaicona, one of the Regents, and he'd said it was okay. I talked to Phil, and the rest was simple. He went out of his way to get here."

"I keep on hearing about this Vaicona. There are two Regents, aren't there?"

Danny nodded. "Arturo Bonatelli is the other one. He's been on vacation for the past two weeks."

"Did Phil ever mention anything to you about selling the circus?"

Lemongello tapped his foot a few times on the floor. It was the gesture of a nervous man who was trying to appear thoughtful. "He first mentioned it to me about six months ago," Danny said at last. "He said he was getting tired of the grind and had enough money to live out a good retirement. I guess all he was waiting for was a good offer."

"Uh-huh. And he got one here, obviously."

"That's right. There's a Mr. Fordamp who bought the circus."

"So I hear; Phil's half and my half."

"I don't know anything about that."

"What's all this business about sealing the country off because of an epidemic?"

"There's meningitis on the other side of the mountain," Danny said easily. "Nothing too serious, but San Marino's whole economy is based on tourism, so they want to make sure nothing happens to any visitor. I'm sure the quarantine will be lifted in a few days. By the way, how did you get—?"

"One more thing, Danny. Doesn't it seem strange to you that

85

Phil would leave without saying good-bye to the people he'd worked with over the years?"

The boy thrust his hands into his pockets and studied my face. I imagined I could hear him making up his next lie in his head.

"The last time I talked to Phil he was pretty strung out," Danny said tightly, avoiding my eyes. "He was really anxious to get started on his retirement. I suppose leaving the way he did was just his way."

"But that wasn't his way," I said evenly. I waited for Danny to say something. He remained silent. "I think somebody's trying to pull a swindle, Danny. What do you think?"

He said something, but I didn't really listen to his answer. I was sure Danny Lemongello was lying; and if he thought at all, he wouldn't have put himself in a situation where he would have to lie. His mouth stopped moving and I slapped him on the back, thanked him, and ushered him out of the trailer.

•　　•　　•

I decided it would be pushing my luck to try talking my way past Marshmallow Mouth again, so I made my exit from the circus through a small patch of weeds in back of Nell's trailer. I climbed out of the valley, then headed toward a police station I had seen on my way through town.

The entrance to the station was manned by a handsome San Marinese policeman who looked more than a little embarrassed about the whole thing. He had a clean-cut face, firm and honest. We nodded to each other as I passed inside.

It wasn't much of a police station as police stations go—small, very old, obviously not intended as a maximum security prison, but as a way station for the occasional drunk who floated in on the cheap San Marinese cognac.

There was a man sitting inside. What I could see of him was dressed in expensive clothes. There was a big bulge under his right armpit. A pair of Gucci shoes with feet in them were propped up on a scarred wooden desk in front of a metal plate that read *Chief*. The other end of him was hidden behind a newspaper. I went and stood in front of the desk. The paper didn't move.

"Who's in charge here?" I asked in Italian.

"I am," came the muffled reply.

"I want to report a missing person."

The paper came down slowly to reveal a pair of ice-cold black eyes. A jagged scar ran from his hairline down across the bridge of his nose to the left side of his mouth. The scar tissue that had formed over the lip had puckered up his mouth into a perpetual leer. His name was Luciano Petrocelli, and he was an unlikely candidate for police chief; I'd last seen his picture in the *New York Times* in connection with an article describing how the Italian police were banishing certain suspected *mafiosi* to a small fishing village on an island off the coast of Sicily. Petrocelli was to have been the leading resident. The climate apparently hadn't agreed with him.

"How'd you get away from the circus?"

I repeated that I wanted to report a missing person.

"There aren't any missing persons in San Marino, buddy. Everybody is accounted for."

"Well, I don't think he's so much missing as kidnapped."

The brows came together and the eyes focused on my chest, like the cold, black barrels of guns.

"There ain't nobody been kidnapped in San Marino, dwarf. You're talking crazy."

"As long as I'm here, I'd like to visit a prisoner."

Petrocelli grunted and put the newspaper back up to his face. I had the feeling he was able to watch me through it. "We don't have any prisoners in San Marino."

"I'm talking about the man called Jandor. He's supposed to have killed somebody. Don't you have him here?"

Petrocelli put the paper to one side and leaned forward in his chair. "He a friend of yours?"

"Yes."

"You've got some pretty dangerous friends, dwarf. Also, you ask too many questions. Why don't you take my advice and get out of San Marino?"

"I can't. You've got the country sealed off, remember? Also, there's a small matter of my missing partner selling a circus that's half mine. What are you going to do about that?"

A vein in the side of Petrocelli's neck was beginning to throb. I'd have ducked if he had a gun in his hand.

"If you're not out of here in one minute, dwarf, I'm going to throw you in the can with your friend."

I was out of the police station in something under a minute, and in the Marinello's souvenir shop in less than ten. Molly greeted me warmly and took me into living quarters in back of the shop to have some cognac with her husband. I passed on the cognac and offered a question instead.

"This is a nice little country you've got here," I said. "What's to prevent somebody from taking it over?"

John Marinello tossed down one slug of cognac and poured another. His eyes were glassy.

"The law," he said. "We have a constitution, like in the United States. We elect our leaders. If they do not obey our laws we get rid of them."

"By voting them out of office, like in the United States?"

John put his glass down. He had a puzzled expression on his face. "That's right. Why?"

"Let's suppose for the sake of argument that someone, for reasons unknown, was in a hurry and didn't want to be bothered with a formality like an election. Let's suppose this person or group wanted to fill all the key posts in San Marino with their own men. How would they go about it?"

Marinello shrugged. "They couldn't. The Regents, with the grand council, appoint all the officials who aren't elected."

"Men can be bought or blackmailed. There are many ways."

"Here that is impossible."

"But what would you do about it?"

"The Italians would help us."

"But only if they were officially asked, right?"

"Yes. What are you getting at?"

I thought I'd been making myself clear. I decided to hit him over the head with the whole package. "I think somebody's already taken over San Marino."

John put his glass down. His cheeks were still flushed, but his eyes cleared a little. "You're not making any sense."

"For openers, your chief of police at the moment is a *mafioso* who was supposed to have been locked up by the Italians. There are hired guns all over the place. You've got no phone service, and the country's sealed off. It seems to me that you've got a problem."

"There's sickness in the country," John said weakly. "That's why we've been isolated."

"Really? Do you know of one single individual who's come down with this sickness?"

"I took it for granted."

"Like everybody else in San Marino."

Marinello put the cork back in the jug of cognac and pushed it away. "I read in the paper where a new chief had been appointed, but I didn't give it much thought. It was a new appointment, and it was made by Albert Vaicona himself."

"There's a second Regent, Arturo Bonatelli. He's supposed to be on vacation. Can Vaicona make appointments by himself?"

"Yes, but the Grand Council has to approve."

"And the Grand Council approved a *mafioso*?"

John shook his head. "Even if what you say is true, why would anybody want to take over San Marino? Our country is a joke to most people."

"I don't know. But I'm convinced that the brains behind it is a man by the name of Victor Fordamp. The circus comes into it somewhere, but I don't know how. It doesn't make any sense for a man like Fordamp to take over San Marino just to give your police chief a place to hide. Petrocelli is a big gun, but I don't think he rates a whole country. In any case, the big question is why your government is going along with it."

"That's assuming this whole plot isn't in your imagination."

"A man was killed while he was talking to me over the telephone, from here, asking for my help. That wasn't my imagination."

John mulled it over, then frowned. "We will have to fight."

"A lot of people could be killed."

Marinello flushed. "We are not cowards."

"Of course not. But I hope you're not fools either. Fordamp and his men probably have enough firepower to outfit a battalion. They haven't used it because they haven't had to. That doesn't mean that they won't start firing if they're pressed. You can't fight bullets with your bare hands. How many guns do you have in San Marino?"

"We have a few hunters with rifles. And the police have their pistols."

"The men I've seen would eat you for breakfast, and all the police are playing follow the leader to Fordamp's men. Somebody has to go for the Italian authorities. It's risky, but not that bad. I got up here by walking through a vineyard. There's no reason someone can't go down the same way."

"I'll gladly do that."

"Not yet. We'll need more to go on than my suspicions. With the way things are in the world today, the Italian government probably won't be too anxious to send troops up the mountain unless we can prove there's a good reason."

John's eyes were cloudy with barely controlled anger. "I will take this man Petrocelli myself. And Fordamp."

"And you'll get yourself killed. You sit tight until you hear from me."

"Where are you going?"

"To look for something to back us up."

· · ·

I slipped back onto the circus grounds and headed for Nell's trailer. The door was slightly ajar. I knocked on it three times.

"Run, Mongo! They're waiting—"

Nell's voice was cut off by the obscene sound of metal striking flesh. I heard Nell groan, then the sound of a man cursing and running toward the door. I crouched down, my back against the trailer, and waited for him. The door burst open and I caught a quick glimpse of Nell huddled by the door, her hand pressed to a deep gash on her cheek where the man standing above me had pistol-whipped her. Nell's beard was matted with blood.

Marshmallow Mouth started down the three steps leading to the ground. I caught him on the second step, grabbing his left ankle and lifting it. The somersault he executed wouldn't have won many diving points, but it looked beautiful to me. Marshmallow Mouth flipped and landed on his back with a delightful smack as the breath went out of him. The automatic pistol he was holding popped out of his hand and landed harmlessly a few feet away.

He was helpless, his eyes glazed, so I didn't follow up with

90

anything fancy; I stepped forward and kicked him in the jaw hard enough to put him on a liquid diet for about three months. The remaining lights in his eyes clicked out.

I picked up the gun and turned to go into the trailer. I froze in a crouch as three men emerged from around the side. The tallest one had hawklike features and bright, cocaine eyes. He was wearing a four-hundred-dollar sharkskin suit that clashed with the dusty circus grounds and the bulky vest he wore beneath it. The two men on either side were wearing guns, both of which were pointed at me.

"Drop your gun, Dr. Frederickson," Fordamp said. "You have a reputation for speed and cleverness. I assure you that my men will not underestimate you. If you even breathe funny you will be shot full of holes."

"And have the whole circus down on your neck?"

Fordamp didn't blink an eye. "Perhaps. But you will be dead. It will be an unfortunate situation for both of us."

I dropped the gun and straightened up. The two gunmen flanked me. I kept my eyes on Fordamp. The expression on his face might have been a grin.

"Dr. Robert Frederickson," Fordamp said in the tone of voice of a man who was about to give a lecture. "Mongo the Magnificent, famous circus headliner, college professor, criminologist, private detective *extraordinaire*."

"You have good sources."

"Of course. A businessman can never know too much about those who might stand in his way. I don't suppose you've come to ask for your job back?"

"I'm here to find out why my partner sold my half of the circus out from under me."

Fordamp smiled again. "How much would you consider taking for your half of the business?"

"I'm not in the mood to sell out. I'd as soon stay partners with you. My guess is that this circus is suddenly going to start making a lot more money that it has been. What's the deal, Fordamp? What do you want with a circus?"

Fordamp made a clucking sound with his tongue. "That's a disappointing ploy coming from someone with your reputation, Dr. Frederickson. I've seen the ownership papers, so I know that you do not own any part of the circus. Still, you are here. My guess is that you've come to interfere in my affairs."

"Why did you kill Roscoe, Fordamp?"

Fordamp absently touched the rectangular bulge in his vest, but said nothing.

"Where's Statler? Did you kill him, too?"

This time I got a reply of sorts; another clucking sound from Fordamp, and a gun barrel on the top of the head from one of Fordamp's goons who had slipped behind me. The pain shot like a lightning bolt from the top of my head to my toes. The ground opened up beneath me, then closed over my head.

•   •   •

I clawed my way back up the sides of a hole that smelled like ether, crawled over the edge, and found myself propped up against a stone wall, staring into the grizzled face of Phil Statler. He had a dead cigar in a mouth framed by a stubble of steel-gray beard that had managed to foil every technological advance in razor blades. He had a look in his pale eyes that he usually reserved for sick elephants. I grinned.

"Hey, Phil, how's business?"

"Mongo," Phil growled, "you turn up in the damndest places."

"I got a call from Roscoe; he said there was trouble, so I flew over. You can see how much help I've been."

Phil made a sound deep in his throat. "If I ever get out of here I'm going to kill a few sons-of-bitches," he said evenly. He might have been talking about buying a new car.

"Phil, Roscoe's dead."

Something passed over Phil's face. He rose slowly and turned away, but not before I caught the glint of tears in his eyes.

Now I could see the rest of the room; it bore a close resemblance to a dungeon. There was a single window with a clear view of nothing but sky, which explained why it was unbarred.

The man standing next to the window had the soft, handsome features of a San Marinese. He had a good deal of stubble on his face, but his dress was still impeccable. He still wore a suit jacket, and his tie was neatly knotted. His gaze was a mixture of curiosity and dignity in the midst of adversity; the whole impression added up to a man used to holding public office.

"Arturo Bonatelli, I presume?"

The man smiled. "*Ciao,*" he said, then added in English: "Pleased to meet you."

Phil eyed the two of us. "You two know each other?"

"Only by reputation," I said. "This is a strange place to take a vacation, Mr. Bonatelli."

Bonatelli grinned wryly. "Is that what they say?"

"That's what they say." I grimaced against the pain, rose and shook Bonatelli's hand. "I'm Robert Frederickson, Mr. Bonatelli. What's happening here?"

Anger glinted in Bonatelli's eyes. The emotion seemed out of place on his features, like an ink smear on a fine painting. "A man is trying to take over my country."

"I know that. Fordamp. Why?"

"I think he intends to turn it into a sanctuary for international criminals."

Things were beginning to fall into place; I kicked myself for not thinking of it earlier.

"Fordamp told us that he only wanted to use San Marino for a little while," Bonatelli continued, "long enough to make plans for getting Luciano Petrocelli out of Europe. Petrocelli has paid Fordamp a lot of money. But if it works once, why should it not work many times?"

"That's why you're here?"

"Yes."

"What about the circus?" Phil said. "There ain't no money in the circus."

"The circus is his transportation vehicle," I said. "Hiding a man in San Marino is one thing; getting him in and out is something else again. It won't work forever, but it will work long enough to make Fordamp a tidy profit. At least Fordamp thinks so." I turned to Bonatelli. "Why didn't the others resist?"

"It isn't because they are cowards," the Regent said quickly. "It is because they fear for their country, and I did not agree with them on which was the best way to meet the threat. You see, despite the plastic souvenirs, San Marino itself is an authentic medieval treasure house. Most of the buildings are irreplaceable,

93

and they contain countless art masterpieces. Without our churches, our art and our castles, we would be nothing more than a joke on a mountain.

"In addition, tourists would no longer come, and our economy would be crippled. Victor Fordamp has placed dynamite charges in many of our buildings, including the castles. He carries an electronic detonator in a vest that he wears, and he has threatened to blow up everything we hold dear if we resist. If you've met him, you know that he always has two armed guards with him. It is impossible to take him by surprise."

Bonatelli was flushed with anger, pacing back and forth in front of the window. "I, too, love everything that is San Marino," he continued. "But I do not believe we can allow ourselves to be blackmailed. Besides, I think Fordamp will blow up everything when he is finished with us anyway; such men cannot abide beauty. I argued that we had to find a way to resist. My opposition was reported to Fordamp, and I was locked up here with Mr. Statler, who refused to sell his circus."

I nodded and walked over to the window. As I'd suspected, we were locked up in one of the castles. I leaned out the window and looked down; the tops of a grove of pine trees were a hundred feet below. As I watched, a thrush winged her way to a nest built in the crevices between the stones that comprised the tower. I tried not to think of the fact that we were sitting on a charge of dynamite that could probably blow us all over the mountainside.

"Why do you suppose they haven't killed the two of you?"

"I'm not sure," Bonatelli said.

"I'm thinking he hasn't gotten around to it," Phil said around his cigar. "Besides, having us locked up here gives him a little added insurance in case he has to start threatening again."

I turned back to Phil and the Regent. "Assuming one of us could get out of here, what do you think would happen to the other two?"

Phil shrugged. "Things could get hairy, I suppose, but it would still be better to have one of us on the outside with a shot at Fordamp. As it is, we're simply sitting here waiting for the place to blow."

"That's obvious," Bonatelli said. There was a trace of impatience in his voice. "But the discussion is academic."

94

Phil removed the cigar from his mouth and spat into a corner. "Nothing's academic with Mongo."

"The door is two feet thick, and it's bolted. We are more than a hundred feet off the ground. How—"

"I think I can get out of here," I said. "Down the wall. But I'll be wasting my time unless there's some way I can convince the Italian authorities that we need them. Mr. Bonatelli, do you have anything I could show them as proof that I've been in contact with you?"

"I have my Regent's ring," Bonatelli said. "They would recognize that, I suppose, but you couldn't possibly climb down that wall. You'd fall to your death."

"He might make it," Phil said, eyeing me. He sounded as if he might be auditioning new talent. "I've seen him do even more amazing things in his act."

"Act?"

"Forget it," I said curtly. "Mr. Bonatelli, may I have your ring?"

The Regent slipped a gold, crested ring off his right hand and handed it to me. His hand trembled, and he had the air of an inexperienced prison warden giving a condemned man his last meal. I put the ring in my pocket, went to the window and climbed out.

Balance and timing, two skills that I had once had in abundance, were essential for the descent I planned to make; I hoped they hadn't atrophied in the five years I'd spent away from the circus.

A cold breeze was blowing off the top of the mountain, drying the rivulets of sweat that had already broken out on my body. I kept my head level, staring straight ahead at the niches in the rocks where I gripped with my fingers as I groped below me with my feet for the next toehold. Finding it, I would brace, then bring one hand down the wall until I found another handhold.

The thrush exploded in a whir of wings somewhere below and to my right. My peripheral vision caught the faces of Phil and Bonatelli at the window above me; Bonatelli was bone white, his mouth gaping open as if the air at the top of the castle was too thin for him; Phil had the calmer expression of a man who has lived with the risks of death and maiming for a long time.

"Take it easy, Mongo," Phil growled softly. "There ain't no net under you."

"Wait until you get my bill for this exercise," I said without looking up. "I'll be able to buy a dozen nets, all fine-spun gold."

"You got a blank check, Mongo. A blank check. Just don't forget that I don't owe you nothin' if you get killed."

I cut the banter short; I was going to need my breath. I was barely a quarter of the way down and already the pain was spreading from the small of my back, around my rib cage through my arms and fingers, numbing them. I'd gashed my right hand, and the blood was welling between my fingers.

Despite the risks of slipping, I was going to have to speed my descent. Otherwise, I was going to run out of strength long before I reached the bottom, which meant that there'd be a neat, dwarf-sized hole at the base of a castle in San Marino.

I started taking chances, accepting toeholds that felt spongy, digging my fingers into dusty pockets in the wall that could give way as soon as I touched them. One did, and for a few brief moments that felt like years I found myself dangling by one hand that had no feeling.

Phil's soft oath wafted down to me. I kept my eyes level, sucked in my breath, and swung back again. My other hand found a grip and my feet found solid footing. The muscles in my belly crawled, as if reaching out by themselves in an attempt to grasp the smooth rocks on the face of the wall. I didn't want to move; I wanted to stay there until all the feeling left and I dropped. I convinced myself that that wasn't positive thinking; I forced myself to calm down and continue groping. Then I could see the tops of trees out of the corner of my eye. I scurried down another twenty feet and fell the rest of the way, banging into the ground with a force that momentarily dazed me.

I half expected to hear a chorus of boos from some circus gallery. All I got was the croaking of a frog in the forest behind me. I shook my head to clear it, then took a quick mental inventory and decided nothing was broken.

I glanced up toward the window. Bonatelli might have been a dead man; he was in exactly the same position—with the same expression on his face—that he'd been in when I'd gone over the window ledge. Phil was standing with his hands clasped over his head.

I got to my feet and slipped into the forest.

It was a clear day, and I could see Italy below me, through breaks in the trees. I needed a messenger. It was only a matter of a few hours before Fordamp would discover that I was missing, and things would start to come apart. On the positive side, Fordamp obviously didn't feel that secure of his position, or he wouldn't have felt the need to cut off the telephones and seal the country.

Regardless of what I did or didn't do, the fact that I had escaped from the castle would increase the pressure on Fordamp. I decided that I'd have to risk upping the ante some more, and hope that things in San Marino wouldn't start exploding.

That decision was given added urgency by a discovery I made in a small glen a few yards in from the tree line. Whoever had shot Danny Lemongello hadn't even bothered to dig a hole for him. Apparently Fordamp had found out that Danny had talked to me; more probably, the boy simply knew too much. Whatever the reason, Danny's body lay sprawled on the grass. His glazed eyes were crossed, as if trying to see into the hole someone had put in the center of his forehead.

•   •   •

Petrocelli didn't look exactly overjoyed to see me. His jaw dropped open when I walked into the police station. He was still fumbling for his gun when I hit him on the side of the head with the heavy glass ashtray he kept on his desk. He slumped forward and his face smacked into the desk top with the satisfying sound of cracking egg shells. I took his keys and went back into the cell block.

Jandor was standing, gripping the bars of his cell, when I came through the connecting door. His eyes widened. He'd put on some weight since I'd last seen him, and it all looked like muscle. He was a broad-shouldered man with surgeon's hands that could flick a blade of steel and shave a rose petal at fifty feet.

"Mongo!"

I grinned and unlocked the cell door. "Exercise time, Jandor."

"What?"

"No time now to tell you how I got here, Jandor. We've got a lot of work to do, and not much time to do it in."

I opened the door of the cell. Jandor didn't move. He seemed dazed; he stared at the open space between us as if it was a barrier he couldn't ever cross.

"You must know about Roscoe and my knife in his neck. How do you know I didn't kill him?"

"I've got a better suspect."

"Petrocelli killed him," Jandor said defensively.

"How do you know?"

"He bragged about it. He thought it was a big joke that I should be locked up for a crime the chief of police committed."

I nodded grimly. "Let's get him into the cell. The walls are pretty thick, and it will probably be a time before anybody comes looking for him."

Jandor went into the office, then dragged Petrocelli back to the cell. Then he paused and looked at me.

"I'd like to hurt him," Jandor said quietly.

"Be my guest."

In one single, fluid motion, Jandor picked the unconscious Petrocelli up and flung him toward the steel bunk at the back of the cell. Petrocelli hit the bunk with the full force of his weight on his right shoulder. I heard it snap. He was going to have some more pain when he woke up. I locked the cell and connecting doors, then motioned Jandor out the back of the jail, into an alley.

I filled Jandor in on what was happening, then gave him the Regent's ring and instructions on what to do with it. Jandor nodded and started off down the hill, into the forest. I headed in the opposite direction, toward the town.

I knocked lightly at the back door of the Marinello's souvenir shop. Molly, her front draped with a spaghetti-splashed apron, came to the door; the apron reminded me that I hadn't eaten anything in close to twenty-four hours. Molly opened the door, but her welcoming smile faded when she saw the expression on my face.

"I have to talk to John, Molly, and I'd like you to hear what I have to say."

Molly, sensing trouble, hesitated a moment, but finally went to the front of the shop to get her husband. I was glad to see that

John Marinello was clear-eyed. We sat around a small table while I told him what had happened to their country.

Molly's face grew progressively sadder and more tense, but she didn't interrupt. John's breathing grew short and sharp. I finished quickly, then paused, searching for my next words.

"I know I have no right to ask you this," I said to both of them, "but I need John's help. Fordamp's trump card is the explosive charges he's planted in the castles and churches. If we take those away from him, he's relatively powerless. Also, it means that he won't be able to blow up your Regent and a friend of mine."

"Why John?" Molly's voice was barely a whisper.

"John said that he used to be a construction worker, specializing in stonemasonry. My guess is that he knows something about explosives."

"I do," John said evenly.

Molly gripped her husband's arm. "The charges could blow up in your face."

"Yes," I said quietly.

John abruptly stood up. "Let's go, Mr. Frederickson. We're wasting time."

I waited, watching Molly. Her answer surprised me. "You go, John. Mr. Frederickson is right; we must fight."

Marinello and I headed for the door. Molly's voice came after us, her words incongruous yet somehow reassuring. "I'll keep your dinner warm, John."

According to John Marinello, finding the explosives wasn't going to be as difficult as I'd first expected. Assuming that the explosive charges had been placed by an expert, they would be found near the architectural centers of the buildings, where they would do the most damage. It came down to a matter of second-guessing the person who had originally planted the charges.

For practice, we started with the most secluded spot we could find: St. Francesco's Church, built in the fourteenth century. John outlined the search procedure he wanted to follow. He cautioned me for the tenth time not to touch anything I might find, then we split up.

Forty-five minutes later John found one of the charges. I rounded the corner of the church and saw him kneeling tensely beside a niche in the foundation wall, near the ground. He glimpsed me out of the corner of his eye and raised his hand, signaling me to stop. Then he reached inside the niche and slowly withdrew a bundle consisting of five sticks of dynamite lashed together. On top of the bundle was a small metal cannister that resembled a miniature soup can with the label torn off.

John set the dynamite gently down on the ground, then motioned me closer. He was shaking his head.

"There's the first charge," John said. "My guess is that there's another one in the same spot on the other side of the building. We'll have to keep looking."

I glanced at my watch. "It's taking too much time. With some luck, Jandor should be back with the Italian authorities in another hour or so. When that happens, I don't want Fordamp to have the option of blowing the place up."

"There's no way to go any faster," John said. "I'm sorry." He didn't have to add that St. Francesco's Church was only one of dozens of potential targets, not including the three castles.

I pointed to the cannister. "That's the ignition device?"

John nodded. "Radio controlled. Fordamp must have the transmitter with him."

"He does. Is there any way we can jam the frequency?"

"We don't have the equipment."

"Can he set them off one at a time?"

John studied the cannister. "I doubt it. I'd say they're set to go off all at once."

It seemed to fit Fordamp's disposition. If he couldn't get what he wanted, he'd leave everything of value in San Marino in ruins.

"How do you disarm it?"

John reached down and unsnapped the cannister from a magnetic clamping device. It seemed simple enough.

"Is there enough there to blow up a castle?"

"Fordamp will have more there."

"Okay. I've got to go to the castles. I've got a friend in one of them."

"I'll go with you," John said, rising to his feet. "A man's life is the most important thing."

I heard a noise behind me and wheeled. Marshmallow Mouth

and another one of Fordamp's men were standing a few feet away, their guns trained on us.

I decided I'd rather die running than propped up against a tree. I made a gesture of resignation, then made as if to toss the dynamite at them.

They reacted as I'd hoped, instinctively stepping backward and throwing their hands up to their faces. I grabbed the detonator away from John, then leaped to one side and sprinted toward the corner of the building. A gun barked three times and bullets ricocheted off the stone, peppering my face with sharp chunks of rock. But there was no cry of pain from behind me, which meant that at least John had had the good sense to stay put. I made it around the corner of the church and sprinted down an alley.

I had the dynamite and the detonator, but they made an unlikely weapon, one that I couldn't even control. Still, it was all I had. I tucked the dynamite under my arm, put the cannister in my pocket, then headed at a trot toward the castle where Phil and the regent were imprisoned. I had to make one last-ditch effort at getting them out.

A moment later I heard my name in English. It was amplified over a loudspeaker."

"Frederickson! It's all over now! Come here! We have your friends!"

·   ·   ·

The sound was coming from the direction of the circus grounds. A few San Marinese stopped and stared around, then moved on. Those who did understand English probably assumed that the words had something to do with circus business.

The message came at me again. More insistent.

I made my way across the town to the high ridge overlooking the field and crouched down in the tall grass. The scene below wasn't encouraging.

Fordamp, flanked by his bodyguards, was standing in the middle of the field. John Marinello had a gun pointed at his gut. Jandor was there, too, his hands tied behind his back. There wasn't going to be any last-minute cavalry charge; I was on my own, and things weren't looking up.

A few San Marinese, attracted by the loudspeaker, appeared on the ridge across from me. They were quickly shooed away by guilty-looking members of the San Marinese police force. Occasionally the men paused and cast glances at a well-dressed San Marinese whom I took to be Alberto Vaicona. Vaicona stood with his head bowed. The police kept dispersing the onlookers.

However, there were a few spectators who weren't so easily scattered. The circus people were coming out of their trailers and gathering in a knot at the western edge of the field. Big Nell was in their midst, moving around and whispering urgently. At a signal from Fordamp, the guards moved toward the circus people, guns drawn. Nell signaled and the circus people moved—but not away, and not in the direction Fordamp had intended; they began to quickly fan out. In a few moments Fordamp and the others were encircled.

Once again the police seemed uncertain of how to react; it was obvious where their sympathies lay, but it was even more obvious where the power lay. Fordamp, keeping an anxious eye on the circle, reached inside his vest and withdrew the transmitter. The device was about the size of a carton of cigarettes, with a red button in the center. Vaicona paled. The Regent walked quickly up to the policemen and spoke to them. Their guns rose.

I glanced over my shoulder at one of the three castles rising into the sky; all that stood between two men and eternity was one man's shaking hand. One push of that red button and the castle would come crumbling to the ground.

The valley below suddenly smelled of death; the tension was building to a peak. Sooner or later someone was going to make a move, and bullets would fly. The button would be pressed. Fordamp was betting everything he had on the one last card he held in his hand, and I couldn't afford to call.

I pulled a few strands of long grass out of the ground and twisted them into a rope of sorts. I replaced the detonator on the dynamite, then lashed the whole package to my belt, at my back, just beneath my shirt. Then, trying not to think of what would happen if Fordamp pushed the button, I stood up and immediately raised my hands in the air.

Even from that distance I could see Fordamp's satisfied grin. He put the transmitter back into his vest, then motioned for me to come down.

Dozens of eyes watched me as I worked my way down the slope. I moved through the circle and heard my name whispered. Big Nell was watching me with wet eyes; I smiled at her and pressed on through.

I moved toward Fordamp, who raised his hand in a signal for me to stop. I stopped. He whispered something to a seemingly indestructable Petrocelli who grinned through his smashed jaw and reached inside the sling on his arm to produce a gun. I had the distinct impression that my death warrant had been issued.

Petrocelli stepped forward, his eyes swimming with hate, and waved his gun toward a grove of trees behind him. It was time to make a move, any move.

I walked forward until I was abreast of Fordamp, then lunged sideways into the man. I locked my fingers around his belt with one hand and struggled to untie the dynamite from my belt with the other.

Fordamp gave me a startled look, then lifted me off the ground and shook me like a rag doll, trying to break my grip.

The ring of circus people was closing in, led by Nell. Petrocelli fired a shot into the air, and they stopped. All except Nell. She walked forward three more steps.

"You can't shoot us all!" Nell shouted at Petrocelli. Then she turned around to face the circle. "If we don't stop them, they're going to kill Mongo!"

Petrocelli got a shot off and Nell spun, grabbing her right shoulder, falling to the ground. Blood spurted from the wound, but she rolled over and started to get up. Petrocelli advanced on her, his gun pointed at her head. He froze when the guns of the San Marinese policemen swung on him.

Fordamp seemed to have forgotten that I was still clinging to his belt. He quickly reached into his vest and withdrew the transmitter again.

"Stop!" Fordamp called in a voice that was none too steady. "Stop instantly, or I'll push the button!"

By then I'd had enough time to untie the bundle of dynamite. I let go of Fordamp's belt, then brought the dynamite around and stuffed it into the bulge of his stomach, something like a quarterback trying to hand a football to a reluctant halfback. Fordamp looked down at his belly and gagged.

103

"You push that button and you end up jelly," I said with a smile.

Fordamp's lips moved; finally sound came. "You'll blow yourself up, too, you fool."

"Getting shot, getting blown up; it's all the same to me, buster. This gives me much more satisfaction." I paused a few moments to let his imagination ponder the problem, then I said, "It's all over, Fordamp. Put the transmitter down on the ground."

Fordamp swallowed hard, then carefully placed the transmitter at his feet. Now it was Petrocelli who thought he saw his ticket out. He let out a cry and leaped toward the box. The policeman's bullet caught him in mid-air, slicing in beneath his shoulder blade and puncturing his heart. I reached down and scooped up the transmitter before Petrocelli's body landed on the spot where it had been.

One of the policeman had cut Jandor's hands free. I walked over and handed the transmitter to him. "Why don't you get this to a safe place?"

"Will do, Mongo. I'm sorry I couldn't make it to—"

"Forget it." I turned to John. "Can you disarm this thing?"

John Marinello nodded. "I think so."

They started off toward the haven of the forest. I turned back toward the center of the field. Vaicona was still standing in the same spot, his shoulders slumped, staring at the ground. I suddenly felt sorry for him; he had only done what he felt was necessary to preserve his country's treasures. Others had disagreed, and now Vaicona had been made to look like a fool, if not a traitor.

I suspected his political career was over.

Big Nell was being attended to. The police had herded all of Fordamp's gorillas into a tight knot and were guarding them; two men were dragging Petrocelli's body away.

Fordamp was still staring at his belly, apparently dazed, which may have explained why he wasn't being guarded. But Fordamp wasn't through yet; his eyes rose and settled on me.

"You!" Fordamp screamed, his eyes seething. "I'll kill you!"

He reached into his vest and came up with a .38. The barrel came around and stopped in a line with my forehead. I stood still and stared.

I was too far away to do anything about it.

Jandor wasn't. He had turned at the sound of Fordamp's voice and sized up the situation in an instant. His hand flew up, disappeared for a moment behind his head, then came forward in a blur of speed.

Fordamp's eyes widened; the gun dropped from his fingers as he reached up and tried desperately to pull the knife out of his throat. A moment later he slumped to the ground, dead.

The valley was suddenly very still. An army of curious faces had begun to appear on the ridge. I stooped down and searched through Fordamp's pockets until I found a ring of keys. Then I turned and walked toward the castle on the hilltop in the distance.

Here's another piece about the attempts of unscrupulous people to manipulate behavior, and Mongo's absolute insistence on carrying on the constant struggle to be the master of his own fate. Perhaps it is also a bit of a meditation on the theme of the "dwarf in all of us." The plot line of this story was incorporated into the novel An Affair of Sorcerers.

Dark Hole on a Silent Planet

Dr. Peter Barnum's craggy, fifty-year-old face was slightly flushed, and I thought I knew why: Barnum didn't like moonlighting college professors or celebrities, and he felt I belonged in both categories. I didn't know how he felt about dwarfs and I didn't care, but I was curious as to what he was doing in my downtown office on a Saturday morning. I took the hand he extended. It felt moist.

"Dr. Frederickson," Barnum said, "do you have a few moments?"

My services not being that much in demand, I invited him to sit down. Barnum perched on the edge of the chair, as if he were waiting for someone to call him to a speaker's platform.

"I'd like to hire you, Dr. Frederickson," Barnum said, rushing. "I mean, as a private detective."

"You didn't have to come down here. You could have seen me at the university."

"I know," he said, waving his hand in the air as though I'd

made a preposterous suggestion. "I prefer it this way. You see, what I have to say must remain in the strictest confidence."

For a change, the air conditioning in the building was working. Still, the few wisps of blond hair that ringed the bald dome of Barnum's head were damp with sweat. A vein throbbed under his ear. I decided to take a little umbrage at his attitude.

"Everything my clients tell me is taken in confidence. It's the way I work."

"But you haven't said whether or not you'll help me."

"You haven't said what it is you want me to help you with. Until you do, I can't commit myself." That wasn't exactly true, but I hoped it would force the issue.

The university president finally passed a hand over his eyes as if trying to erase a bad vision, then leaned back in the chair. "I'm sorry," he said after a few moments. "I've been rude. I didn't want to risk having us seen talking to each other at great length at the university. It might have seemed strange."

"Strange to whom?"

Slowly, Barnum raised his eyes to mine. "I would like you to investigate one of your colleagues, Dr. Vincent Smathers."

I let out a low, mental whistle. I was beginning to understand Barnum's penchant for secrecy. Vincent Smathers was the university's most recent prize catch, an experimental psychologist who was a Nobel Prize winner. University presidents don't normally make a habit of investigating their Nobel Prize winners. The usual procedure is to create a specially endowed $100,000 chair, which was what had been done for Smathers.

"What's the problem?"

Barnum shrugged his shoulders. "I don't know," he said at last. "Perhaps I'm being overly suspicious."

"Suspicious about what?"

"Dr. Smathers brought with him an assistant, Dr. Chiang Kee. Dr. Kee, in turn, brought two assistants with him, also Chinese. Quite frankly, those two men don't look like people with university backgrounds."

"Neither do I."

Barnum flushed. "I suppose you're implying—"

"I'm not implying anything," I said. I was feeling a little abrasive. "I'm saying that you, better than anybody else, should

107

know that you can't judge a man by his looks. I'm sure Smathers knows what he's doing. I just don't want you to waste the university's money."

Barnum thought about that for a moment. "I suppose I am on edge," he said distantly. "Ever since they found that man's body on the campus—"

"I have a brother who's a detective in the New York Police Department, so I'm able to keep track of these things. Nobody has accused anybody at the university of killing him, if that's what you're worried about. He was fresh off the Bowery."

"Yes, but there's still the question of what a Bowery derelict was doing on the campus."

"This is New York," I said, as if that explained everything. "Do you think there's some connection between Smathers and the killing?"

"Oh, *no!*" Barnum said quickly. "But the university has come under increasing scrutiny, simply because the body was found there. I have to make sure that everything . . . appears as it should."

"Besides the Chinese, what else doesn't appear as it should?"

Barnum took a deep breath. "There is the matter of the hundred-thousand-dollar yearly endowment Dr. Smathers receives for the academic chair he holds. While it's true that a man of Dr. Smathers' proven administrative abilities is not normally expected to—"

He was filibustering against his own thoughts. I cut him short. "You don't know what's happening to the money."

Barnum looked relieved. "That's right," he said. The rest seemed to come easier. "I believe you know Mr. Haley in the English Department?"

I said I did. Fred Haley and I had shared a few cups of coffee together.

"Mr. Haley swears to me that he's seen Dr. Kee before, in Korea. As you probably know, Mr. Haley was a POW. He tells me that Dr. Kee—who was using a different name then—was an enemy interrogator, in charge of the brainwashing program to which all of the POWs were subjected. He had a reputation for brutality, psychological and physical."

I mulled that over in my mind. Fred Haley was not a man

given to wild accusations. At least he was no more paranoid than anybody else who has to live and/or work in New York.

"It wouldn't be the first time a former enemy had come to work in the United States," I said. "Often it works to our benefit, as in the case of Von Braun. He changed his name to keep people from rattling the skeletons in his closet. It's possible everything's on the up-and-up."

"Yes, it's possible. But since the good name of the university is involved, don't you feel it's worth some investigation?"

I said I thought it was. We discussed the mundane subject of fees and I told him I'd look into it.

•   •   •

I checked into my university office, did some paperwork, then locked up and headed across the campus toward Marten Hall, an older building which houses the Psychology Department.

It soon became apparent that one doesn't just walk in and strike up a conversation with a Nobel Prize winner; Smathers' security system would have shamed the nearest missile-tracking base. His first line of defense was his secretary, a 250-pound, hawk-faced woman who had somehow escaped the last pro football draft. The nameplate on her desk said Mrs. Pfatt. It really did.

She stopped torturing her typewriter long enough for me to introduce myself as one of Smathers' university colleagues, a criminologist who wanted to consult with Dr. Smathers on a question of criminal psychology, if you please.

I was told Dr. Smathers had no time for consultations. The typewriter groaned and clacked.

"In that case, perhaps I could speak with Dr. Kee."

I was told Dr. Kee had no time for consultations.

I left Mrs. Pfatt and walked down a long corridor lined on both sides with classrooms. A few undergraduate classes were in session, filled with sleepy-looking freshmen. Everything looked distressingly in order. Most of the students in the building recognized me and waved. I smiled and waved back.

Marten Hall has four floors, and I assumed Smathers had his private offices and research labs on the top one. I worked my way up the floors as casually as possible. The third floor was mostly offices and laboratories sparsely populated on a Saturday morning with a few graduate researchers. I headed toward the stairway at the end of the corridor, stopped and stared. Somebody had installed a heavy steel door across the entrance to the stairs. NO ADMITTANCE—AUTHORIZED PERSONNEL ONLY was stenciled in red paint across the door.

Less money should have been spent on material and more on the lock; I got out my set of skeleton keys and hit on the third try. I pushed the door open. A narrow flight of stairs snaked up and twisted to the left, out of sight. I was beginning to understand where much of the first year's $100,000 had gone; the inside of the door, as well as the walls and ceiling of the staircase, had been soundproofed. It seemed a curious expense for a Psychology Department; mental processes just don't make that much noise.

I climbed the stairs and found myself at the end of a long corridor, expensively refinished with glassed-in offices on one side and closed doors on the other. I pushed one of the doors and it swung open. I stepped in, closed the door behind me and turned on the lights.

It was a laboratory, large, heavily soundproofed. There was an array of monitoring machines, computers and other sophisticated equipment lined up against the walls. All had wires leading to a large, water-filled tank in one corner of the lab. The tank looked like an aquarium designed to hold a baby whale. It was at least ten feet long, three feet wide and four feet deep. Electrode nodes were built into the glass walls of the tank, along with black rubber straps that now floated on the surface.

I poked around the machines for a while, but couldn't figure out what they were supposed to do. I turned off the lights, went out of the lab and walked quietly down the corridor, glancing in the other rooms with the closed doors. They were all labs, similar to the one in which I had been. The offices on my left were all empty—except for the last one.

The Chinese caught me out of the corner of his eye. He was the original Captain Flash, out of his chair and standing in front of me in a lot less time than it would have taken Superman to find a phone booth. I should have listened to Barnum's sermonette on first impressions; the man in front of me looked like a refugee from some tong war. Somebody had tried to use his head as a whetstone; the whole right side of his face was a sheet of white, rippled scar tissue. The right eye was stitched shut, unseeing, but the other eye was perfectly good, and it was obvious that he had all the moves. He was crouched now, perfectly balanced on the balls of his feet, his calloused hands rigid and extended in front of him like knife blades.

I smiled and gave him a cheery good morning. He must have taken it as a Chinese insult, or maybe he just didn't like dwarfs. He grabbed my right shoulder and threw me over his hip. I bounced off the wall and fell to the floor, where I stayed, eyes half-closed, watching him. He came forward in the same crouch, his hands in front of him. This guy could kill.

I waited until he was just above me, then snapped my left leg out, catching him on the side of the knee with the instep of my shoe. The joint snapped. His eyes flecked with pain and he toppled backward. He didn't stay down for long. Somehow he managed to get up on his one good leg and, dragging the smashed one behind him, he came toward me.

The karate had surprised him, but that was finished. I had a black belt, but so, obviously, did he. This time he meant to kill.

His arm darted out like a snake's tongue, the deadly knuckle of his middle finger aiming for my forehead. An ear-splitting scream deafened me as I ducked. The missile that was his hand went over my head and smashed into the wall behind me. I came up with my head into his solar plexus. He grunted as he rose into the air, then screamed when he came down on the bad leg. He crumpled over on his side.

The man was finished, staring up at me with hatred and unspeakable pain forming a second skin over his eye. I suddenly felt sick to my stomach. I went back down the stairs and headed for my office.

It didn't take Smathers long to get there. He burst through the office door, long brown hair flowing behind him, his face the color of chalk. He barely managed to bring himself to a halt in front of my desk. He stood there, trembling with rage, literally speechless. A tall, thin man with pale, exhausted eyes, he leaned on the desk and finally managed to speak.

"What were you doing in my private laboratories?"

"I got lost looking for the men's room."

111

Smathers' rage was probably more justified than my sarcasm, but he looked fairly ridiculous. His tongue worked its way back and forth across his lips. "You, sir, are a liar!"

"Okay, Dr. Smathers," I said testily. "The reason is quite simple. I was looking for you or Dr. Kee. I wanted to consult on a professional matter."

"My secretary told you that neither Dr. Kee nor I have time for such matters."

"I don't like doing business through other people's secretaries."

"The door to the laboratories was locked!"

"Not when I got there, it wasn't," I lied. "Talk to your keeper of the keys; the door was open when I walked by, so I just went up. The next thing I knew I was face to face with Fu Manchu."

"Do you realize that that man may never walk properly again?"

"He was trying to kill me. If you or your associates want to press charges, go ahead. We'll take it up with the president. Barnum might like to find out what's so important to you that you feel the need to keep it locked behind two inches of steel."

That backed him up. He took his hands off the top of my desk and straightened up, making a conscious effort to control himself. "I don't think there's any need for that," he said. "We're both professionals. I have no desire to get you into trouble and, quite frankly, I can't spare the time from my work that bringing charges against you would entail."

"Just what would that work be?" I asked casually.

"Surely you can appreciate the fact that I don't care to discuss my private affairs with you."

"Sorry, I was just making conversation. I couldn't help but be curious as to what kind of research requires a human watchdog like the one that came after me."

Smathers made a nervous gesture with his hand. "Quite frankly, Dr. Kee and I are involved in research into some of the more bizarre human mental aberrations. On occasion, we have potentially dangerous people on that floor. Tse Tsu thought you might have been one of them. He overreacted in simply doing his job."

"What are those water tanks for?"

Gates clanged shut behind Smathers' eyes. "You've been spying!"

"Not at all. I just happened to be looking around for you and noticed the tanks. Naturally, I was curious."

"You will not come up there again, Dr. Frederickson."

"Interesting man, this colleague of yours. Did you know that Dr. Kee used to be an officer in the Peoples' Liberation Army in North Korea? I understand he was a brainwashing specialist."

Smathers flushed. "That's slanderous. Who told you this?"

"It's just a rumor. Haven't you heard it?"

"I wouldn't pay any attention to such a story."

"Why not? The war's over."

Smathers was either tired of talking or didn't like the turn the conversation had taken. He gave me a long, hard stare. "Please don't interfere in my affairs anymore, Dr. Frederickson."

I wanted to talk some more, but Smathers had already turned and was walking out of my office. He slammed the door behind him. I picked up the phone and dialed Barnum's office. After running a gauntlet of secretaries, I finally got to hear the Big Man himself.

"This is Frederickson," I said. I considered telling him about the incident—and the laboratories—in Marten Hall, then decided against it. "I have a nagging feeling that you left out parts of the story."

"I can't imagine what you're talking about." Barnum's voice was arch, restrained. I'd hurt his dignity.

"What did Smathers win his Nobel Prize for?"

"He did pioneering work in sensory deprivation. He's the top authority in his field."

"Sensory deprivation; that's artificially taking away all a man's senses—sight, sound, smell, touch, taste?"

"That's correct."

"To what end?"

"No end. That's what the experimentation was all about: to determine the effects. NASA was interested in it for a while because of its possible relation to interplanetary space travel, but they gave it up when it became apparent that it was too dangerous for the volunteers involved."

I remembered Smathers' comment about dangerous people in his laboratories. I'd assumed he'd been making excuses for his

113

Chinese gorilla. Now I wondered; but I wasn't ready to accuse him of anything, at least not yet.

"Where did he come from?"

"Platte Institute. Near Boston."

"I know where it is. How did he come here? Platte takes good care of its prize winners. It's hard for me to believe they wouldn't have matched any offer you made."

I took the long silence at the other end of the line as an answer of sorts, a justification for the nagging itch at the back of my mind.

"There's some question about it, isn't there?" I pressed.

"There's no question that Dr. Smathers is a Nobel Prize winner," Barnum said. He sounded irritated. "They're not exactly a dime a dozen, you know."

"So you don't ask questions when one wants to leave one place and come to another?"

"No," Barnum said after a long pause. "But he came with the highest recommendations."

"I'm sure he did. Now, what you want to know is how you came to get a Nobel Prize winner at what amounts to bargain basement prices."

Again, a long pause, then: "Have you found out anything?"

"I'll get back to you."

.   •   •   •

Barnum was, after all, my client, and I wasn't quite sure why I'd held back on him. Perhaps it was because Smathers was a colleague, and scientists—especially brilliant ones—take enough nonsense from administrators as it is. I *had* been nosing around some very expensive equipment in an area that had clearly been off-limits to me. I wanted to do some more digging before I started telling tales.

I went to the Liberal Arts building and looked around for Fred Haley. I wanted some more information on the other, nonscholarly side of Dr. Kee. It would have to wait; Haley was away for the weekend.

The walk wasn't entirely wasted, as I managed to latch onto Jim Larkin, a former student of mine who was now a graduate fellow in experimental psychology. He accepted my offer of a cup of coffee and we went downstairs to the Student Union. I gradually steered the conversation around to Dr. Vincent Smathers.

"Strange man," Jim said. Coming from him, it was hard to tell whether this was a complaint or a compliment. Probably it was neither. Jim was a young man with an almost fanatic devotion to the notion of live and let live. "All the graduate fellows were assured before he came here that we'd have access to him, that he wouldn't be just a high-priced name for the university to print in its alumni newsletter. However . . ."

"I take it that it didn't work out that way?"

"Smathers showed up at exactly one of our graduate seminars, and that was it."

"Interesting. What do you suppose he does with his time?"

"I haven't the slightest idea," Jim said. A braless co-ed, who shouldn't have been, had entered the cafeteria and was bobbing along the tables. I made a stab at getting Jim's attention back.

"What happens to a man when he undergoes sensory deprivation?"

Jim turned back to me. "That's Dr. Smathers' field."

"I know."

"Well, simply put, he goes out of his mind. To be more precise, his mind goes out of him. You take away all a man's sensory landmarks and he becomes like a baby, with no past, present, or future, at least while he's undergoing the deprivation. He becomes very suggestible."

"You mean he's brainwashed?"

Jim made a face. "That's an old-fashioned term."

"Uh-huh. Is it like brainwashing?"

"I suppose so."

"How do you go about this sensory deprivation?"

"The first thing you need is a controlled medium in which to support the man's body."

"Like water?"

"Yeah, water's good. What are you getting at, Dr. Frederickson?"

"Just curious," I said with a straight face. "What do you think of Smathers' Chinese helpers?"

Jim shrugged noncommittally. "I'll tell you this," he said after

115

some thought, "I think there's some strange business going on in that department."

"What kind of strange business?"

"You heard about that guy who was shot on campus? The old Bowery bum?"

I said I had.

"I saw him in Marten Hall one day. He was walking with one of Dr. Smathers' assistants, one of those Chinese guys."

•　　　•　　　•

Garth, as usual, was chin-deep in paperwork. My brother, all six-feet-plus of him, was sitting behind a desk which might have fit me, merrily clacking away at a typewriter, vintage nineteenth century. His face was grim; his face was always grim when he was doing paperwork. He didn't bother looking up.

"Look what the ants dragged in. What's happening, Mongo?"

"I just wanted to drop in and say hello to my brother."

"You're here to pump information," Garth said evenly. He hit the wrong key and swore.

"There was an old man killed on the university campus a few weeks back. Shot."

Garth frowned. "I don't recall it."

"You probably had fifty murders the same day. In any case, I'd like a look at the file."

"Why?"

"C'mon, Garth. I'm on a fishing expedition."

Garth leaned back in his chair and stared at me. His eyes were hard. "You're beginning to take our relationship for granted, Mongo. This is a police station, a public agency, and you're a private citizen. You can't just walk in here and ask to look at a confidential file." He paused. Something moved behind his eyes. "You got a lead on this thing?"

"I'm groping around in the dark, Garth. Maybe yes, maybe no. I don't want to talk about it, not yet. And I happen to know that that precious file is buried somewhere. The New York Police Department doesn't have time to investigate the death of some Bowery bum. Sure, you did an autopsy because it's required by law in a murder case, but it's never going to be investigated because you just don't have the manpower. It's not going to hurt to let me look at the file."

Garth's eyes flashed and the bald spot on top of his head reddened. "You've got a lot of lip today, brother."

"It's the truth, and you know it. Besides, you owe me a couple. Let me see the file, Garth."

Garth hesitated a moment, then got up and disappeared into another room. He returned a few moments later with the file. I thanked him, but Garth said nothing. He went back to his typing and I went over to a corner with the file.

The dead man's name was Bayard T. Manning, and his only known address had been a flophouse on the Bowery. Everything was covered in three short paragraphs. The most interesting part was the results of the autopsy, covered in the last paragraph. Manning had been a dedicated alcoholic; cirrhosis of the liver had set in years before, and his brain had been just about pickled. The curious thing was that he'd been off the juice for at least a month, according to the pathologist's report. Not a drop. Bone dry. The texture of his skin indicated that he'd spent a great deal of time in water just before his death. He'd been holding a transistor tube in his hand when he was killed.

Also, his eardrums had been punctured.

Some legwork had been done; a cursory investigation of his usual haunts had turned up the fact that he hadn't been seen in a month.

I had a pretty good idea where he'd been.

•   •   •

I put in a restless Sunday reading the *New York Times* and trying to watch the Jets. My file on the case was building, spinning a web around Vincent Smathers. If the web got any tighter, Smathers was going to be eaten by some very nasty spiders, the kind that hatch in a man's mind when he has to spend the rest of his life in prison.

That bothered me. Why should a Nobel Prize winner jeopardize his whole reputation and future by enmeshing himself in a set of circumstances that could destroy him? It was easy to pin any possible blame on the shadowy Kee, but Kee was Smathers' responsibility, assuming a crime had been committed. In fact, I wanted to make very sure I knew what I was talking about before I brought in the police or turned Smathers' future over to a pedantic, professional fund-raiser like Barnum.

I made it to half-time in the ball game, then went to the phone and called Fred Haley's home on the outside chance that he might have returned early. There was no answer. I had nothing better to do, so I drove out to the suburban town where Haley lived. I'd wait for him.

Haley's car was in the driveway of his house. I parked my car behind his, went up the flagstone walk in front of the house and knocked at the door. I waited thirty seconds, then knocked again. There was still no answer.

Something cold crawled up my back. I went around to the back of the house and knocked on that door. I got the same response. I got out my skeleton keys and let myself in.

Fred Haley hadn't gone anywhere that weekend. His body lay on the floor of his study, very stiff with rigor mortis. I guessed he'd been dead at least two days. The odd angle of his head told me he'd died of a broken neck.

I spent the next two hours answering questions, avoiding speculation on possible connections between Haley's death and his knowledge of Chiang Kee's background. It could very well be that Haley had been killed by a burglar he'd surprised. The ransacked house pointed to it—except that Fred Haley, as far as I knew, was no slouch at defending himself; and he was supposed to have left on a Friday afternoon, which was a strange time for a burglar to be prowling around.

That much I told the police. The detective in charge dutifully noted my opinions in his notebook and went about his business; Garth showed up later and backed me into a corner. I got him off my back by promising to come in to see him with everything I knew, after I made one more stop. That didn't do much to pacify him, but it gave me time to catch one of the shuttle flights out of Kennedy Airport to Boston.

I knew it was useless trying to talk to any of the officials at Platte. If they talked to me at all, they'd have nothing but glowing reports for Smathers. That was the way the academic game was played; screw up, and you were asked to resign; resign, and nobody has anything but good things to say about you.

I went to the best source of information I could find, the janitor who worked in the Psychology Department.

•　　•　　•

I landed back at Kennedy at one the next afternoon and got my car out of the parking lot. It was time to report to Garth, and then to Barnum to warn him about the approaching storm. Instead, I put in a call to Garth's office and left a message for him to meet me at my university office in an hour. Then I drove back to the campus and parked in front of Marten Hall.

Mrs. Pfatt was in her usual good form; she looked as though she'd gained weight during her day off. "I told you before that Dr. Smathers does not see visitors."

"He'll see me this time," I said pointedly. "You tell him I just came back from Platte Institute."

Mrs. Pfatt bridled a bit, but she finally called Smathers on the intercom. Her face went through a series of changes as she talked to him. She hung up the phone and stared at me as though I'd just performed a miracle.

"Dr. Smathers will see you, Dr. Frederickson," she said with a new ring of respect in her voice. "He's in his laboratories upstairs. He'd like you to come up."

I went up. The steel door was unlocked. I opened it and went up the soundproofed stairway. Smathers was in the first office. I made a point of checking to make sure that the other offices and labs were empty, then went in to see him.

"You know," he said without looking at me.

"I know that you got pressured to leave Platte because you insisted on performing experiments that had been legally and medically forbidden to you."

"Why are you doing this to me?"

I showed him a photostat of my license. "Besides being a criminology professor, I'm also a private detective. I was hired to investigate you."

"Who hired you?"

"Sorry. I won't tell you that."

The fire in Smathers' eyes went out as quickly as it had flared. "They were fools," he said hollowly. "I'm surrounded by fools.

119

I'm on the verge of a very important discovery—a profound medical breakthrough—and they will not leave me alone."

"You've discovered a cure for the common cold?"

"Don't mock me, Dr. Frederickson. I can cure drug addiction and alcoholism, along with a number of other things that plague modern man."

"You do all this by puncturing a man's eardrums?"

His eyes dropped. "You know about that, too?"

"I can guess that Bayard T. Manning was the subject for some of your experiments. Willingly or unwillingly, I don't know. I do know he ended up dead."

"Manning was paid," Smathers said. "You see, I *have* discovered a cure for alcoholism. Alcoholism, like drug addiction, is primarily a psychological problem, despite the physical changes that take place as a result of dependence. The problem is one of the *mind*. I can literally remake a mind, erase those problems—"

"By erasing his mind."

"That's simplistic! To begin with, the minds of the people I'm talking about have been rendered worthless anyway. These men and women are no good to themselves, or to anyone else. Don't moralize to me!"

"The thought never crossed my mind."

Smathers took a deep breath. "Sensory deprivation, combined with other forms of therapy, can literally destroy a man's craving for drugs and alcohol. It can remove the root psychological causes and make a man or woman whole again, a rational, intelligent human being." He paused, picked up a pencil and began to roll it back and forth between his thumb and forefinger. Guilt was beginning to rise in his voice, like steam from a hot spring. "Manning originally came here of his own accord, in exchange for the money we offered him. Part of our treatment involved sound therapy, the use of certain tones as a therapeutic device. One day while Manning was on the machine he became frightened and touched some controls. The resulting frequencies punctured his eardrums. We would have treated him, but he escaped soon after that. I knew he would probably go to the authorities, so I was getting ready to go myself. When I heard he'd been killed, there didn't seem much point."

"Convenient, wasn't it?"

Smathers' head jerked around. "What does that mean?"

His indignation had the ring of sincerity. I sidestepped. "Did it ever occur to you that the same techniques you use to treat drug addiction could be used to alter a man's political beliefs and behavior?"

"Don't be melodramatic, Frederickson. I'm a scientist, not a politician."

"How did you team up with Dr. Kee?"

"I don't think I have to answer any more of your questions."

"That's right, you don't."

He answered it anyway. "I knew that Dr. Kee had worked for the Chinese Army during the Korean War. That seemed irrelevant now. He is an expert in induced aberrational psychology. He is the only man in the world who knows enough to assist me."

"How did he come to assist you?"

"I was at a conference in Poland and it was made known to me through intermediaries that Kee wished to come to the United States and work with me. I jumped at the chance. He came to me soon after that."

I grunted. "Smathers, your brilliance is matched only by your naïveté." I expected him to get angry, but he didn't. Perhaps it was all coming home to him now; his blind passion for his work had pulled him down a long, very dark passageway, and only now was he beginning to see the ugly things at the end. "I'll bet that a little checking would turn up the fact that Kee is in this country illegally, hiding behind your reputation. He's here brushing up on the latest brainwashing techniques so he can go home and use them on his own people."

"You realize, my work is very important. Perhaps you don't fully understand *how* important."

I gave him the tag line. "I think Kee killed two men."

"Impossible!"

"I think he killed Manning, and I think he killed Fred Haley, an English professor who knew who Kee really was."

Smathers' face suddenly drained of color. "Mr. Haley was here just the other day. I saw him talking to . . ." He let it trail off. "What do you want me to do?"

"I want you to turn yourself in to the authorities before they

121

come after you. My brother is a detective in the New York Police Department. He's waiting for me right now in my office. He doesn't know anything about this yet. You come and tell him your story. Things may end up easier for you."

"Why should you want to help me?"

"Because I respect any man who's been awarded the Nobel Prize. Also, if your work is as important as you say it is, I'd like to see it continued. If it's true that your only crime is being incredibly stupid, perhaps you can rebuild your career when all the debts have been paid."

I hadn't heard a sound, but the sudden jerk of Smathers' head and the look of alarm on his face was warning enough. I half turned in my seat and glimpsed a very large Chinese poised behind me. His eyes were great pools of darkness set in a field of flesh that might have been fine, yellow porcelain. I didn't get that much time to study him; his hand flicked forward and landed on the nape of my neck. Everything went dark . . .

•   •   •

It stayed dark. Something was rapping on the inside of my head, not hard or painfully, but persistently, with a sound like a pencil eraser on soft wood. Then I realized it was only the blood pulsing through my veins. I listened for a few moments, and then it was gone, replaced by a voice.

"Dr. Frederickson. Robert. This is Dr. Kee." The voice came from everywhere and nowhere. It started from somewhere back of my eyes and undulated out, filling my head—or what I thought was my head. There was simply no more *head*, no toes, no fingers, no body. There was only my mind, and I wondered how long that was going to last; all things disappear when you end up in one of Smathers' fish tanks.

"I am your friend," the voice continued. "There has been a very great misunderstanding on your part. That will be corrected. You will learn to love my voice—and then you will learn to love me. My voice will be your only contact with reality, and you will look forward to hearing it. Soon you will pay careful attention to what I have to say."

I waited for more. There wasn't any more. After a while, I wished there were, just as Kee had predicted. I cursed, slowly, methodically. My voice came back to me muffled, as from a great distance.

I tried to visualize myself: I would be floating in one of the tanks, the saline water warmed exactly to body temperature. My arms and legs would be strapped together, loose enough to allow for circulation, but tight enough to restrict any kind of movement. I imagined my head was encased in some kind of black hood into which oxygen was pumped; naturally, the hood had earphones. There were probably tubes stuck in my body through which I was being fed intravenously.

The next thought that occurred to me was that I'd be there forever, living in absolute darkness. Smathers and Kee would never take me out; they would go away and lock the steel door behind them. I would be left floating . . . floating forever, until I died, and rotted, and my bones sank to the bottom of the tank.

I found I was crying. I could just barely feel the tears sliding down my cheeks. I thought of my mother, a beautiful woman who had loved me as I was and who, with my brother, had kept me whole during the nightmare years of my childhood and adolescence.

I tried to sleep. Maybe I did. It was impossible to tell; sleeping and waking were all the same. Then the voice came again.

"Hello, Robert."

"Go to hell," I said; or maybe I only thought I said it.

"You've been with us for twenty-four hours now, Robert, I know you've missed my voice. I hope you've had time to think about your mistakes, your bad thinking."

I tried to match the voice to the face I'd seen in Smathers' office. The voice was like the face, smooth, unemotional, capable of sudden, unexpected violence.

"You should give some thought to—"

The voice broke off in midsentence. I strained, listening for the rest, but then I realized that the sudden break was all part of the game. The voice would be my only link with reality, and soon I would be willing to do anything it asked of me. My mind screamed, and I backed away from the terrible need, backed down into myself.

I found myself on a plain, stretching off to nothing. There was no horizon, only a black pit directly in front of me. I backed up, and the pit moved forward. It yawned before me like a dark hole on a silent planet.

There were sounds in the hole, wailing winds, screams, groans; and the hole was myself, the deepest part of me. That was where Kee wanted to push me, to trap me—and then remake me.

I was losing my mind.

The torment ended simply, even ludicrously, with a mouthful of water. My first reaction was that they'd decided to scrap the whole brainwashing business and just drown me. I didn't care; anything was better than the terrible silence. Then somebody was holding my head above the surface, ripping off the black rubber mask. The light hit my eyes like razor blades. I screwed them shut and turned my head away. Hands reached down and loosened the straps on my arms and legs. Needles were pulled from my body. Still keeping my eyes closed, I planted my feet on the bottom of the tank and pushed, propelling myself over the side. I landed hard on my back and the breath whistled out of me. The hands reached down and grabbed me under the armpits.

"Get up, Dr. Frederickson!"

I opened my eyes a crack and the blurred image of Smathers flooded in. He pulled me to my feet and I promptly fell down again. After being held absolutely motionless for twenty-four hours, my legs weren't working, but now my eyes were growing accustomed to the light.

"What's the matter? You have a change of heart?" I asked Smathers.

He was white. His flesh trembled.

"I . . . I must have been out of my mind. I don't know what . . . I just couldn't let him do this to you. Can you walk?"

"No. Did you have anything to do with the killings of Manning and Haley?"

"No. I swear to you I knew nothing about them."

"But you let Kee talk you into this."

"I saw everything I'd worked for crumbling around me. If you only knew how *close* I am to controlling the reactions! Dr. Kee convinced me that you could be made to forget everything, perhaps even be made to work for us."

"You were willing to work with a murderer?"

Smathers dropped his eyes. "My work is . . . very important to me. It is possible that many men's lives could be salvaged."

"At the cost of turning me into a vegetable. Forget it, pal. You're

124

no Albert Schweitzer. The first thing you have to learn is that *one* man's life is the most important thing; one life, many lives, it's all the same thing. It wouldn't have worked anyway. My brother would have eventually tracked me down. He might have been too late, but he'd have been here. And my brother isn't exactly used to hearing me talk like a robot." My legs were beginning to feel slightly more solid than a plate of mashed potatoes. I tried getting up on them. They still weren't ready to carry me to a world record in the hundred-yard dash, but they worked.

I looked around for something to cover my nakedness, didn't see anything, decided that modesty was not an appropriate concern at the moment. "Let's get out of here."

Smathers grabbed my arm and I shook his hand off. I felt almost normal. We started toward the door. A huge electronic monitoring machine off to the right blinked, as if welcoming me back to the real world at last.

I should have taken it as a warning. Kee suddenly appeared in the door. Behind him was the healthy half of the Tong Twins. Kee didn't take long to size up the situation; his eyes flicked back and forth between Smathers and me. Then he made a sound in his throat and put his hand back in the direction of his helper; the helper put a .38 in it. Kee flicked his wrist and fired a bullet through Smathers' forehead. Smathers flipped backward and landed on the floor with the sound that only heavy sacks and dead men make. The bullet continued on through his skull and shattered the tank behind him. A few hundred gallons of water roared out through the ruptured glass and hit me full in the back, sweeping me across the floor and bringing me up hard against the monitor. I cringed, waiting for the next bullet. It didn't come.

Kee had other plans for me—like framing me for Smathers' murder. In a way, it made sense; if he could knock me unconscious and place the gun in my hand, it might just confuse the issue long enough for him to slip back over whatever border he'd crossed in the first place. At least Kee seemed to have it figured that way. He was half smiling as he advanced on me. Brother Tong was waiting in back of him, his hands on his hips like a referee.

In my present condition I was no match for either of them.

Still, it was time to do something—like jump up on the monitor and pull some wires. That's what I did.

The machine whirred and popped, sending up clouds of black, acrid smoke. The live wires in my hand sputtered like Fourth of July sparklers. I spun a mental prayer wheel, something concerning proper insulation in the machine I was standing on, then threw the wires into the water on the floor.

Kee had good reflexes; he leaped at the same time I dropped the wires and managed to land on a dry spot near the wall at the opposite side of the room. Brother Tong wasn't so lucky. He tried walking on water and didn't get far. The scream was burned out of his throat by a few hundred thousand volts of electricity. Already dead, he danced around for a few seconds, then fell on his face. His body gradually stopped twitching as the electricity locked his joints and muscles. There was a smell in the air like fried pork.

The gun had fallen in the middle of the floor, out of everybody's reach. That was fine with me, because Kee had problems of his own; the water was gradually working its way over to his tiny island of dry wood. He was backed up against the wall, his arms stretched out to either side of him, as though trying to claw holes in the plaster. I sat down, crossed my legs and smiled at him.

"Win a few, lose a few," I said.

For the first time, emotion showed in his eyes. There was fear, and there was hate, a lot of hate. I shouldn't have goaded him; it was too inspirational. The main power switch was a good ten feet away, but I'd already seen the strength he had in his legs. He gave a tremendous yell, leaped straight up in the air, planted his feet against the wall and dove for the power switch.

I knew he was going to make it even before he did, and the gun was closer to him than it was to me. His fingertips hit the control switch, plunging the floor into darkness. I heard his body hit the water and I hit the floor at the same time. I raced down the corridor, toward the stairs. I could hear Kee splashing behind me, and there was no doubt in my mind that he had the gun. I caromed off the wall at the end of the corridor, scampered down the stairs and hit the steel door.

Naturally, it was locked. There wasn't going to be any naked dwarf running through the sacred corridors of Marten Hall.

I spun and crouched in the darkness, trying to make myself as small a target as possible. The frame business was finished; there were one too many bodies to explain. That meant Kee would want me out of the way as quickly and efficiently as possible. It was going to be like shooting a dwarf in a barrel.

I held my breath and waited for the crash of the gun. All I heard was a dull click. The water had fouled the firing mechanism of the gun. I waited.

I could hear Kee descending the stairs slowly. The job I'd done on his two assistants had given him some respect, but that wasn't enough. Even if I hadn't spent the last twenty-four hours under water, I'd have been no match for Kee. On the other hand, I couldn't just sit and wait for him to beat my brains out.

I waited a few seconds, then lunged upward, sweeping my hand in the general direction where I hoped his ankle would be. I got lucky. I caught his ankle and yanked. He went backward, landing on his back on the stairs. There was no way of getting by him; both his hands were deadly weapons, and he'd have broken every bone in my body by the time I got halfway past. But I had the angle on his midsection. I stiffened my fingers and drove them as hard as I could into his groin. That took the power out of a kick that would have killed me. His heel bounced off my rib cage, and I felt something snap inside.

Kee was doubled over, his shape just barely visible in the darkness. I could go past him now, but that would just mean playing cat and mouse up in the darkness of the laboratories, and that was a game I knew I eventually had to lose. I had to attack.

Trying to ignore the pain in my side, and hoping that the sudden movement wouldn't pierce any of my machinery, I moved around in front of him and clapped my hands over both his ears. He screamed and half rose, which was exactly the position for which I was waiting. He was off balance now, his concentration gone. I grabbed a handful of hair and yanked. Kee plummeted down into the darkness. He came up hard against the steel door, and there was a single, sharp sound. I didn't have to go down to know that Kee was dead, his neck broken.

I tasted blood and I was getting dizzy. I sat down on a step and braced my arm against my broken rib. I stared down into the darkness. Eventually someone would open the door. It would probably be Garth, and he would probably want to know what I was doing sitting naked in the darkness with a dead body.

I strongly suspect that "religious faith," by which I mean a sincere, even profound belief in the supernatural and not just an adherence to form inspired by social or political pressure, may have an actual genetic basis in the human species, and that I'm missing the appropriate genetic marker. I have always been at once intrigued and appalled by the pervasiveness of superstition in our "modern" societies, whether it be represented by a professor of physics praying to a Deity of Choice on Saturday or Sunday, the wife of a president in twentieth-century America seeking advice from an astrologer, or somebody reading runes in a basement. I get the same eerie chill when I pass a church, synagogue, ashram, or any other "house of worship" that I imagine an archaeologist must experience when unearthing some ancient "temple to the gods" in Peru or Mexico.

The notion that "you are what you believe," and should therefore be very careful about what you allow yourself to believe, comes to play an ever-increasing role in my journeys with Mongo, and begins to surface for the first time in the following story. It is a tale I would treat slightly differently if I were writing it today, but it shows the initial interest in a theme that, many years later, I will treat at great length in the three novels I think of as the Valhalla Trilogy (The Beasts of Valhalla, Two Songs This Archangel Sings, The Cold Smell of Sacred Stone), *and with what I intended to be a blunderbuss in* Second Horseman Out of Eden.

Later, this story will also be incorporated into An Affair of Sorcerers, *the first novel to grow out of my amazement before the fact that people really will believe the damnedest things—and usually pay the price.*

The Healer

The man waiting for me in my downtown office looked like a movie star who didn't want to be recognized. After he took off his hat, dark glasses and leather overcoat he still looked like a movie star. He also looked like a certain famous Southern senator.

"Dr. Frederickson," he said, extending a large, sinewy hand. "I've been doing so much reading about you in the past few days, I feel I already know you. I must say it's a distinct pleasure. I'm Bill Younger."

"Senator," I said, shaking the hand and motioning him toward the chair in front of my desk.

Younger, with his boyish, forty-five-year-old face and full head of brown, neatly cut hair, looked good. Except for the fear in his eyes, he might have been ready to step into a television studio. "Why the background check, Senator?"

He half smiled. "I used to take my daughter to see you perform when you were with the circus."

"That was a long time ago, Senator." It was six years. It seemed a hundred.

The smile faded. "You're famous. I wanted to see if you were also discreet. My sources tell me your credentials are impeccable. You seem to have a penchant for unusual cases."

"Unusual cases seem to have a penchant for me. You'd be amazed how few people feel the need for a dwarf private detective."

Younger didn't seem to be listening. "You've heard of Esteban Morales?"

I said I hadn't. The senator seemed surprised. "I was away for the summer," I added.

The senator nodded absently, then rose and began to pace back and forth in front of the desk. The activity seemed to relax him. "Esteban is one of my constituents, so I'm quite familiar with his work. He's a healer."

129

"A doctor?"

"No, not a doctor. A psychic healer. He heals with his hands. His mind." He cast a quick look in my direction to gauge my reaction. He must have been satisfied with what he saw because he went on. "There are a number of good psychic healers in this country. Those who are familiar with this kind of phenomenon consider Esteban the best, although his work does not receive much publicity. There are considerable . . . pressures."

"Why did you assume I'd heard of him?"

"He spent the past summer at the university where you teach. He'd agreed to participate in a research project."

"What kind of research project?"

"I'm not sure. It was something in microbiology. I think a Dr. Mason was heading the project."

I nodded. Janet Mason is a friend of mine.

"The project was never finished," Younger continued. "Esteban is now in jail awaiting trail for murder." He added almost parenthetically, "Your brother was the arresting officer."

I was beginning to get the notion that it was more than my natural dwarf charm that had attracted Senator Younger. "Who is this Esteban Morales accused of killing?"

"A physician by the name of Robert Edmonston."

"Why?"

The senator suddenly stopped pacing and planted his hands firmly on top of my desk. He seemed extremely agitated. "The papers reported that Edmonston filed a complaint against Esteban. Practicing medicine without a license. The police think Esteban killed him because of it."

"They'd need more than thoughts to book him."

"They . . . found Esteban in the office with the body. Edmonston had been dead only a few minutes. His throat had been cut with a knife they found dissolving in a vial of acid." The first words had come hard for Younger. The rest came easier. "If charges had been filed against Esteban, it wouldn't have been the first time. These are the things Esteban has to put up with. He's always taken the enmity of the medical establishment in stride. Esteban is not a killer—he's a healer. He couldn't kill anyone!" He suddenly straightened up, then slumped into the chair behind him. "I'm sorry," he said quietly. "I must seem overwrought."

130

"How do you feel I can help you, Senator?"

"You must clear Esteban," Younger said. His voice was steady but intense. "Either prove he didn't do it, or that someone else did."

I looked at him to see if he might, just possibly, be joking. He wasn't. "That's a pretty tall order, Senator. And it could get expensive. On the other hand, you've got the whole New York City Police Department set up to do that work for free."

The senator shook his head. "I want one man—you—to devote himself to nothing but this case. You work at the university. You have contacts. You may be able to find out something the police couldn't, or didn't care to look for. After all, the police have other things besides Esteban's case to occupy their attention."

"I wouldn't argue with that."

"This is *most* important to me, Dr. Frederickson," the senator said, jabbing his finger in the air for emphasis. "I will double your usual fee."

"That won't be nec—"

"At the least, I must have access to Esteban if you fail. Perhaps your brother could arrange that. I am willing to donate ten thousand dollars to any cause your brother deems worthy."

"Hold on, Senator. Overwrought or not, I wouldn't mention that kind of arrangement to Garth. He might interpret it as a bribe offer. Very embarrassing."

"It *will* be a bribe offer!"

I thought about that for a few seconds, then said, "You certainly do a lot for your constituents, Senator. I'm surprised you're not president."

I must have sounded snide. The flesh on the senator's face blanched bone-white, then filled with blood. His eyes flashed. Still, somewhere in their depths, the fear remained. His words came out in a forced whisper. "If Esteban Morales is not released, my daughter will die."

I felt a chill, and wasn't sure whether it was because I believed him or because of the possibility that a United States senator and presidential hopeful was a madman. I settled for something in between and tried to regulate my tone of voice accordingly. "I don't understand, Senator."

131

"Really? I thought I was making myself perfectly clear. My daughter's life is totally dependent on Esteban Morales." He took a deep breath. "My daughter Linda has cystic fibrosis, Dr. Frederickson. As you may know, medical doctors consider cystic fibrosis incurable. The normal pattern is for a sufferer to die in his or her early teens—usually from pulmonary complications. Esteban has been treating my daughter all her life, and she is now twenty-four. But Linda needs him again. Her lungs are filling with fluid."

I was beginning to understand how the medical establishment might get a little nervous at Esteban Morales' activities, and a psychic warning light was flashing in my brain. Senator or no, this didn't sound like the kind of case in which I liked to get involved. If Morales were a hoaxer—or a killer—I had no desire to be the bearer of bad tidings to a man with the senator's emotional investment.

"How does Morales treat your daughter? With drugs?"

Younger shook his head. "He just . . . *touches* her. He moves his hands up and down her body. Sometimes he looks like he's in a trance, but he isn't. It's . . . very hard to explain. You have to see him do it."

"How much does he charge for these treatments?"

The senator looked surprised. "Esteban doesn't charge anything. Most psychic healers—the real ones—won't take money. They feel it interferes with whatever it is they do." He laughed shortly, without humor. "Esteban prefers to live simply, off Social Security, a pension check, and a few gifts—small ones—from his friends. He's a retired metal shop foreman."

Esteban Morales didn't exactly fit the mental picture I'd drawn of him, and my picture of the senator was still hazy. "Senator," I said, tapping my fingers lightly on the desk, "why don't you hold a press conference and describe what you feel Esteban Morales has done for your daughter? It could do you more good than hiring a private detective. Coming from you, I guarantee it will get the police moving."

Younger smiled thinly. "Or get me locked up in Bellevue. At the least, I would be voted out of office, perhaps recalled. My state is in the so-called Bible Belt, and there would be a great deal of misunderstanding. Esteban is not a religious man in my

132

constituents' sense of the word. He does not claim to receive his powers from God. Even if he did, it wouldn't make much difference." The smile got thinner. "I've found that most religious people prefer their miracles well aged. You'll forgive me if I sound selfish, but I would like to try to save Linda's life without demolishing my career. If all else fails, I will hold a press conference. Will you take the job?"

I told him I'd see what I could find out.

•   •   •

It looked like a large photographic negative. In its center was a dark outline of a hand with the fingers outstretched. The tips of the fingers were surrounded by waves of color—pink, red and violet—undulating outward to a distance of an inch or two from the hand itself. The effect was oddly beautiful and very mysterious.

"What the hell is it?"

"It's a Kirlian photograph," Dr. Janet Mason said. She seemed pleased with my reaction. "The technique is named after a Russian who invented it about thirty years ago. The Russians, by the way, are far ahead of us in this field."

I looked at her. Janet Mason is a handsome woman in her early fifties. Her shiny gray hair was drawn back into a severe bun, highlighting the fine features of her face. You didn't need a special technique to be aware of her sex appeal. She is a tough-minded scientist who, rumor has it, had gone through a long string of lab-assistant lovers. Her work left her little time for anything else. Janet Mason has been liberated a long time. I like her.

"Uh, what field?"

"Psychic research: healing, ESP, clairvoyance, that sort of thing. Kirlian photography, for example, purports to record what is known as the human *aura*, part of the energy that all living things radiate. The technique itself is quite simple. You put an individual into a circuit with an unexposed photographic plate and have the person touch the plate with some part of his body." She pointed to the print I was holding. "That's what you end up with."

"Morales'?"

"Mine. That's an 'average' aura, if you will." She reached into the drawer of her desk and took out another set of photographs. She looked through them, then handed one to me. "This is Esteban's."

I glanced at the print. It looked the same as the first one, and I told her so.

"That's Esteban at rest, you might say. He's not thinking about healing." She handed me another photograph. "Here he is with his batteries charged."

The print startled me. The bands of color were erupting out from the fingers, especially the index and middle fingers. The apogee of the waves was somewhere off the print; they looked like sun storms.

"You won't find that in the others," Janet continued. "With most people, thinking about healing makes very little difference."

"So what does it mean?"

She smiled disarmingly. "Mongo, I'm a scientist. I deal in facts. The fact of the matter is that Esteban Morales takes one hell of a Kirlian photograph. The implication is that he can literally radiate extra amounts of energy at will."

"Do you think he can heal people?"

She took a long time to answer. "There's no doubt in *my* mind that he can," she said at last. I considered it a rather startling confession. "And he's not dealing with psychosomatic disorders. Esteban has been involved in other research projects, at different universities. In one, a strip of skin was removed surgically from the backs of monkeys. The monkeys were divided into two groups. Esteban simply handled the monkeys in one group. Those monkeys healed twice as fast as the ones he didn't handle." She smiled wanly. "Plants are supposed to grow faster when he waters them."

"What did you have him working on?"

"Enzymes," Janet said with a hint of pride. "The perfect research model; no personalities involved. You see, enzymes are the basic chemicals of the body. If Esteban could heal, the reasoning went, he should be able to affect pure enzymes. He can."

"The results were good?"

She laughed lightly. "Spectacular. Irradiated—'injured'— enzymes break down at specific rates in certain chemical solutions. The less damaged they are, the slower their rate of breakdown. What we did was to take test tubes full of enzymes—supplied by a commercial lab—and irradiate them. Then we gave Esteban half of the samples to handle. The samples he handled broke down at a statistically significant *lesser* rate then the ones he didn't handle." She paused again, then said, "Ninety-nine and nine-tenths percent of the population can't affect the enzymes one way or the other. On the other hand, a very few people can make the enzymes break down *faster*."

"'Negative' healers?"

"Right. Pretty hairy, huh?"

I laughed. "It's incredible. Why haven't I heard anything about it? I mean, here's a man who may be able to heal people with his hands, and nobody's heard of him. I would think Morales would make headlines in every newspaper in the country."

Janet gave me the kind of smile I suspected she normally reserved for some particularly naive student. "It's next to impossible just to get funding for this kind of research, what's more publicity. Psychic healing is thought of as, well, *occult*."

"You mean like acupuncture?"

It was Janet's turn to laugh. "You make my point. You know how long it took Western scientists and doctors to get around to taking acupuncture seriously. Psychic healing just doesn't fit into the currently accepted pattern of scientific thinking. When you do get a study done, none of the journals want to publish it."

"I understand that Dr. Edmonston filed a complaint against Morales. Is that true?"

"That's what the police said. I have no reason to doubt it. Edmonston was never happy about his part in the project. Now I'm beginning to wonder about Dr. Johnson. I'm still waiting for his anecdotal reports."

"What project? What reports? What Dr. Johnson?"

Janet looked surprised. "You don't know about that?"

"I got all my information from my client. Obviously, he didn't know. Was there some kind of tie-in between Morales and Edmonston?"

"I would say so." She replaced the Kirlian photographs in her desk drawer. "We actually needed Esteban only about an hour or so a day, when he handled samples. The rest of the time we were involved in computer analysis. We decided it might be interesting to see what Esteban could do with some real patients, under medical supervision. We wanted to get a physician's point of view. We put some feelers out into the medical community and got a cold shoulder—except for Dr. Johnson, who incidentally happened to be Robert Edmonston's partner. I get the impression the two of them had a big argument over using Esteban, and Rolfe Johnson eventually won. We worked out a plan where Esteban would go to their offices after finishing here. They would refer certain patients—who volunteered—to him. These particular patients were in no immediate danger, but they would eventually require hospitalization. These patients would report how they felt to Edmonston and Johnson after their sessions with Esteban. The two doctors would then make up anecdotal reports. Not very scientific, but we thought it might make an interesting footnote to the main study."

"And you haven't seen these reports?"

"No. I think Dr. Johnson is stalling."

"Why would he do that after he agreed to participate in the project?"

"I don't know. Maybe he's had second thoughts after the murder. Or maybe he's simply afraid his colleagues will laugh at him."

I wondered. It still seemed a curious shift in attitude. It also occurred to me that I would like to see the list of patients that had been referred to Morales. It just might contain the name of someone with a motive to kill Edmonston—and try to pin it on Esteban Morales. "Tell me some more about Edmonston and Johnson," I said. "You mentioned the fact they were partners."

Janet took a cigarette from her purse, and I supplied a match. She studied me through a cloud of smoke. "Is this confidential?"

"If you say so."

"Johnson and Edmonston were very much into the modern big-business aspect of medicine. It's what a lot of doctors are doing these days: labs, ancillary patient centers, private, profit-making hospitals. Dr. Johnson's skills seemed to be more in the area of administration of their enterprises. As a matter of fact, he'd be about the last person I'd expect to be interested in psychic healing. There were rumors to the effect they were going public in a few months."

"Doctors go public?"

"Sure. They build up a network of the types of facilities I mentioned, incorporate, then sell stocks."

"How'd they get along?"

"Who knows? I assume they got along as well as any other business partners. They were different, though."

"How so?"

"Edmonston was the older of the two men. I suspect he was attracted to Johnson because of Johnson's ideas in the areas I mentioned. Edmonston was rumored to be a good doctor, but he was brooding. No sense of humor. Johnson had a lighter, happy-go-lucky side. Obviously, he was also the more adventurous of the two."

"What was the basis of Edmonston's complaint?"

"Dr. Edmonston claimed that Esteban was giving his patients drugs."

I thought about that. It certainly didn't fit in with what the senator had told me. "Janet, doesn't it strike you as odd that two doctors like Johnson and Edmonston would agree to work with a psychic healer? Aside from philosophic differences, they sound like busy men."

"Oh, yes. I really can't explain Dr. Johnson's enthusiasm. As I told you, Dr. Edmonston was against the project from the beginning. He didn't want to waste his time on what he considered to be superstitious nonsense." She paused, then added, "He must have given off some bad vibrations."

"Why do you say that?"

"I'm not sure. Toward the end of the experiment something was affecting Esteban's concentration. He wasn't getting the same results he had earlier. And before you ask, I don't know why he was upset. I broached the subject once and he made it clear he didn't want to discuss it."

"Do you think he killed Edmonston?"

She laughed shortly, without humor. "Uh-uh, Mongo. That's your department. I deal in enzymes; they're much simpler than people."

"C'mon, Janet. You spent an entire summer working with him.

He must have left some kind of impression. Do you think Esteban Morales is the kind of man who would slit somebody's throat?"

She looked at me a long time. Finally she said, "Esteban Morales is probably the gentlest, most loving person I've ever met. And that's all you're going to get from me. Except that I wish you luck."

I nodded my thanks, then rose and started for the door.

"Mongo?"

I turned with my hand on the doorknob. Janet was now sitting on the edge of her desk, exposing a generous portion of her very shapely legs. They were the best looking fifty-year-old legs I'd ever seen—and on a very pretty woman.

"You have to come and see me more often," she continued evenly. "I don't have that many dwarf colleagues."

I winked broadly. "See you, kid."

.   .   .

"Of course I was curious," Dr. Rolfe Johnson said. "That's why I was so anxious to participate in the project in the first place. I like to consider myself open-minded."

I studied Johnson. He was a boyish thirty-seven, outrageously good-looking, with Nordic blue eyes and a full head of blond hair. I was impressed by his enthusiasm, somewhat puzzled by his agreeing to see me within twenty minutes of my phone call. For a busy doctor-businessman he seemed very free with his time—or very anxious to nail the lid on Esteban Morales. He was just a little too eager to please me.

"Dr. Edmonston wasn't?"

Johnson cleared his throat. "Well, I didn't mean that. Robert was a . . . traditionalist. You will find that most doctors are just not that *curious*. He considered working with Mr. Morales an unnecessary drain on our time. I thought it was worth it."

"Why? What was in it for you?"

He looked slightly hurt. "I considered it a purely scientific inquiry. After all, no doctor ever actually *heals* anyone. Nor does any medicine. The body heals itself, and all any doctor can do is to try to stimulate the body to do its job. From his advance publicity, Esteban Morales was a man who could do that without benefit of drugs or scalpels. I wanted to see if it was true."

"Was it?"

Johnson snorted. "Of course not. It was all mumbo jumbo. Oh, he certainly had a psychosomatic effect on some people—but they had to believe in him. From what I could see, the effects of what he was doing were at most ephemeral, and extremely short-lived. I suppose that's why he panicked."

"Panicked?"

Johnson's eyebrows lifted. "The police haven't told you?"

"I'm running ahead of myself. I haven't talked to the police yet. I assume you're talking about the drugs Morales is supposed to have administered."

"Oh, not *supposed* to. I *saw* him, and it was reported to me by the patient."

"What patient?"

He clucked his tongue. "Surely you can appreciate the fact that I can't give out patients' names."

"Sure. You told Edmonston?"

"It was his patient. And he insisted on filing the complaint himself." He shook his head. "Dr. Mason would have been doing everyone a favor if she hadn't insisted on having the university bail him out."

"Uh-huh. Can you tell me what happened the night Dr. Edmonston died? What you know."

He thought about it for a while. At least he looked like he was thinking about it. "Dr. Edmonston and I always met on Thursday nights. There were records to be kept, decisions to be made, and there just wasn't enough time during the week. On that night I was a few minutes late." He shook his head. "Those few minutes may have cost Robert his life."

"Maybe. What was Morales doing there?"

"I'm sure I don't know. Obviously, he was enraged with Robert. He must have found out about the Thursday night meetings while he was working with us, and decided that would be a good time to kill Dr. Edmonston."

"But if he knew about the meetings, he'd know you'd be there."

Johnson glanced impatiently at his watch. "I am not privy to

139

what went on in Esteban Morales' mind. After all, as you must know, he is almost completely illiterate. A stupid man. Perhaps he simply wasn't thinking straight . . . if he ever does." He rose abruptly. "I'm afraid I've given you all the time I can afford. I've talked to you in the interests of obtaining justice for Dr. Edmonston. I'd hoped you would see that you were wasting your time investigating the matter."

The interview was obviously over.

•   •   •

Johnson's story stunk. The problem was how to get someone else to sniff around it. With a prime suspect like Morales in the net, the New York police weren't about to complicate matters for themselves before they had to, meaning before the senator either got Morales a good lawyer or laid his own career on the line. My job was to prevent that necessity, which meant, at the least, getting Morales out on bail. To do that I was going to have to start raising some doubts.

It was time to talk to Morales.

I stopped off at a drive-in for dinner, took out three hamburgers and a chocolate milk shake intended as a bribe for my outrageously oversized brother. The food wasn't enough. A half hour later, after threats, shouts and appeals to familial loyalty, I was transformed from a dwarf private detective to a dwarf lawyer and taken to see Esteban Morales. The guard assigned to me thought it was funny as hell.

Esteban Morales looked like an abandoned extra from *Viva Zapata*. He wore a battered, broad-brimmed straw hat to cover a full head of long, matted gray hair. He wore shapeless corduroy pants and a bulky, torn red sweater. Squatting down on the cell's dirty cot, his back to the wall, he looked forlorn and lonely. He looked up as I entered. His eyes were a deep, wet brown. Something moved in their depths as he looked at me. Whatever it was—curiosity, perhaps—quickly passed.

I went over to him and held out my hand. "Hello, Mr. Morales. My name is Robert Frederickson. My friends call me Mongo."

Morales shook for my hand. For an old man, his grip was

140

surprisingly firm. "Glad to meet you, Mr. Mongo," he said in a thickly accented voice. "You lawyer?"

"No. A private detective. I'd like to try to help you."

"Who hire you?"

"A friend of yours." I mouthed the word "senator" so the guard wouldn't hear me. Morales' eyes lit up. "Your friend feels that his daughter needs you. I'm going to try to get you out, at least on bail."

Morales lifted his large hands slowly and studied the palms. I remembered Janet Mason's Kirlian photographs; I wondered what mysterious force was in those hands, and what its source was. "I help Linda if I can get to see her," he said quietly. "I must touch." He suddenly looked up. "I no kill anybody, Mr. Mongo. I never hurt anybody."

"What happened that night?"

The hands pressed together, dropped between his knees. "Dr. Edmonston no like me. I can tell that. He think I phony. Still he let me help his patients, and I grateful to him for that."

"Do you think you actually helped any of them?"

Morales smiled disarmingly, like a child who has done something of which he is proud. "I know I did. And the patients, they know. They tell me, and they tell Dr. Edmonston and Dr. Johnson."

"Did you give drugs to anybody?"

"No, Mr. Mongo." He lifted his hands. "My power is here, in my hands. All drugs bad for body."

"Why do you think Dr. Edmonston said you did?"

He shook his head in obvious bewilderment. "One day the police pick me up at university. They say I under arrest for pretending to be doctor. I no understand. Dr. Mason get me out. Then I get message same day—"

"A Thursday?"

"I think so. The message say that Dr. Edmonston want to see me that night at seven-thirty. I want to know why he mad at me, so I decide to go. I come in and find him dead. Somebody cut throat. Dr. Johnson come in a few minutes later. He think I do it. He call police . . ." His voice trailed off, punctuated by a gesture that included the cell and the unseen world outside. It was an elegant gesture.

"How did you get into the office, Esteban?"

"The lights are on and door open. When nobody answer knock, I walk in."

I nodded. Esteban Morales was either a monumental acting talent or a man impossible not to believe. "Do you have any idea why Dr. Edmonston wanted to talk to you?"

"No, Mr. Mongo. I thought maybe he sorry he call police."

"How do you do what you do, Esteban?" The question was meant to surprise him. It didn't. He simply smiled.

"You think I play tricks, Mr. Mongo?"

"What I think doesn't matter."

"They why you ask?"

"I'm curious."

"Then I answer." Again he lifted his hands, stared at them. "The body make music, Mr. Mongo. A healthy body make good music. I can hear through my hands. A sick body make bad music. My hands . . . I can make music good, make it sound like I know it should." He paused, shook his head. "Not easy to explain, Mr. Mongo."

"Why were you upset near the end of the project, Esteban?"

"Who told you I upset?"

"Dr. Mason. She said you were having a difficult time affecting the enzymes."

He took a long time to answer. "I don't think it right to talk about it."

"Talk about what, Esteban? How can I help you if you won't level with me?"

"I know many things about people, but I don't speak about them," he said almost to himself. "What make me unhappy have nothing to do with my trouble."

"Why don't you let me decide that?"

Again, it took him a long time to answer. "I guess it no make difference any longer."

"*What* doesn't make a difference any longer, Esteban?"

He looked up at me. "Dr. Edmonston was dying. Of cancer."

"Dr. Edmonston told you that?"

"Oh, no. Dr. Edmonston no tell anyone. He not want anyone to know. But I know."

"How, Esteban? How did you know?"

He pointed to his eyes. "I see, Mr. Mongo. I see the aura. Dr. Edmonston's aura brown-black. Flicker. He dying of cancer. I know he have five, maybe six more months to live." He lowered his eyes and shook his head. "I tell him I know. I tell him I want to help. He get very mad at me. He tell me to mind my own business. That upset me. It upset me to be around people in pain who no want my help."

My mouth was suddenly very dry. I swallowed hard. "You say you *saw* this aura?" I remembered the Kirlian photographs Janet Mason had shown me and I could feel a prickling at the back of my neck.

"Yes," Morales said simply. "I see aura."

"Can you see *anybody's* aura?" I had raised my voice a few notches so that the guard could hear. I shot a quick glance in his direction. He was smirking, which meant we were coming in loud and clear. That was good . . . maybe.

"Usually. Mostly I see sick people's aura, because that what I look for."

"Can you see mine?" I asked.

His eyes slowly came up and met mine. They held. It was a moment of unexpected, embarrassing intimacy, and I knew what he was going to say before he said it.

Esteban Morales didn't smile. "I can see yours, Mr. Mongo," he said softly.

He was going to say something else but I cut him off. I was feeling a little light-headed and I wanted to get the next part of the production over as quickly as possible. I could sympathize with Dr. Edmonston.

I pressed the guard and he reluctantly admitted he'd overheard the last part of our conversation. Then I asked him to get Garth.

Garth arrived looking suspicious. Garth always looks suspicious when I send for him. He nodded briefly at Esteban, then looked at me. "What's up, Mongo?"

"I just want you to sit here for a minute and listen to something."

"Mongo, I've got *reports!*"

I ignored him and he leaned back against the bars of the cell and began to tap his foot impatiently. I turned to Esteban

143

Morales. "Esteban," I said quietly, "will you tell my brother what an aura is?"

Morales described the human aura, and I followed up by describing the Kirlian photographs Janet Mason had shown me: what they were, and what they purported to show. Garth's foot continued its monotonous tapping. Once he glanced at his watch.

"Esteban," I said, "how does my brother look? I mean his aura."

"Oh, he fine," Esteban said, puzzled. "Aura a good, healthy pink."

"What about me?"

Morales dropped his eyes and shook his head mutely.

The foot-tapping in the corner had stopped. Suddenly Garth was beside me, gripping my arm. "Mongo, what the hell is this all about?"

"Just listen, Garth. I need a witness." I took a deep breath, then started in again on Morales. "Esteban," I whispered, "I asked you a question. Can you see my aura? Can you see my aura, Esteban? Damn it, if you can, say so! I may be able to help you. If you can see my aura you have to say so!"

Esteban Morales slowly lifted his head. His eyes were filled with pain. "I cannot help you, Mr. Mongo."

Garth gripped my arm even tighter. "Mongo—"

"I'm all right, Garth. Esteban, tell me what it is you see."

The healer took a long, shuddering breath. "You are dying, Mr. Mongo. Your mind is sharp, but your body is—" He gestured toward me. "Your body is the way it is. It is the same inside. I cannot change that. I cannot help. I am sorry."

"Don't be," I said. I was caught between conflicting emotions, exultation at coming up a winner and bitterness at what Morales' statement was costing me. I decided to spin the wheel again. "Can you tell about how many years I have left, Esteban?"

"I cannot say," Morales said in a choked voice. "And if I could, I would not. No human should suffer the burden of knowing the time of his death. Why you make me say those things about you dying?"

I spun on Garth. I hoped I had my smile on straight. "Well, brother, how does Esteban's opinion compare with the medical authorities'?"

Garth shook his head. His voice was hollow. "Your clients get a lot for their money, Mongo."

"How about getting hold of a lawyer and arranging a bail hearing for Esteban. Like tomorrow?"

"I can get a public defender in here, Mongo," Garth said in the same tone. "But you haven't proved anything."

"Was there an autopsy done on Edmonston?"

"Yeah. The report is probably filed away by now. What about it?"

"Well, that autopsy will show that Edmonston was dying of cancer, and I can prove that Esteban knew it. I just gave you a demonstration of what he can do."

"It still doesn't prove anything," Garth said tightly. "Mongo, I wish it did."

"All I want is Esteban out on bail—and the cops dusting a few more corners. All I want to show is that Esteban knew Edmonston was dying, fast. It wouldn't have made any sense for Esteban to kill him. And I think I can bring a surprise character witness. A heavy. Will you talk to the judge?"

"Yeah, I'll talk to the judge." Again, Garth gripped my arm. "You sure you're all right? You're white as chalk."

"I'm all right. Hell, we're all dying, aren't we?" My laugh turned short and bitter. "When you've been dying as long as I have, you get used to it. I need a phone."

I didn't wait for an answer. I walked quickly out of the cell and used the first phone I found to call the senator. Then I hurried outside and lit a cigarette. It tasted lousy.

. . .

Two days later Garth popped his head into my office. "He confessed. I thought you'd want to know."

I pushed aside the criminology lecture on which I'd been working. "Who confessed?"

Garth came in and closed the door. "Johnson, of course. He came into his office this morning and found us searching through his records. He just managed to ask to see the warrant before he folded. Told the whole story twice, once for us and once for the DA. What an amateur!"

I was vaguely surprised to find myself monumentally uninter-

145

ested. My job had been finished the day before when the senator and I had walked in a back door of the courthouse to meet with Garth and the sitting judge. Forty-five minutes later Esteban Morales had been out on bail and on his way to meet with Linda Younger. Rolfe Johnson had been my prime suspect five minutes after I'd begun to talk to him, and there'd been no doubt in my mind that the police would nail him, once they decided to go to the bother.

"What was his motive?" I asked.

"Johnson's forte was business. No question about it. He just couldn't cut it as a murderer . . . or a doctor. He had at least a dozen malpractice suits filed against him. Edmonston was getting tired of having a flunky as a partner. Johnson was becoming an increasing embarrassment and was hurting the medical side of the business. Patients, after all, are the bottom line. Edmonston had the original practice and a controlling interest in their corporation. He was going to cut Johnson adrift, and Johnson found out about it.

"Johnson, with all his troubles, knew that he was finished if Edmonston dissolved the partnership. When Dr. Mason told him about Morales, Johnson had a notion that he just might be able to use the situation to his own advantage. After all, what better patsy than an illiterate psychic healer?"

"Johnson sent the message to Esteban, didn't he?"

"Sure. First, he admitted lying to Edmonston about Esteban giving drugs to one of Edmonston's patients, then he told how he maneuvered Edmonston into filing a complaint. He figured the university would bail Esteban out, and a motive would have been established. It wasn't much, but Johnson didn't figure he needed much. After all, he assumed Esteban was crazy and that any jury would know he was crazy. He picked his day, then left a message in the name of Edmonston for Esteban to come to the offices that night. He asked Edmonston to come forty-five minutes early, and he killed him, then waited for Esteban to show up to take the rap. Pretty crude, but then Johnson isn't that imaginative."

"Didn't the feedback from the patients give him any pause?"

Garth laughed. "From what I can gather from his statement,

146

Johnson never paid any attention to the reports. Edmonston did most of the interviewing."

"There seems to be a touch of irony there," I said dryly.

"There seems to be. Well, I've got a car running downstairs. Like I said, I thought you'd want to know."

"Thanks, Garth."

He paused with his hand on the knob and looked at me for a long time. I knew we were thinking about the same thing, words spoken in a jail cell, a very private family secret shared by two brothers. For a moment I was afraid he was going to say something that would embarrass both of us. He didn't.

"See you," Garth said.

"See you."

That Theme again—and another story I would treat slightly differently if I were writing it today. This piece, too, was eventually to be incorporated into An Affair of Sorcerers.

The idea for "Falling Star," and for most of the occult pieces in this collection, grew out of my friendship with a man who was, and still is, a very successful and highly influential tarot reader and palmist. I liked the man very much, considered his choice of profession absurd. Other people didn't find his work so ridiculous. On a wall in the foyer of his brownstone were framed palm prints of the rich and famous, names virtually anyone would recognize, who came to him on a regular basis for palm and tarot readings and advice on how to lead their lives—rock stars, heiresses, politicians, and the wives of politicians. These people believed *that the answers to their problems could be found in the lines of their hands, the layout of the tarot cards, and my friend's interpretation of these things. These powerful people acted on his advice, just as Nancy Reagan heeded the strictures of her astrologer.*

Now, my friend is a kind, sensitive, and responsible person who wields his considerable power with great care. But as I studied the palm prints of the people on the wall, I couldn't help but reflect on the havoc he could wreak in people's lives if he were not so kind and responsible. Now I wish I had been more ambitious and come up with the idea of an astrologer able to reach directly into the White House in order to influence a president's behavior, but at the time I would have dismissed the idea as patently ridiculous.

Falling Star

I don't usually get clients walking into my university office, but I wasn't complaining. That's the kind of attitude somebody in my position develops after a while.

My visitor was a big man with a swarthy complexion, wearing expensive shoes and suit, diamond pinkie rings, and show biz written all over him. He had red hair and milky blue eyes that did a double take between me and the nameplate on my desk.

"I'm looking for Dr. Frederickson."

"I'm Frederickson."

"You're a dwarf."

"You've got something against dwarfs?" I must have sounded nasty.

He flushed and extended his hand. "Sorry," he said. "My name is Sandor Peth. I need a private detective. Your brother suggested I come and talk to you."

That raised a mental eyebrow. I wondered what business Peth had had with Garth. I shook Peth's hand and motioned him to a chair.

Peth reached into his suit jacket and took out a neatly folded piece of paper. He unfolded it, handed it across the desk to me, and said, "I brought this along for what it's worth. I think it could be important."

I studied the paper. There were two concentric circles divided into twelve sections by intersecting lines. The sections were filled with symbols and notes that were meaningless to me.

I placed the paper to one side. "What is it?"

"A horoscope."

I didn't say anything. The thought crossed my mind that Garth might be having a little fun with me.

Peth cleared his throat. "Have you ever heard of Harley Davidson?"

"Sure. He's a famous motorcycle."

Peth smiled. "He's a rock star. At least he used to be."

"Used to be?"

The smile faded. "Harley's in trouble."

"What kind of trouble?"

Peth lighted a cigar and stared at me through the smoke. His milky eyes fascinated me; they were like mirrors, reflecting all and revealing nothing. "I want you to know that I don't believe in none of this stuff, but Harley does. That's the point."

"What does Harley believe in, and what's the point?"

"Astrology, witchcraft, all sorts of occult nonsense. Harley's no different from lots of people in the business who won't get out of bed in the morning unless their astrologer tells them it's okay. But Harley got into it a lot deeper. He got mixed up with a bad-news astrologer by the name of Borrn. Borrn's the one who cast that horoscope. Whatever's in it scared the hell out of Harley, messed his mind. So far, he's missed two recording dates and one concert. No promoter's going to put up with that stuff for long. Harley's on his way out."

"What's your interest in Harley?" I asked.

"I was Harley's manager up to a week ago," Peth said evenly. "He fired me."

"On Borrn's advice?"

"Probably."

"A neutral observer might call your interest sour grapes."

"I don't need Harley. If you don't believe me, check with my accountants. I've got a whole stable of rock stars. I like Harley and I hate to see him get messed up like this. He's made me a bundle, and I figure maybe I owe him some."

I nodded. It seemed a sincere enough statement. "How do you think I can help, Mr. Peth?"

"I want to nail Borrn. It may be the only way to save Harley from himself."

"Harley may not want to be saved."

"I just want to make sure he has all the facts. I don't think he does now."

"I'm not in the business of 'nailing' people. I just investigate. If you think Borrn's into something illegal, you should go to the police."

"I did. That's how I met your brother. He said that as far as he knew Borrn was clean. He told me he couldn't do anything unless there was a complaint, which there hasn't been. I want to find out if there's a basis for a complaint. I can afford to tilt at a few windmills. How about it? Will you take the job?"

I took another look at the expensive shoes and diamond pinkie rings. "I get one hundred fifty dollars a day, plus expenses. You don't get charged for the time I'm teaching."

Peth took out a wad of bills and lightened it enough to keep me busy for a few days. "Borrn operates out of a store-front down on the Lower East Side," Peth said, handing me the money. "That's about all I know, except for what I've already told you." He rose and started to leave.

"Just a minute," I said. Peth turned and looked at me inquiringly. "You said Garth told you he thought Borrn was clean. Did he say how he knew that? Astrologers aren't his usual meat and potatoes."

Something that might have been amusement glinted in Peth's eyes. "They are now," he said. "Didn't you know? He's been assigned to a special unit keeping tabs on the New York occult underground."

I hadn't known. For some reason I found the notion enormously funny, but I waited for Peth to leave before I laughed out loud.

Peth had left the horoscope behind. I picked it up and stuffed it into my pocket along with my newfound wealth.

•　　•　　•

At the precinct station house I found Garth torturing a typewriter in the cubicle he called an office. He looked tired. Garth always looks tired. He is a cop who takes his work seriously.

"Abracadabra!" I cried, jumping out from behind one of the partitions and flinging my arms wide.

Garth managed to hide his amusement very well. He stopped typing and looked up at me. "I see Peth found you."

"Yeah. Thanks for the business."

"Why don't you say it a little louder? Maybe you can get me brought up on departmental charges."

I sat down on the edge of his desk and grinned. "I understand you're using the taxpayers' money to chase witches."

"Witches, warlocks, Satanists and sacrificial murderers," Garth said evenly. "As a matter of fact, the man Peth wants you to investigate is a witch as well as an astrologer."

I'd been kidding. Garth wasn't. "You mean 'warlock,' don't you?"

"No, I mean a witch. A witch is a witch, male or female. The term 'warlock' has a bad connotation among the knowledgeable. A warlock is a traitor, or a loner. Like a *magus* or ceremonial magician."

"A who?"

"Never mind. You don't want to hear about it."

What Garth meant was that he didn't want to talk about it. I asked him why.

"I'm not prepared to talk about it," Garth said quietly, staring at the backs of his hands. "At least not yet. I'll tell you, Mongo, you and I come from a background with a certain set of preconceptions that we call 'reality.' It's hard giving up those notions."

"Hey, brother, you sound like you're starting to take this stuff pretty seriously. Are the practitioners of the Black Arts getting to you?"

"What do you know about magic?"

"I'm allergic to rabbits."

"It isn't all black," Garth said, ignoring my crack. "Witchcraft, or Wicca, is recognized as an organized religion in New York State. The parent organization is called Friends of the Craft."

"I'm not sure I get the point."

Garth pressed his hands flat on the desk in front of him. He continued to stare at them. "I'm not sure there is a point."

I was growing a little impatient. "What can you tell me about this Borrn character?"

"He's supposed to be a good astrologer, and there aren't that many good ones around. I don't know anything else, except that he's never been involved in any of our investigations. That's why I sent Peth to you."

"What about a bunko angle? It's possible that Borrn could be milking Davidson. If he's using scare tactics, that's extortion."

Garth threw up his hands. "Then Davidson will just have to file a complaint. We're not running a baby-sitting service." He thought about what I'd said for a few moments, then added, "It's true that some of these guys are bunko artists, con men. They get an impressionable type, come up with a few shrewd insights, scare the hell out of him with a lot of mumbo jumbo, then start giving bad advice."

"Do any of them give good advice?"

Garth looked at me strangely. "I've seen some things that are hard to explain, and I've *heard* of things that are impossible to explain. I know very little because I get told very little. The occult underground is a very secret society. Secrecy is part of the Witch's Pyramid."

"There you go again."

"Never mind again. If you want to know more you should talk to one of your colleagues at the university."

I tried to think of one of my colleagues who might know something about the occult. I came up zero. "Who would that be?"

"Dr. Jones."

"*Uranus* Jones?"

"That's the one."

Uranus was more than a colleague; she was a friend. She was also one of the most levelheaded, *together* people I'd ever met. I shook my head. "You must have your signals crossed. Uranus isn't an astrologer, she's an astronomer. And one of the best in the business."

Garth grunted. "You may know her as an astronomer. In the circles I travel in lately, she's a living legend. She's cut an awful lot of corners for me, helping to track lost kids who get involved in the occult, that kind of thing. She's opened doors I wouldn't even be able to find on my own. Or wouldn't know existed. You wouldn't believe her reputation." He stared off into space for a few moments, as though considering his next words. "She's supposed to be psychic, and a materializing medium."

"There you go—"

"You know what a psychic is. A materializing medium is a person who can make objects appear in another person's hand—by willing it."

I found Uranus in her offices in the university's Hall of Sciences. The rooms were cluttered with charts, telescope parts, and other astronomical paraphernalia. Uranus was bent over a blowup of a new star cluster she had discovered. Her hair, strawberry blond in old photographs she had shared with me, was now a burnished silver. I knew she was fifty, but she had the face and body of a woman in her early thirties, and the eyes of a teen-ager.

She glanced up and smiled when I entered. "Mongo! How nice to see you!"

"Hello, darlin'." I went over to her desk and looked at the photograph. "How do you think those stars are going to affect my behavior this year?"

Uranus casually pushed the photo to one side, leaned back in her chair, folded her hands in her lap and stared at me. "Who have you been talking to?"

"A certain cop who's a little in awe of you. Didn't you know Garth is my brother?"

"I did."

"Well, how come you never talked to *me* about any of these hidden talents of yours? Heaven knows we've sat through enough boring faculty parties together."

"What would have been your reaction?"

I envisioned myself choking on a Scotch sour. She had a point, and I decided not to pursue it. "Uranus, I'd like to ask you a few questions."

"As a criminologist or private detective?"

"Private detective. I need some help."

"All right. What do you want to know?"

"For openers, darlin', what's a nice astrologer like you doing in a place like this?"

That caught her off guard and she laughed. "Astronomy evolved from astrology," she said, pointing to the charts and photographs strewn around her office. "The one is much older than the other."

"I'm not sure what that means."

"It may mean," Uranus said easily, "that any man who rejects

154

out-of-hand the tools that other men have found useful for thousands of years is a fool." She paused, then slowly drew a circle in the air with her index finger. "We live in a circle of light that we call Science. Obviously, I believe in science. But I also know that the circle of light expands slowly, illuminating things that are in the surrounding darkness. The atom, the force of gravity, the fact that the earth is round—all were very 'unscientific' concepts at one time. There are still unbelievably powerful forces out in that darkness we temporarily call the Occult, Mongo. The ancients knew about and used these forces instinctively. Most modern men—at least in the West—are not so wise. Science can be thought of as a means of *getting things done*. But there are other ways. For example, taking an airplane is a perfectly reasonable and efficient means of getting to, say, Europe. There are men and women alive today who can make the same journey—and report their observations—without ever leaving their living rooms. It's called astral projection."

"Are you one of those people?"

Uranus ignored the question. "The Magi mentioned in the Bible were astrologers," she said. "Our word 'magician' comes from *magi*. The 'star' they saw in the east was actually an astrological configuration that they knew how to interpret. And look where it led them. Jesus may have been the greatest ceremonial magician who's ever lived. He—with his disciples— numbered thirteen, the classic number of the witch's coven. Each of the disciples displays the characteristics of one of the twelve signs of the Zodiac. The sign of the early Christians was the fish. Pisces is symbolized by fish, and Jesus lived in the age of Pisces."

I meant to laugh; it came out a nervous chuckle. I remembered Garth's comment on preconceptions. "You'd better not let your friendly neighborhood clergy hear you talking like that."

Uranus smiled. "Everything I've said is common knowledge to anyone who's done his theological homework. It's a matter of difference of opinion over interpretation." She paused and touched my hand. "In any case, you can no longer claim that I don't discuss these things with you. What did you want to see me about, Mongo?"

I took out the horoscope Peth had given me and handed it to her. "I'd like you to read this for me."

Uranus smoothed the paper flat on the desk and studied it. After a few moments she looked up at me. "Is this yours, Mongo?"

I shook my head.

"I'm glad. I don't have time to do a thorough reading, but at a glance I'd say this person is in trouble."

"How do you know that?"

Uranus motioned me closer to the desk and pointed to the two circles. "The inner circle is the natal horoscope," she said, "the position of the sun, moon and planets in the sky at this person's birth. There are no severe afflictions—bad signs—in it. He or she probably has a marked talent in art or music, although that talent is used rather superficially, in a popular vein. But the chart indicates considerable success."

I swallowed hard and found that my mouth was dry. "Where does the trouble come in?"

"The outer circle is a synthesis—the horoscope projected up to the present time. Saturn—an evil, constricting influence—is in very bad conjunction with the other planets. There is a bad grouping in Scorpio, the sign of the occult. There are a number of other afflictions indicated, including a bad conjunction in the house of the secret enemy. I would say that whoever this is has reached a most important crossroad in his life, and the situation is fraught with danger. May I ask whose horoscope this is?"

I felt light-headed. I wrenched my brain back into gear. "A rock star by the name of Harley Davidson."

Uranus choked off a cry as her hand flew to her mouth.

"You know him?"

Uranus shuddered. "His real name is Bob Greenfield. Bob was one of my students a few years back. Tall, likable boy. Black hair, angular features. Maybe you remember him."

I didn't, which wasn't unusual. The university is a big place. I briefly told Uranus the story Peth had given me.

Uranus' eyes clouded and her face aged perceptibly. "Borrn is an evil man," she said quietly. "Bob would be no match for him."

"His ex-manager seems to think the same thing. He hired me to try to get something on Borrn."

Uranus shook her head. "You'll fail. And you'll be running a great personal risk if you try. Borrn is exceedingly dangerous."

"If he's criminal, maybe I can prove it."

"No. Evil is not necessarily criminal. There's a difference."

I didn't argue the point. I understood it all too well.

"Borrn is a gifted astrologer and palmist," Uranus continued. "There's also a rumor to the effect that he's a member of a supersecret coven of witches."

"Garth mentioned that."

"Garth must be developing some other good contacts; or someone is deliberately trying to mislead him. I'm not sure if the rumor is true, but it probably is. If so, it could explain a lot of things."

"Like what?"

"The influence you claim Borrn has over Bob. It could be the coven's cone of power acting on him."

"Cone of power?"

"An influence coming from a powerful collective will. That's the purpose of a coven: to form a collective will. There's no telling what they want with Bob. It could be a homosexual angle—Bob's a handsome boy—or it could simply be money."

I cleared my throat. "I'm sorry, Uranus, but I don't believe that 'cone of power' number."

Uranus seemed distracted, and I couldn't tell whether she hadn't heard or was merely ignoring my comment. "We should go and talk to Bob," she said at last.

"We?"

"He wouldn't talk to you. He would to me. I know the language."

I considered it for a moment, then reached for the phone, intending to call Peth. "I'll find out where he lives."

Uranus was already halfway to the door. "I know where he lives; we kept in touch up until a few months ago." She paused and stared at me. I was still standing by her desk, trying to sort things out. The urgency in her eyes hummed in her voice. "I really think we should hurry, Mongo."

•　　　•　　　•

The place where Harley Davidson had once lived was a three-story brownstone in a fashionable section of Greenwich

157

Village. Nobody answered the bell, and it took me half an hour to work my way through the double lock on the door.

Harley Davidson was out, and he wouldn't be back. He'd left his body behind on the floor of his bedroom, filled with sleeping pills.

I picked my way through the empty plastic vials on the floor and called Garth. Uranus sat down on the edge of Davidson's bed and began to cry softly. I began to poke around. The first thing that caught my attention was what appeared to be a notebook on a night stand. It had metal covers and was inscribed with strange symbols. I used a handkerchief to pick it up and carry it over to where Uranus was sitting. Her sobbing had subsided and she was staring off into space, beyond a young man's corpse, at what was and what might have been.

I touched her gently on the shoulder and showed her the notebook. "Darlin', do you know what this is?"

She glanced at the notebook. "It's a witch's diary," she said distantly. Her voice had the quality of an echo. "All initiates start one, and fill it the rest of their lives. It usually contains personal experiences, spells, and coven secrets."

I grunted, opened the book and started to leaf through it. There wasn't much in it that made any sense to me; I decided the obfuscation was probably intentional, designed to preserve its contents from prying eyes like my own. Borrn's name was mentioned a number of times, along with a list of various ceremonies in which Davidson had participated.

"Borrn seems to be the coven leader, judging by all this," I said.

Uranus said nothing, nor did she exhibit any interest in the notebook. I didn't press her on it. I asked a question instead. "What's 'scrying'?"

"Is that mentioned in there?"

"A number of times."

"Scrying is a method of divination," Uranus said hollowly, "of looking into the future or discovering secrets. It usually involves crystal gazing, but flame or water can also be used. Bob would have been nowhere near the point where he could scry."

"Who *is* at that point?"

I must have made a face, or the tone of my voice wasn't right. Uranus suddenly snapped, "Don't mock what you don't understand! I do it all the time!" She punctuated the outburst with a long sigh; it was an apology, unasked for and unneeded. "With the locked door and empty pill bottles, it's an obvious suicide. It's finished, Mongo. What's your interest now?"

It was a good question, one I'd been asking myself. Maybe it was the fact that a lot of Sandor Peth's money was still rustling around in my pocket. It seemed a shame to give it back, and if I were going to keep it I had to work for it.

"There's a point of law called psychological coercion," I said. "If it can be shown that Borrn or any other member of his coven influenced Davidson to take his own life, it's a criminal offense. Probably impossible to prove, but worth looking into."

"Leave it, Mongo. Please. No good will come out of your investigating Borrn. I know you don't believe this, but you can't imagine the misery he could cause you."

I didn't say anything. I was tired of warnings, tired of unwanted glimpses into the dark attics of men's minds. There was the body of the boy on the floor, shot out of the tree of life by invisible bullets of what had to be superstition. Those bullets had found their mark in a bright, talented and rich boy who had exploded under their impact, plunging from the rarefied atmosphere of celebrity to end as a cold, graying hulk, like a falling star.

Uranus suddenly gripped my arm. "Bob shouldn't have had something like this."

I looked at her. The grief in her eyes had been replaced by something else. She looked as if she had just waked from sleep, passing from a nightmare into something worse.

"Why not? You told me Borrn was a witch. Under the circumstances, wouldn't it have been natural for Davidson to become a member of Borrn's coven?"

"No. It would have been virtually impossible. I told you that a coven is made up of thirteen members. Thirteen is a magic number of sorts. No coven would take in a fourteenth member."

"Maybe somebody died or decided to join the Elks instead."

Uranus shook her head. "Not at the level at which this coven operated. You don't just 'leave' a coven like that. And, even if a member had died, they would never choose a boy like Bob to take his place. Borrn's coven is highly skilled. They would never accept an initiate."

"Maybe the book belongs to somebody else."

"I doubt it. A witch's diary is his most precious possession. He almost never lets it out of his sight."

I put the book back in its place and started for the door. "Garth should be here in a few minutes," I said. "You fill him in. I'll talk to him later."

"Where will I tell him you've gone?"

"Tell him I've gone to have my fortune told."

•   •   •

It took a bit of looking, but I finally found Borrn's store-front operation. It was the only open door in a narrow alley bounded on both sides by crumbling warehouses with boarded-up windows. I went through it.

The room was small and cramped, permeated by the smell of incense. Borrn sat in the middle of it like a spider in the middle of an invisible web that was no less deadly for the fact that I couldn't see it. In front of him was a plain wooden table on which was a crystal ball. It was the only *exotica* in the room; the rest consisted of bookshelves filled with books, most of which looked well-worn. I wondered whether he actually read them, or had picked them up in a secondhand bookstore. Borrn himself was dressed in a very unmystical outfit consisting of faded denims and dungaree jacket. I felt vaguely disappointed, like a boy who'd peeked into a clown's dressing room.

Borrn rose as I entered. He was not a big man, but he had presence, the kind of self-assurance that comes from being able to make a living doing what you like and being good at it. He was short and stocky, with brown hair and piercing black eyes.

"Can I help you?" His voice was soft, almost lilting, like the swish of a garrote before it bites into flesh.

I gave him a phony name. Business or no, I didn't want my name popping up at a later date on some astrologer's list of clients. "I hear you tell fortunes."

I'd offended him. Borrn sat back down and crossed his arms over his chest. "I do not 'tell fortunes,' as you put it. I advise you to look on Forty-second Street."

160

"What do you do?"

"If you are serious, I will read your palm. I charge twenty-five dollars for a one-hour consultation. However, I do not think you are serious. You would have known that I am not a fortune-teller."

"What do you call palm reading?"

"The palm is a map of your past and an indication of what your future may hold. It does not tell your destiny; *you* decide your destiny."

"It still sounds like the same thing."

"It is not. If I tell you there is a red light two blocks from here, that does not affect your freedom to decide to stop for it or to run it."

"It sounds a little complicated to me. How about doing my horoscope?"

He motioned me to sit down. I did.

"I believe your horoscope would be useless to you," he said in the tone of a doctor criticizing a medication. "I'm sure it will come as no surprise to you to be told that you're a dwarf. Your horoscope would probably show a great affliction in the physical area, but the rest might not necessarily hold true. A horoscope is like an insurance company's actuary tables. You differ markedly from the norm; your dwarfism—the immediacy of it—would consistently influence your life far more than the planets."

"All right," I said, holding out my hand, "see what you can do with that."

"Are you right-handed?"

"Yes."

"Then this hand is the record of what you have done with your natural talents. The left is your subconscious, your potential. Later we will compare the two."

He took my right hand and began to manipulate it, bending the fingers back and forth, pressing the mounds of flesh at the base of the palm and fingers. He had a soft, delicate touch. To this point he had been rather pleasant, a natural psychologist; I had to remind myself that the worst evil often comes in the nicest packages.

"Were you once in the circus?"

The question startled me, until I reflected on the logic of it. "Sure," I said evenly. "We call it 'Dwarfs' Heaven.'"

Borrn shook his head. He seemed puzzled. "But you weren't there in the capacity of a clown, or a freak. You were important, had a wonderful reputation and considerable publicity. I . . . see great coordination and drive. I would have to say that you were an acrobat. Or a tumbler." He looked up at me. "Is that right?"

I decided Borrn had one hell of an act. I resisted the impulse to look at my own hand. "What else does it say?"

Borrn turned his attention back to my hand. "The head line is very long and complex. I would say that you have—or once had—multiple careers. You have a great deal of intelligence, and may be a teacher, probably at an advanced level, as your hand shows that you are impatient with stupidity. Also, you are dying."

The last went through me like a jolt of electricity. I yanked my hand away. "It comes with the package," I said tightly. "That's why you don't see many dwarfs in old-age homes. Did Harley Davidson's hand say the same thing?"

That gave Borrn a little jolt of his own, but he had remarkable control. Something flashed in his eyes, then went out, leaving his eyes looking like two cold lumps of coal. The effect was startling, as though he had suddenly contracted and was watching me from somewhere deep inside himself, far behind the dull eyes I was watching. "Who are you?" he asked. "What do you want?"

"Davidson was one of your clients. Did you know that he's dead?"

"I do not discuss my clients," Borrn said in a voice that was so low it was barely audible. "Get out."

"You may have to discuss Davidson with the police. I think you may have had something to do with his death. What did you tell him that would make him want to take his own life?"

I expected some kind of reaction and got none. I knew instinctively that Borrn was not going to say more. He sat very still, like some kind of statue executed in perfect detail, but still without life. Again, I had the impression that he had retreated to somewhere deep within himself to a trancelike state where, as far as I was concerned, he had left the room and would not be coming back. I swallowed hard. His eyes were blank, looking at and beyond me. I suddenly knew that he could stay that way for hours if he chose to do so. Nothing I could say or do would have the slightest impact on him.

It was the most effective brush-off I'd ever seen. I got up and left.

I didn't go far. It had been a long day, and I'd covered a lot of territory, geographic and emotional; but there was still a way to go, and I was anxious to get to the end of whatever road it was I was traveling on. Borrn had gotten to me in a way he probably hadn't anticipated. He'd known too much about me. That meant one of two things: He had actually seen things in my palm, or he had a dossier. To me it was no contest. I wanted to find the dossier, then find out who had given it to him, and why.

I killed what remained of the afternoon in a local bar over beer and a steak sandwich. Then I went out and bought a penlight and a navy blue sheet. Finally I went back to the alley. It was dark.

It took me all of thirty seconds to burgle my way into the store-front. I shrouded myself with the sheet to hide the light from the penlight and began to go through Borrn's rather extensive library. I wasn't sure what I was looking for; whatever it was, I didn't find it. Most of the books were highly technical treatises on astrology, replete with countless charts and tables that made my eyes water. That was it, except for a crumbling copy of something called the *Kabala* and other books on mysticism. There were no personal papers or records of any kind.

I sat down in Borrn's chair and tried to think. I'd apparently struck out in Borrn's office, and I doubted strongly that I would find any "Borrn" listed in the telephone directory. Besides, judging from what Uranus and Garth had said, I wasn't going to get any information from people in the neighborhood who might have any.

I raised a good dwarf chuckle by reflecting on the fact that I might just have to "scry" up some answers. I reached out and touched the crystal ball in front of me. It was heavy leaded glass. I absently pushed at it and heard a soft click behind me. I turned and whistled softly.

A section of one of the bookcases had slid open to reveal a short corridor leading to what appeared to be a large chamber.

Light from the secret chamber was pouring out into the storefront and splashing onto the street. I quickly rose from the chair and went through the opening.

I'd been worried about getting the door shut, and I realized too late that I'd confused my priorities. The heavy steel door sighed shut as I passed through the opening. It came up flush against the wall with a very solid and ominous click. I looked for some way to get the door open and couldn't find it. It was a double-security system, primarily designed to keep intruders out but, failing that, designed to insure that they stayed in. Since there seemed to be no way out, I went in.

The setup inside was impressive. The interior of the warehouse behind Borrn's store-front had been gutted and reconstructed to form a huge, circular chamber. The walls and ceiling were solid and soundproofed; the floor was concrete. I estimated the construction costs to be in excess of a half million dollars. Borrn didn't get that kind of money from doing mystical manicures.

The job wasn't completed yet. There was a gaping hole high on the north wall, with ropes and scaffolding hanging down from it. That would be the conduit for the building supplies.

There was a large crater in the middle of the floor, about twenty feet in diameter. I walked over and looked in. It was perhaps six feet deep, covered at the bottom with large gas jets. The ceiling above was blackened, and there were air vents placed at strategic points around the chamber to allow for circulation. The whole thing reminded me of a crematorium.

There were twelve cubicles built around the perimeter of the chamber, and I could see from where I was standing that they were living quarters of sorts, complete with cots, small libraries and black-draped, candle-covered altars; but it was the thirteenth cubicle built into the north wall in which I was interested. It was at least twice as large as the others, and was draped in red: that would be Borrn's. I walked in.

I was a slow learner. The cubicle was rigged in the same manner as the store-front; I had no sooner stepped over the threshold than a steel door dropped from a hidden receptacle in the ceiling. Obviously, arrangements for walking out had to be made before walking in. I decided that didn't bode well for my immediate future.

I began a systematic search of the room. It didn't take me long to strike pay dirt. This time there were personal notes and correspondence written in a language I could understand.

Two things became very clear: Borrn was not the leader of the coven, and Harley Davidson had, indeed, had a "secret enemy."

The door sighed open an hour or so later. Sandor Peth stood in the doorway, staring down at me where I sat on the bed. Borrn and the rest of the coven stood slightly behind him. All were dressed in crimson, hooded robes adorned with mystic symbols. The lights had been turned out in the large chamber, and there was a loud hissing sound; firelight flickered and danced like heat lightning.

I looked at Peth. "Dr. Livingstone, I presume?"

Peth's milky blue eyes didn't change. "You are a very persistent man, Dr. Frederickson," he said evenly. "And fast. I'm afraid I seriously underestimated you."

I motioned to the firelight behind him. "Rather newfangled, isn't it?"

"One of the exigencies of living in New York City."

"You want to tell me what this is all about?"

"Like in the movies?"

"Like in the movies."

Peth motioned to Borrn, who came forward and searched me. I didn't put up any resistance. It wasn't the time. I wanted to find out what Peth had to say—if anything. Also, I thought resistance might be offensive to the thirteen of them.

"All right," Peth said when Borrn had finished with me and stepped back into the group. He entered the room and sat down on a chair across from me. "First, why don't you tell me what you've surmised so far?"

"You killed Davidson, and you were trying to cover your tracks."

"The second part of your statement is correct. But I—or we—did not kill Davidson; we caused him to die."

"An interesting legal point."

"Yes. I suppose it is."

"How'd you do it?"

Peth motioned to himself and the others, as though the answer were obvious. There was a faint ringing in my ears.

"You're telling me you put a spell on him?" I decided he was crazy, and I told him so.

Peth shrugged. "You asked me what this was all about, and I am trying to tell you. Of course, the fact that we caused Harley to take his own life is unprovable. However, the papers in this room, which I'm sure you've seen, do prove intent to do harm, and could prove embarrassing in a courtroom. I'm truly sorry you proved to be so conscientious."

"Why did Davidson have to die?"

"We depend on people—you would probably call them 'victims'—for our financial resources. All of us, in one way or another, are involved with people, and these people unwittingly provide financial support for our activities."

"What activities?"

"Simply put, the accumulation of power that will enable us to control even more people. As you know, fame and fortune in the rock-music business is ephemeral. Harley was at the peak of his earning powers. The power which you scoffed at had enabled me to secure Harley's power of attorney and convince him to sign a will leaving all of his rather large list of investments to me. Also, I had managed to buy a million dollars' worth of insurance, without a suicide clause, on Harley's life. Very expensive, but I knew I wouldn't have that many premiums to pay. At that point Harley became more valuable to us dead than alive."

"And that's when Borrn went to work on his head?"

"We all participated in the process. We knew that Harley would eventually kill himself, but we did not know when or how. If I had known he would do it the way he did—by swallowing pills inside a locked house, as reported on the radio—I would not have proceeded the way I did. However, I knew that I, as the beneficiary of very large sums of money, would come under a great deal of suspicion. That's why I went to your brother. I anticipated his reaction and thought that would be the end of it, with my innocence established in his mind. However, when he suggested that I come to you, I felt I had to take the suggestion."

"You did some pretty thorough research on me first."

Peth looked surprised. "No. As a matter of fact, I didn't. I should have. If I had, Borrn would have been prepared for your visit, and you would not be in the position you find yourself. As

166

it was, Borrn did not know you were a dwarf—I hadn't had a chance to tell him—and you gave him a false name."

"You're lying. Why? It's a small point."

Again, Peth looked surprised. Suddenly he laughed. "Borrn gave you a reading, didn't he?"

Something was stirring deep inside my mind; it was blind, soft and furry, with sharp teeth. I ran away from it. "You took Davidson into your coven, right?"

"Borrn made Davidson think he was a part of the coven—in which I, obviously, was the missing member. Of course he was never really a part. All of the ceremonies he took part in were actually part of a magical attack on his deep mind."

I'd heard enough to convince me that some kind of legal case could be made against Peth, Borrn and the others, and the papers I'd hidden inside my shirt would give me a shot at proving it. At the least, New York City would be rid of one particular supercoven composed of thirteen megalomaniac cranks. There remained only the slight difficulty of finding a way to get past thirteen men, and out of a sealed room. I tried not to let that depress me.

"What happens now?"

"Must I state the obvious?"

"You'd be a fool to kill me."

"Really? Why is that? I think we would be fools not to kill you. The fire is very hot. It will leave no trace of you. You will simply have disappeared."

"My brother knows I'm investigating Borrn. He'll find this place."

"Oh, I don't think so."

"Somebody's building it."

"Haitians, who appreciate our powers. They are afraid of voodoo spells. They would tear their own tongues out before they told anybody about this place. It's true that Borrn will be investigated, but I have no doubt that he will come out of it clean."

"People know he's a witch."

That shook him. "How is that?"

I decided against mentioning Garth or Uranus. "It's in his witch's diary. Davidson's."

Peth was silent for a long time. Whatever he'd finally decided wasn't going to be shared with me. He rose from his chair and gave a slight nod of his head. As one, the twelve figures outside the door entered the room and began to fan out around me. Their movements were slow, almost mechanical; it was like seeing a guillotine blade descend in slow motion.

I smiled in what I hoped was a disarming manner, and gathered my legs beneath me. I focused my gaze on Peth's solar plexus. I couldn't fight thirteen men, but a few of them were going to discover that I was one deadly dwarf. Peth would be my first candidate for instruction.

"O Pentacle of Might, be thou fortress and defense to Robert Frederickson against all enemies, seen and unseen, in every magical work!"

Uranus' voice drifted down from the darkness in the outer chamber. Before all the lights went out I caught the looks of utter astonishment on the faces of the coven members. I was a little surprised myself, but not so much that I forgot the way out of the room. I lunged forward in the darkness, caromed off a few sheeted bodies and landed on my face on the concrete outside. I got back up on my feet and raced off to my left, taking cover in the darkness, beyond the firelight. I'd traded in one trap for a new, slightly larger one; as long as the lights remained out, a few people were going to pay a heavy price for trying to find me.

That left me to meditate on the question of what Uranus was doing in the building.

Peth and the others seemed to be preoccupied by the same question. I watched as they slowly emerged from the darkness to spread out in a circle around the raging fire. Peth stood at their head, gazing up toward the spot where the hole in the north wall would be.

"Who are you?" Peth asked in a whisper that carried throughout the chamber.

"All wise Great One, Great Ruler of Storms, Master of the Heavenly Chamber, Great King of the Powers of the Sky, be here, we pray thee, and guard this place from all dangers approaching from the west!"

Peth and the others knew a few rhymes of their own. There

was no visible signal of any kind, but their voices rose in a chorus that made chills ripple through my body:

"Amodeus, Calamitor, Usor! You who sow confusion, where are you? You who infuse fear and hate and enmity, I command you by the power of Disalone and Her Horned Consort to go!

"So mote it be!

"So mote it be!"

There was a pause, then Uranus' voice again, soft, drifting like a sonic feather:

"Four corners in this house for Holy Angels. Christ Jesus be in our midst. God be in this place and keep us safe."

The response was a blast of psychic hate:

"It is not our hands which do this deed, but that of Amodeus the Horned One!

"The trespasser must die!

"So mote it be!

"So mote it be!"

I was watching a duel of sorcerers, and I felt thrown back in time a thousand years, thrown to the ground at the mouth of a cave in which moved dark, strange shapes.

There was a long silence. Peth made a motion with his hand and the other members of the coven turned and started to fan out. It was dwarf-hunting time.

"Stop!" Uranus' voice was weaker, ragged, as though she were short of breath. The movement of the coven members stopped. "I am Uranus Jones, and Dr. Frederickson is under my protection. You have heard of me and know of my powers."

Peth's voice drifted softly through the room, waxing and waning like some invisible moon. "I have heard of you, Uranus Jones. You are a member of our family, a unit of the Universal Mind. Respect our wishes. This is not your concern. Leave us. So mote it be."

Again, the faint, muted tones: "I repeat that Dr. Frederickson is under my protection. You harm him at your own peril."

Her voice drifted off strangely. The muscles in my stomach began to flutter uncontrollably. There was movement to my left.

"Mongo! Shoot the leader if anyone moves again!"

Uranus' voice seemed stronger now, as though she had

successfully passed through some great ordeal. I liked her suggestion, except that I didn't have a gun, and Peth knew it.

"He doesn't have a gun," Peth said, underlining my thoughts. I wondered why he sounded so uncertain.

"He does now," Uranus said. "Open the doors and let him pass."

It was the beginning of an argument between two other parties that I was going to lose. It seemed a good time to excuse myself from the debate.

I remembered the scaffolding hanging from the hole in the north wall, and tried to picture in my mind exactly where it would be. I knew it was about ten feet off the ground, and I would need tremendous momentum if I hoped to reach it.

Circus time. I shoved off the wall and sprinted across the floor, getting up a good head of steam. Somebody reached out for me and missed. Twenty feet from where I judged the wall to be I launched into a series of cartwheels, then, on the last turn, planted my feet on the floor and hurled myself up into the air.

At the apogee of my leap my hands touched wood. I gripped the edge of the scaffold; I scrambled up onto the platform, shinnied up the rope and dropped over the concrete cornice onto a pile of building supplies.

The entire escape had taken less than fifteen seconds.

I could see Uranus now in the glow of the firelight reflected off the walls. She was slumped against a girder, next to a large circuit breaker; her appearance frightened me more than anything that had happened previously. She appeared to have aged into an old woman, devoid of energy; her beautiful, silver hair hung in wisps from her head.

I ran over to her and grabbed her around the waist.

"Fire exit," she gasped. "Off to the left."

I started to my left, pulling Uranus after me. I'd expected to hear a furor from below or, at the least, a few well-chosen curses. There was silence.

"Why the hell didn't you tell me about this place?" I whispered through clenched teeth. "It would have saved everybody a lot of trouble."

"Scry," Uranus sighed in the same broken voice that had so frightened me before. "Knew . . . felt . . . you in trouble. Called Garth but afraid . . . there wasn't . . . time."

170

She seemed to be regaining her strength. I released her and she scrambled along beside me. I found the window she had come through. We both went out, then started down the fire escape.

"The gun," Uranus said. "Do you have it? They may try to come after us."

"I don't have a gun."

Uranus said nothing. I could hear the sirens of Garth's cavalry coming to the rescue. Judging from the sound, they were closing fast.

"Let's go watch the show," I said, starting down the alley leading to the front of the building.

Uranus grabbed my wrist and pulled me into the darkness beside the building. She looked herself again, though still pale; it was as though she had passed through a near-fatal illness in a matter of only a few minutes.

"I can't go with you," she said.

"Why the hell not? Knowing Garth, he'll have an army of cops with him."

"That's not the point. I don't want to answer questions. I don't want anyone to know exactly what happened in that building tonight."

"Peth will tell them."

"No, he won't. And none of the others will either. I must beg you not to speak, Mongo, for the sake of our friendship. When I called Garth I told him simply that I had a hunch about you and the warehouse. Garth has learned to trust my hunches."

"This is no time for games," I said impatiently. "How did you know where I was?"

She ignored my question. "There will be reporters out there, questions that I'm not prepared to answer. I would no longer be able to carry on my work at the university, and you know how important that is to me. It's my link with the . . . rest of the world. Please, Mongo. Don't take that away from me."

She turned and ran off into the darkness without waiting for an answer. I walked slowly toward the flashing lights at the front of the building.

The proverbial mop-up of Peth and his crew was decidedly anticlimactic. When Garth and the other policemen broke down the secret door the members of the coven were waiting calmly.

Their robes and, presumably, all of the records had been consigned to the gas-fed bonfire still roaring from the pit in the center of the floor. They offered no resistance.

As Uranus had predicted, no one mentioned her presence in the building earlier. For some reason I didn't fully understand, I didn't either.

I was exhausted, and my head felt as though it had been stuffed with rotting cotton. Still, I managed to drag myself down to the police station, where I turned over the papers I had taken and made some kind of statement. Then I went home and poured myself a tumbler of Scotch. I wanted desperately to sleep, but there were still a lot of things on my mind.

There was nothing that had happened which could not be explained by a few good guesses and a lot of abnormal psychology emanating from some very sick minds. I needed the Scotch because I realized that Uranus possessed one of those sick minds. A woman I loved was, in my opinion, desperately ill, and I had to find the courage to confront her with this opinion, to suggest that she see a psychiatrist.

Having resolved this, I slipped off my jacket and threw it toward the bed. Only at the last moment did I realize that it somehow seemed heavier than it should. The jacket slid across the smooth bedspread and fell to the floor on the opposite side with a heavy, metallic clunk. The sound shrieked in my ears, echoing down to the very roots of my soul.

Whatever was in the jacket, I didn't want to know about it. I raced around the bed, picked up the jacket and in the same motion sent it hurtling toward the window. The weighted cloth shattered the glass and dropped from sight.

I stood, shaking uncontrollably and breathing hard as the cool wind whistled through the broken pane. Even as a tremendous surge of relief flowed through me, I knew that throwing away the jacket was no answer. If, indeed, there were the forces outside the "circle of light" Uranus had mentioned, it would do no good for me to deny it: I would merely remain ignorant of their existence. If the jacket was lost, I'd spend the rest of my life wondering what had been in the pocket—and how it had gotten there.

I drained off the Scotch, then went back into the night.

This story, also incorporated into An Affair of Sorcerers, *is the one I would approach* most *differently if I were writing the piece now instead of this introduction to it. This is the closest I ever came to acceding to the possibility that there "might be something there," when all that is there is our fear and ignorance. Today I would like to believe, and perhaps even argue, that the story is really about how fear alone can most definitely kill, and about the tendency of superstitious people who insist on "taking things on faith"—even when all objective evidence points to the contrary—to be their own executioners intellectually, spiritually, and often physically. The naked text is there, but I would still like to believe that I was writing about the terrible cost of the dues for membership in some belief systems.*

Book of Shadows

It had been a long day with absolutely nothing accomplished. I'd spent most of it grading a depressing set of mid-term papers that led me to wonder what I'd been teaching all semester in my graduate criminology seminar. After that I'd needed a drink.

Instead of doing the perfectly sensible thing and repairing to the local pub, I'd made the mistake of calling my answering service, which informed me there was a real live client waiting for me in my downtown office. The Yellow Pages the man had picked my name out of didn't mention the fact that this particular private detective was a dwarf: One look at me and the man decided he didn't really need a private detective after all.

With my sensitive ego in psychic shreds, I headed home. I

planned to quickly make up for my past sobriety and spend an electronically lobotomized evening in front of the television.

I perked up when I saw the little girl waiting for me outside my apartment. Kathy Marsten was a small friend of mine from 4D, down the hall. With her blond hair and blue eyes, dressed in a frilly white dress and holding a bright red patent leather purse, she looked positively beatific. I laughed to myself as I recalled that it had taken me two of her seven years to convince her that I wasn't a potential playmate.

"Kathy, Kathy, Kathy!" I said, picking her up and setting her down in a manner usually guaranteed to produce Instant Giggle. "How's my girl today?"

"Hello, Mr. Mongo," she said very seriously.

"Why the good clothes? You look beautiful, but I'd think you'd be out playing with your friends by this time."

"I came here right after school, Mr. Mongo. I've been waiting for you. I was getting afraid I wouldn't see you before my daddy came home. I wanted to ask you something."

Now the tears came. I reached down and brushed them away, suddenly realizing that this was no child's game. "What did you want to ask me, Kathy?"

She sniffled, then regained control of herself in a manner that reminded me of someone much older. "My daddy says that you sometimes help people for money."

"That's right, Kathy. Can I help you?"

Her words came in a rush. "I want you to get my daddy's book of shadows back from Daniel so Daddy will be happy again. But you mustn't tell Daddy. He'd be awful mad at me if he knew I told anybody. But he just *has* to get it back or something terrible will happen. I just know it."

"Kathy, slow down and tell me what a 'book of shadows' is. Who's Daniel?"

But she wasn't listening. Kathy was crying again, fumbling in her red purse. "I've got money for you," she stammered. "I've been saving my allowance and milk money."

Before I could say anything the little girl had taken out a handful of small change and pressed it into my palm. I started to give it back, then stopped when I heard footsteps come up behind me.

"Kathy!" a thin voice said. "There you are!"

The girl gave me one long, piercing look that was a plea to keep her secret. Then she quickly brushed away her tears and smiled at the person standing behind me. "Hi, Daddy! I fell and hurt myself. Mr. Mongo was making me feel better."

I straightened up and turned to face Jim Marsten. He seemed much paler and thinner since I'd last seen him, but perhaps it was my imagination. The fact of the matter was that I knew Kathy much better than I knew either of her parents. We knew each other's names, occasionally exchanged greetings in the hall, and that was it. Marsten was a tall man, the near side of thirty, prematurely balding. The high dome of his forehead accentuated the dark, sunken hollows of his eye sockets. He looked like a man who was caving in.

"Hello, Mongo," Marsten said.

I absently slipped the money Kathy had given me into my pocket and shook the hand that was extended to me. "Hi, Jim. Good to see you."

"Thanks for taking care of my daughter." He looked at Kathy. "Are you all right now?"

Kathy nodded her head. Her money felt heavy in my pocket; I felt foolish. By the time I realized I probably had no right to help a seven-year-old child keep secrets from her father, Jim Marsten had taken the hand of his daughter and was leading her off down the hall. Kathy looked back at me once and her lips silently formed the word *please*.

When they were gone I took Kathy's money out of my pocket and counted it. There was fifty-seven cents.

•   •   •

I must have looked shaky. My brother Garth poured me a second double Scotch and brought it over to where I was sitting. I took a pull at it, then set the glass aside and swore.

Garth shook his head. "It can all be explained, Mongo," he said. "There's a rational explanation for everything."

"Is there?" I asked without any real feeling. "Let's hear one."

•   •   •

Someone was calling my name: a child's voice, crying, afraid, a small wave from some dark, deep ocean lapping at the shore of my mind. Then I was running down a long tunnel, slipping and falling on the soft, oily surface, struggling to reach the small, frail figure at the other end. The figure of Kathy seemed to recede with each step I took, and still I ran. Kathy was dressed in a long, flowing white gown, buttoned to the neck, covered with strange, twisted shapes. Suddenly she was before me. As I reached out to take her in my arms she burst into flames.

I sat bolt upright in bed, drenched in sweat. My first reaction was relief when I realized I had only been dreaming. Then came terror: I smelled smoke.

Or thought I smelled smoke. Part of the dream? I started to reach for my cigarettes, then froze. There *was* smoke. I leaped out of bed, quickly checked the apartment. Nothing was burning. I threw open the door of the apartment and stepped out into the hall. Smoke was seeping from beneath the door of the Marstens' apartment.

I sprinted to the end of the hall and broke the fire box there. Then I ran back and tried the door to 4D. It was locked. I didn't waste time knocking. I braced against the opposite wall, ran two steps forward, kipped in the air and kicked out at the door just above the lock. The door rattled. I picked myself off the floor and repeated the process. This time the door sprung open wide.

The first thing that hit me was the stench. The inside of the apartment, filled with thick, greenish smoke, smelled like a sewer.

There was a bright, furnace glow to my right, coming from the bedroom. I started toward it, then stopped when I saw Kathy lying on the couch.

She was dressed in the same gown I had seen in the dream.

I bent over her. She seemed to be breathing regularly but was completely unconscious, not responding to either my voice or touch. I picked her up and carried her out into the hall, laid her down on the carpet and went back into the apartment.

There was nothing I could do there. I stood in the door of the bedroom and gazed in horror at the bed that had become a funeral pyre. The naked bodies of Jim and Becky Marsten were barely discernible inside the deadly ring of fire. The bodies, blackened and shriveling, were locked together in some terrible and final act of love. And death.

• • •

"They were using combustible chemicals as part of their ritual," *Garth said, lighting a cigarette and studying me. "They started* *fooling with candles and the room went up. It's obvious."*

"Is it? The fire was out by the time the Fire Department got there. *And there wasn't that much damage to the floor."*

"Typical of some kinds of chemical fires, Mongo. You know that."

"I saw the fire: it was too bright, too even. And I did hear Kathy's *voice calling me. She was crying for help."*

"In your dream?"

"In my dream."

My brother Garth is a cop. He took a long time to answer, and I *sensed that he was embarrassed. "The mind plays tricks, Mongo."*

I had a few thoughts on that subject: I washed them away with a *mouthful of Scotch.*

• • •

"Excuse me, Doctor. How's the girl? Kathy Marsten?"

The doctor was Puerto Rican, frail, and walked with a limp. He had a full head of thick black hair and large, brown eyes that weren't yet calloused over by the pain one encounters in a New York City hospital. He was a young man. The tag on his white smock said his name was Rivera. He looked somewhat surprised to find a dwarf standing in front of him.

"Who are you?"

"My name's Frederickson."

The eyes narrowed. "I've seen your picture. They call you Mongo. Ex-circus performer, college professor, private—"

"I asked you how the girl was."

"Are you a relative?"

"No. Friend of the family. I brought her in."

He hesitated, then led me to a small alcove at the end of the corridor. I didn't like the look of the way he walked and held his head: too sad, a little desperate.

"My name is Rivera," he said. "Juan Rivera."

"I saw the name tag, Doctor."

"Kathy is dying."

Just like that. I passed my hand over my eyes. "Of what?"

177

Rivera shrugged his shoulders. It was an odd gesture, filled with helplessness and bitter irony. "We don't know," he said, his eyes clouding. "There's no sign of smoke inhalation, which, of course, was the first thing we looked for. Since then we've run every conceivable test. Nothing. There's no sign of physical injury. She's just . . . *dying*. All the machines can tell us is that her vital signs are dropping at an alarming rate. If the drop continues at its present rate, Kathy Marsten will be dead in two to three days."

"She hasn't regained consciousness?"

"No. She's in a deep coma."

"Can't you operate?"

Juan Rivera's laugh was short, sharp, bitter, belied by the anguish in his eyes. "Operate on *what*? Don't you understand? Modern medicine says there's nothing wrong with that girl. She's merely dying."

Rivera swallowed hard. "There must be something in her background: an allergy, some obscure hereditary disease. That information is vital." He suddenly reached into his hip pocket and drew out his wallet. "You're a private detective. I want to hire you to find some relative of Kathy's that knows something about her medical history."

I held up my hand. "No thanks. I only take on one client at a time."

Rivera looked puzzled. "You won't help?"

"The girl hired me to find something for her. I figure that covers finding a way to save her life. Do you still have the gown she was wearing when I brought her in?"

"The one with the pictures?"

"Right. I wonder if you'd give it to me."

"Why?"

"I'd rather not say right now, Dr. Rivera. I think the symbols on that gown mean something. They could provide a clue to what's wrong with Kathy."

"They're designs," he said somewhat impatiently. "A child's nightgown. What can it have to do with Kathy's illness?"

"Maybe nothing. But I won't know for sure unless you give it to me."

"Hypnosis."

"Hypnosis?! C'mon, Garth. You're reaching."

"Trauma, then. After all, she did watch her parents burn to death."

"Maybe. She was unconscious when I found her."

"God knows what else she was forced to watch."

"And take part in," I added.

"Assuming she did see her parents die, don't you think that—along with everything else—might not be enough to shock a girl to death?"

"I don't know, Garth. You're the one with all the explanations."

"God, Mongo, you don't believe that stuff Daniel told you?!"

"I believe the Marstens believed. And Daniel."

• • •

"You're right, Mongo. They are occult symbols."

I watched Dr. Uranus Jones as she continued to finger the satin gown, examining every inch of it. Uranus was a handsome women in her early fifties—good-looking enough to have carried on a string of affairs with a procession of lab assistants twenty years her junior, or so rumor had it. Her gray-streaked blond hair was drawn back into a ponytail, which made her look younger.

The walls of her university office were covered with astronomical charts, many of which she had designed herself. It was an appropriate decor for the office of one of the world's most prominent astronomers. But I wasn't there to discuss astronomy.

Uranus had a rather interesting dual career. As far as I knew, I was the only one of Uranus' colleagues at the university who knew that Uranus was also a top astrologer and medium, with a near legendary reputation in the New York occult underground.

"What do they mean?"

"They look like symbols for the ascending order of demons," she said quietly.

"What does it mean as far as the Marstens are concerned?"

Uranus took a long time to answer. "My guess is that the Marstens were witches practicing the black side of their craft. I'd say they were into demonology and Satanism, and they were trying to summon up a demon. Probably Belial, judging from the symbols on this gown. From what you've told me, I'd speculate that the Marstens were using a ritual that rebounded on them. The rebound killed them."

"Rebound?"

"The evil. It rebounded and killed them. They weren't able to control the power released by the ritual. That's the inherent danger of ceremonial magic."

"What 'power'?"

"The power of Belial. I assume that's who they were trying to summon. He killed them before they could exercise the necessary control."

I studied Uranus in an attempt to see if she was joking. There wasn't a trace of a smile on her face. "Do you believe that, Uranus?"

She avoided my eyes. "I'm not a ceremonial magician, Mongo."

"That's not an answer."

"It wasn't meant to be. You asked about the symbols on the robe, and I'm responding in the context of ceremonial magic. I'm describing to you a system of belief. It's up to you to decide whether that system could have anything to do with the fact that Kathy Marsten is dying. It's your responsibility to choose what avenue to pursue, and, from what I understand, you don't have much time."

I wasn't sure there was a choice. According to Dr. Juan Rivera, the practitioners of the system called medicine had just about played out their string. I risked nothing but making a fool out of myself. Kathy had considerably more to lose. There was a sudden ringing in my ears.

"All right. Within the context of ceremonial magic, why is Kathy dying?"

Uranus looked at me for a long time, then said: "Belial is claiming a bride."

"Come again."

"The gown: It means that the child was to be a part of the ritual. My guess is that her parents were offering her up to Belial in exchange for whatever it was they wanted. He killed her parents, and now he's taking her."

"You're saying that Kathy is possessed?"

"Within the context of ceremonial magic, yes. And she will have to be exorcised if you hope to save her. To do that, you will need to know the *exact* steps in the ritual the Marstens were using. Needless to say, that's not something you're likely to find in the public library. And I don't mean that to sound flippant. Assuming that such a ritual does exist, it would have taken the Marstens years to research from some of the rarest manuscripts in the world."

The ringing in my ears was growing louder. I shook my head in an attempt to clear it. It didn't do any good. "God, Uranus," I whispered, "this is the twentieth century. I only have a little time. How can I justify using it to chase . . . demons?"

"You can't, Mongo. Not in your belief system. Because demons don't exist in your belief system. But they did in the Marstens', and Kathy Marsten is dying."

"Yes," I said distantly. "Kathy Marsten is dying."

"Consider the possibility that you are what you believe. What you believe affects you. The witch and the ceremonial magician perceive evil in personal terms. Belial, for example. Most men today prefer other names for evil . . . Buchenwald, My Lai."

∙   ∙   ∙

"She was talking about the mind of man," I said. "That's where the demons are. It's where they've always been. The question is whether or not evil can be personified. Can it be made to assume a shape? Can it be controlled?"

Garth shook his head impatiently. "That's all crazy talk, Mongo. You're too close to it now. Give it some more time and you'll know it's crazy. There's an explanation for everything that happened. There aren't any such things as demons, and you damn well know it."

"Of course there aren't any such things as demons," I said, lifting my glass. "Let's drink to that."

∙   ∙   ∙

"Uranus, what's a 'book of shadows'?"

She looked surprised. "A book of shadows is a witch's diary. It's a record of spells, omens. It's a very private thing, and is usually seen only by members of the witch's coven."

"A few hours before the fire Kathy Marsten asked me to get

181

back her father's book of shadows. She said it had been taken by a man named Daniel."

Something moved in the depths of Uranus' eyes. "I know of Daniel," she said quietly. "He's a ceremonial magician."

"Meaning precisely what?" I asked.

"A man who has great control over his own mind, and the minds of others. Some would say the ceremonial magician can control matter, create or destroy life. The ceremonial magician stands on the peak of the mountain called the occult. He is a man who has achieved much. He works alone, and he is dangerous. If he took someone's book of shadows, it was for a reason."

"Then there could have been bad blood between this Daniel and the Marstens?"

"If not before Daniel took the book, then certainly after."

I didn't want to ask the next question. I asked it anyway. "Do you think one of these ceremonial magicians could start a fire without actually being in the room?"

"Yes," Uranus said evenly. "I think so."

"I want to talk to this Daniel."

"He won't talk to you, Mongo. You'll be wasting your time."

"You get me to him and let me worry about the conversation."

•　　•　　•

A Philadelphia bank seemed like an odd place to look for a ceremonial magician. But then nobody had claimed that Daniel could change lead into gold, and even ceremonial magicians had to eat. It looked like this particular magician was eating well. He was sitting in a bank vice-president's chair.

He looked the part; that is, he looked more like a bank vice-president than a master of the occult arts, whatever such a master looks like. Maybe I'd been expecting Orson Welles. In any case, he matched the description Uranus had given me; about six feet, early forties, close-cropped, steely gray hair with matching eyes. He wore a conservatively cut, gray-striped suit. There was a Christmas Club sign to one side of his desk, and beside that a name plate that identified him as Mr. Richard Bannon.

I stopped at the side of the desk and waited for him to look up from his papers. "Yes, sir?" It was an announcer's voice, deep, rich and well modulated.

"Daniel?"

I looked for a reaction. There wasn't any. The gray eyes remained impassive, almost blank, as though he were looking straight through me. I might have been speaking a foreign language. He waited a few seconds, then said: "Excuse me?"

"You are Daniel," I said. "That's your witch name. I want to talk to you."

I watched his right hand drop below the desk for a moment, then resurface. I figured I had five to ten seconds, and intended to use every one of them. "You listen good," I said, leaning toward him until my face was only inches from his. "There's a little girl dying a couple of hours away from here. If I even *suspect* you had anything to do with it, I'm going to come down on you. Hard. For starters, I'm going to make sure the stockholders of this bank find out about your hobbies. Then, if that doesn't make me feel better, maybe I'll kill you."

Time was up. I could feel the bank guard's hand pressing on my elbow. Daniel suddenly raised his hand. "It's all right, John," he said, looking at me. "I pressed the button by mistake. Dr. Frederickson is a customer."

The hand came off my elbow, there was a murmured apology, then the sound of receding footsteps. I never took my eyes off Daniel. He rose and gestured toward an office behind him. "Follow me, please."

I followed him into the softly lit, richly carpeted office. He closed the door and began to speak almost immediately. "You are to take this as a threat," he said in a voice barely above a whisper. "I know who you are; your career is familiar to me. I do not know how you know of me; I know of no person who would have dared tell you about me. But no matter. There is absolutely nothing—*nothing*—you can do to me. But I can . . . inflict. You will discover that to your surprise and sorrow if you came to trifle with me."

It was an impressive speech, delivered as it was in a soft monotone. I smiled. "I want to ask a couple of questions. You answer them right and you can go back to changing people into frogs, or whatever it is you do."

183

"I will answer nothing."

"Why did you steal Jim Marsten's book of shadows?"

Daniel blinked. That was all, but from him I considered it a major concession. "You have a great deal of information, Dr. Frederickson. I'm impressed. Who have you been speaking to?"

"What do you know about the girl? Kathy Marsten."

His eyes narrowed. "Why?" Suddenly he paled. "Is that the little girl you—?"

"She's dying," I said bluntly. "Fast."

His tongue darted out and touched his lips. "What are you talking about?"

I told him. His impassive, stony facade began to crack before my eyes. He abruptly turned his back on me and walked across the room to a window, where he stood staring out over the bank's parking lot. Once I thought I saw his shoulders heave, but I couldn't be sure. His reaction wasn't exactly what I'd expected. He asked my about my role, and I told him that, too.

"I will need help," he said distantly. Then he turned and looked directly at me. "I will need *your* help. There is no time to get anyone else. We must leave immediately. There are things I must get."

"Daniel, or Bannon, or whatever you call yourself, what the hell is this all about?"

"Kathy Marsten is my niece," he said after a long pause. "Becky Marsten is—was—my sister."

"Then I'd say you have some explaining to do. Do you know why Kathy is dying?"

"I owe you no explanations," he said evenly. He studied me for a moment, then added, "But I will explain anyway, because the time will come when I will ask you to do exactly as I say, when I say it, with no discussion and no questions."

"You're out of your mind. Why should I agree to do that?"

"Because you love Kathy and you want to save her life. In order to do that, you and I must touch a dimension of existence the Christians call hell. To do that and survive you will have to do exactly as I say."

I nodded. I hoped it looked noncommittal. "I'm listening."

Daniel's words came rapidly now, in an almost mechanical

voice. He was obviously a man in a hurry, and I could tell his mind was elsewhere.

"I don't know the extent of your knowledge about witchcraft," he said, "but witchcraft is undoubtedly not what you think it is. It is a religion: a very old religion—an Earth religion. The Marstens and the Bannons have practiced witchcraft for generations. You will find witches in every walk of life."

For a moment I thought I saw him smile. He continued: "Some witches—some magicians—even become bank vice-presidents. For most of the Blessed, witchcraft and magic are a means to higher wisdom, toward becoming a better person. But there *is* a dark side to it, as there is to every other religion. I'm sure you're familiar with the Inquisition, not to mention the Salem witch trials where human beings were burned alive."

He paused, then went on: "In any case, Jim Marsten became interested in the black arts, in demonology, about two years ago. He was warned of the possible consequences to him and to his family. He chose to ignore these warnings. At a certain point I tried to get my sister to leave Jim, but she had already been corrupted by the dreams he had laid out for her. Then I discovered that they intended to try to summon the demon Belial. That ceremony involves the spiritual sacrifice of a child, and I knew that child would be Kathy.

"I knew there was no way I could reason with them—they were beyond that. But I could stop them, and I did—or I thought I did. I knew there was one place, and only one place, where the ceremony would have been recorded."

"The book of shadows," I whispered.

"That's right. A witch's holiest book. I took it."

"How?"

"How I do what I do is not important. Please remember that. What is important is that Jim and Becky apparently tried to proceed without the exact ritual in hand. They paid for it with their lives. Belial was released into our dimension, and he is sucking Kathy's life away from her."

It was crazy. Maybe I was going crazy. I heard myself asking, "How do you know you can succeed where the Marstens failed? What is your power? And where does it lie?"

"First, I know the ritual. That is absolutely essential for the

185

exorcism." Again, there was a fleeting grimace around his mouth that might have been a half-smile. "I am a ceremonial magician, Dr. Frederickson. You come from an academic background, and you understand that to move up in your world requires study, perseverance . . . and talent. The same holds true in mine. If you wish, you may think of a ceremonial magician as a witch with a Ph.D."

I tried to think of something to say and couldn't. I'd run out of options: I'd called Dr. Rivera that morning and been told that Kathy was now perilously near death. So I was along for the ride with the ceremonial magician, straddling a nightmare train of terror that I couldn't stop.

And I knew I was going to do anything the man called Daniel asked me to do.

•   •   •

At exactly twenty minutes of midnight, as instructed, I parked my car across from the hospital and got out. I lifted Bannon's knapsack from the rear seat, strapped it on my back, then headed across the street. I went around to the back of the hospital and started climbing the fire escape that would take me to Kathy's room, where I had left Bannon four hours before.

I stopped at the third floor, leaned over the steel railing and peered into the window on my right. There was a small night light on over the bed and I could see Kathy's head sticking up above the covers of her bed. Her face was as white as the sheet tucked up under her chin.

Bannon was lying on the floor beside the bed. He was stripped to the waist. His eyes were closed and his breathing was deep and regular. Sweat was pouring off his body, running in thick rivulets to soak into the towels he had placed under him.

Suddenly the door opened and a young, pretty nurse stepped into the room. Bannon was in silent motion even as the nurse reached for the light switch. He rolled in one fluid motion that carried him under the bed. He quickly reached out, wiped the floor with the towels, then drew them in after him.

The night nurse went up to Kathy's bed and drew back the covers. It was then that I could see a series of wires and electrodes attached to her arms and chest. The nurse felt Kathy's forehead, then checked what must have been a battery of instruments on the other side of the bed, out of my line of vision.

She gave what appeared to be a satisfied nod, recorded the information on a clipboard at the foot of the bed, then turned out the lights and left the room. I tapped on the window.

Bannon emerged from the beneath the bed. He was no longer sweating, but he looked pale and haggard, like a man who had finished a marathon wrestling match. He came to the window and opened it. I climbed through. He immediately began removing the knapsack from my shoulders with deft fingers.

"What time is it?" he croaked in a hoarse voice.

I glanced at the luminous dial on my watch. "Five minutes to twelve."

"We must hurry. The ceremony must begin at exactly midnight. Your watch shows the exact time?"

"Yeah. I checked it out a half hour ago." I was beginning to have second thoughts, to feel like the face on the front page of the morning's edition of some of the country's more sensational tabloids. "What happens if someone else shows up?"

"This is not the time to think about that." He paused, then added, "I think we will have time. The nurses have noted an improvement in Kathy's condition."

I resisted the impulse to clap my hands. "If she's better, what are we doing here?"

Bannon grunted. "She only seems better because I made it appear that way. But the effect is short-lived. Belial must be driven from her mind. Now, let's get busy."

Bannon quickly opened the knapsack and emptied its contents on the floor. There was a white hooded robe, a dagger with occult symbols carved into the ivory handle, two slender white candles in pewter candleholders. In addition there was a charred stick, a heavy lead cup, and numerous small containers, which I assumed contained incense.

The last object out of the sack was a thick volume of papers bound between two engraved metal covers. The symbols inscribed on the covers were the same as those I had seen on Kathy's gown. It was Jim Marsten's book of shadows.

Bannon donned the robe, then opened a small container filled with blue powder. He bent over and spilled the powder out in a thin stream, forming a large circle around the bed. When he had completed that, he drew a second, smaller circle at the foot of the bed, on a tangent with the first circle.

In his costume, he seemed a completely different man. No longer did there seem to be any relationship between the banker and the man—the witch—before me. He was no longer Bannon. He was Daniel.

"Time?" he asked in a strange, hollow voice.

"One minute of."

He placed the candles on either side of the foot of the bed and lit them. "You must stand with me inside the second circle," he said as he arranged the other items in front of him. "No matter what happens, remain inside the circle." He picked up the book of shadows and opened it to a section near the back, then handed it to me.

The book was much heavier than one would have suspected from looking at it. The metal was cold. The writing, in purple ink, looked like a series of child's scrawls. It was completely illegible to me. "Turn the page quickly when I nod my head," Daniel continued. "And remember *not* to step out of the circle—not under any circumstances."

"Look, Daniel—" I started to say.

"No," he said sharply, turning his head away from me. I tried to look at his face beneath the hood and couldn't find it. "There is no time for discussion. Simply do as I say. If you do not, you may die. Remember that."

I allowed myself to be led into the circle, and I held the book out in front me, slightly to the side so that Daniel could read it in the dim glow from the candles and night light. Daniel picked up the dagger and held it out stiffly in front of him while he removed a single egg from the pocket of his robe and placed it carefully on a spot equidistant between the two candles. Then he began to chant:

"Amen, ever and forever, glory the and power the, Kingdom the is Thine for, evil from us deliver, But—"

It was a few moments before I realized that Daniel was reciting the Lord's Prayer backwards. I felt a chill. The book of shadows seemed to be gaining weight, and my arms had begun to tremble. I gripped the book even tighter.

Daniel finished the inverted prayer. He stiffened, described a pentagram in the air with his arm, then stuck his dagger into the middle of it. Finally he placed his left palm in the center of the book.

"I command thee, O Book of Shadows, be useful unto me, who shall have recourse for the success of this matter. In the name of the Father, Son and Holy Ghost! In the name of Yahweh and Allah! In the name of Jesus Christ, let this demon come forth to be banished!"

He turned slowly, taking care to remain in the circle, continuing to describe pentagrams in the air. My eyes were drawn inexorably to the candles: There was no draft in the room, and yet I was positive I had seen them flicker.

"Belial! Hear me where thee dwell! Restore the sanctity of this virgin child! Leave us without delay! Enter this phial! Enter this phial! Enter this phial!"

There was no question: The candle flames were flickering. Daniel leaned over the book and began to chant from it. It was all gibberish to me, but delivered as it was in a low, even voice, the precisely articulated words gripped my mind, flashing me back over the centuries.

Daniel finished abruptly and stabbed the center of the book three times. Kathy's head began to glow with blue-white light.

I blinked hard, but the halo remained. There was an intense pain in my chest, and I suddenly realized that I had been holding my breath. I let it out slowly. Something was hammering on the inside of my skull. Fear.

Daniel pointed with the tip of the dagger toward the egg. "Enter this phial! Enter this phial! Enter this phial!"

The light flashed, then leaped from Kathy's head to the ceiling, where it pulsated and shimmered like ball lightning. And then the room was filled with an almost unbearable stench, like some fetid gas loosed from the bowels of hell.

The light had begun to glow. Daniel folded his arms across his chest and bowed his head. "Go in peace unto your place, Belial," he whispered. Then came the nod of the head. Somehow I remembered to turn the page.

There was more chanting that I couldn't understand, delivered in the same soft voice. There was a different quality to Daniel's voice now, a note of triumph. He finished the chant, paused, then whispered: "May there be peace between me and thee. Belial, go in peace unto—"

Suddenly the door flew open and the lights came on. I wheeled and froze. There was a ringing in my ears. Dr. Juan Rivera stood in the doorway.

"What in God's name—?!"

I started toward him, but suddenly Daniel's hand was on my shoulder, holding me firm. "Stay!" he commanded.

Daniel was halfway across the room when the sphere of light began to glow brighter. He stopped and stiffened, thrusting both arms straight out into the air in Rivera's direction. No word was spoken, and Daniel was still at least ten feet away from the door. Still, Dr. Rivera slumped against the wall, then fell to the floor unconscious.

The light skittered across the ceiling, stopped directly above the white-coated figure. Daniel leaped the rest of the distance, at the same time digging in his robe. He came up with another container. He ripped it open and began to spray a blue powder over Rivera.

There was a sharp hissing sound and the light shot from the ceiling to Daniel's head and shoulders. Daniel stiffened, then arched backward and fell hard against the floor, where he writhed in pain, his head now glowing brightly.

"Jesus!" I murmured, stepping out of the circle and starting toward him. "Oh, Jesus!"

"*Stay back!*"

Instinctively, I made a cross with my forearms, holding them out in front of me like some talisman. "Jesus! Jesus! Jesus!"

And then I was beside him. I grabbed hold of the material of his sleeve and dragged him back across the floor, inside the circle. Again there was a hissing sound, and the light shot to the ceiling. I continued to whisper: "Jesus!"

Daniel's voice, tortured and twisted out of shape now, came up under my own, like some strange, vocal counterpoint.

"Go in peace, Belial. Let there be peace between thee and me. Enter the phial!"

There was an almost blinding flash, and the light expanded, then contracted, shooting in a needle shaft over our heads and

190

into the egg. The egg seemed to explode silently in slow motion, its pieces smoking, then dissolving in the air.

Kathy Marsten suddenly sat bolt upright in bed. Her eyes widened, and for a moment I thought she was going to speak. Her mouth moved, but no sound came out. Then she collapsed over on her side. I tasted terror.

"It's over," Daniel said. I could barely hear him.

·   ·   ·

It was a long time before Garth could bring himself to say anything. "You claim you saw all this?"

"Yes."

There was another long pause, then: "One of three things has to be true. For openers, either you've really fallen out of your tree, or you were hypnotized. I like the hypnosis theory best. Like I said before, it would also explain the girl's reaction."

"Really? How?" I found I wasn't much interested in "logical" explanations.

"I'm willing to buy the notion that this Bannon—or 'Daniel'—had something on the ball mentally. He hypnotized the girl, probably with her parents' help, and put her into a deep coma. It can be done, you know. Then he got you up into that room and ran the same number on you. Remember, you said the girl seemed to be coming out of it anyway."

"Why?"

"Huh?"

"Why? What was Daniel's motive? What you're saying simply doesn't make any sense. And don't try to tell me it does."

"How the hell should I know what his motive was?" Garth said impatiently. It was the cop in him coming out: He was having a hard time making his case. He went on: "Daniel was obviously crazy. Crazy people don't need motives for doing crazy things."

"What about Rivera?"

"What about him?"

"He doesn't remember a thing. He called me the next day to tell me Kathy had made what he called a miraculous recovery. I pumped him a little, gently. Nothing. I don't think he even knows he passed out."

"Which brings us to the third possibility."

"I can't wait to hear this one."

Garth paused for emphasis. "You were never up in that room, Mongo."

"No kidding?"

"Goddamn it, you listen to me and listen to me good! It never happened! That business in the room never happened!" He paused and came up for breath. He continued a little more calmly, "You didn't hear yourself on that phone: I did. I'd say you were damn near hysterical. When I got there I found you unconscious next to the phone booth."

"Back to square one: I fell out of my tree."

"Why not? It happens to the best of us from time to time. You were under a lot of pressure. You'd seen two neighbors burn to death, saved a little girl only to feel that she was in danger of dying. That, along with the witchcraft business, pushed you over the brink for just a few moments."

"Who pushed Daniel?" I said as calmly as I could. Garth was beginning to get to me. I was beginning to feel he had a specific purpose in mind, and I was hoping he'd get to it.

"Nobody pushed Daniel. Daniel fell. It's as simple as that. It blew your circuits. I think you dreamed the rest when you passed out after calling me."

"But you must admit that Daniel was real."

Garth gave a wry smile. "Of course Daniel was real. The coroner's office can testify to that. No, what I personally think may have happened is that he committed suicide. The death of his sister, his niece's illness, unhinged him. Unfortunately, you happened to see him fall and the shock . . . upset your nerves. Made you imagine the whole thing."

Suddenly I knew the point of the conversation. "You didn't include me in your report, did you?"

He shook his head. "Only as the caller . . . a passerby." He looked up. "You start telling people you tried to break into—or did break into—that hospital, and you'll end up with charges filed against you. There goes your license. Second, I don't want to see my brother locked up in the Bellevue loony bin."

"You're not so sure, are you, Garth?"

He avoided my eyes. "It doesn't make any difference, Mongo. You said the materials Daniel used are gone."

I glanced at my watch and was amazed to find that only twelve minutes had passed since I'd climbed through the window. Daniel had gotten slowly to his feet and laid Kathy back on her pillow. He still wore the robe, and no part of his flesh was visible.

"We . . . must bring everything out with us," he whispered in a strained voice. "Clean . . . everything."

There was no time to think, just do. I quickly checked Dr. Rivera. He was still unconscious, but breathing regularly. I heard footsteps outside in the hall. They paused by the door and I tensed. After a few seconds the footsteps moved on.

I used Daniel's towels to erase all traces of the blue powder he had used. When I finished I found him waiting for me by the window. He had replaced the objects in the knapsack and held that in one hand, the book of shadows in the other. I still could not see any part of his face or hands.

He handed me the knapsack, then motioned for me to go through the window first. I climbed through, balanced on the ledge outside, then swung over onto the fire escape. Then I turned back and offered my hand. He shook his head.

I frowned. "Don't you want to take that robe off?"

He shook his head again. "Go ahead," he mumbled. "I'll be right behind you." There was something in his voice that frightened me, but I turned and started down the fire escape.

"*Frederickson!*"

The texture of the voice—the despair and terror—spun me around like a physical force. He was suspended in space, one hand gripping the fire escape railing, the other holding the book of shadows out to me. Both hands were covered with blood.

"*Destroy,*" he managed to say. "*Destroy everything.*"

The book of shadows dropped to the grate and I grabbed for Daniel. His hood slipped off, revealing a head covered with blood.

The ceremonial magician Daniel was bleeding from every pore in his body: Blood poured from his nose, his mouth, his ears. His eyes.

And then he was gone, dropping silently into the darkness to be crushed on the pavement below.

193

Totally devoid of rational thought, a series of primitive screams bubbling in my throat, I picked up the book of shadows and half fell, half ran down the fire escape. I dropped the last few feet and raced to the white-shrouded body. It didn't take me more than a moment to confirm that the hospital would be of no use to Daniel.

I was the one who needed help.

I vaguely remembered a pay telephone booth across the street from the hospital. I raced down the alleyway toward the street, pausing only long enough to hurl the knapsack into one of the hospital's huge garbage disposal bins. It was only as I neared the street that I realized I was still holding the book of shadows.

I wouldn't remember telephoning my brother, or passing out.

•   •   •

I got up from the chair and pretended to stretch. "Okay, Garth, it's over. And if that's it, I'm going to throw you out. I've got a long drive to Pennsylvania tomorrow. I've traced some of Kathy's relatives."

"Witches?"

"Sure. But I wouldn't worry about it. The coven leader also happens to be mayor of the town. His brother is chief of police. A nice, typical American family."

Garth's eyes narrowed. "You're kidding."

"No, I'm not kidding."

Garth rose and walked to the door, where he turned and looked at me. "You sure you're all right?"

"Garth, get the hell out."

"Yeah. I'll see you."

"I'll see you."

I closed the door behind Garth, then went into the bedroom and sat down on the bed. I took a deep breath, then opened the drawer in the night stand and brought out the book of shadows. It was still covered with Daniel's bloody prints.

I brushed dirt off one corner and opened it to the pages Daniel had read from. The writing was still totally incomprehensible to me. But Daniel had been able to read it. Undoubtedly, there were others.

I wondered what some of my colleagues at the university

194

would think of the book of shadows, of Belial. Summoning up a demon would make an interesting research project.

I glanced at the night stand and the small pile of change there. Fifty-seven cents.

I ripped the pages out of the book, tossed them in a metal wastebasket and threw a lighted match after them. There was nothing unusual about the flame.

Aha! A nice, innocent, straightforward animal story. It is a piece that draws on Mongo's circus background while showing his almost mystical way with large and dangerous creatures, a theme that will not be fully explored until twenty years later, in a yet-to-be published novel.

Tiger in the Snow

I don't like working blind, and there aren't many men who can get me to drop everything and fly three thousand miles across the country on the strength of no more than a round-trip airline ticket and a barely legible note.

But Phil Statler was one of those men. I owed Phil.

He was waiting for me at the Seattle airport. Dressed in an ancient, patched sweater and shapeless slacks, his full lips wrapped around a dead cigar, Phil was not likely to be taken for one of the world's most successful circus entrepreneurs, which he was.

"You look ugly as ever," I said, shaking the huge, gnarled hand extended to me, "only older."

Phil didn't smile. "Thanks for coming, Mongo."

"What's the matter? All the phones broken around here?"

"I wasn't sure you'd come if you knew what it was about."

"Hey, that's great! That's one of the most exciting pitches I've ever heard!" Phil had jammed his hands into his pockets and was staring at his feet. "Okay," I continued seriously, "so I'm here. You got trouble?"

"Sam's loose."

The chill that ran through me had nothing to do with the Washington winter. "He kill anybody?"

196

"Not yet."

"My God, if Sam's loose in the city—"

"He ain't in the city."

"Where, then?"

"Let's take a ride," Phil said as he stooped and picked up my bag.

●   ●   ●

"He's somewhere out there."

I gazed in the direction of Statler's pointing finger, out across a broad, open expanse of crusted snow that glittered blue-white under the noon sun. Beyond the snow, forest hogged the horizon, stretching east and west as far as I could see.

"How do you know he's up there?"

"He was spotted. Some guy down in Ramsey."

"That's the town we just passed through?"

Phil Statler nodded. I leaned back against the Jeep and pulled the collar of my sheepskin coat up around my ears. "Okay, Phil," I said, "I'm beginning to get the picture. You're missing a six-hundred-pound Bengal tiger and you want me to employ my natural cunning to track him down. What would you suggest I say to Sam if I find him? He may not want to come back, you know."

Now, a man with a missing tiger needs a laugh, or at least a smile. But Statler simply continued to stare at me for what seemed a very long time. When he did finally speak, his hoarse, gravelly voice was a strange counterpoint to the tears in his eyes.

"It don't make no difference he didn't hurt anybody, Mongo," he said. The tears were already beginning to freeze on his cheeks, but he made no move to wipe them away. "They're going to kill Sam. The people in the county got their minds set. Okay. But if Sam's gotta' be killed I want it to be done by somebody he knows, somebody who cares about him. That's why I asked you to come, and that's why I didn't tell you what it was about. I want to see a man's face when I'm asking him to risk his life."

"I don't understand. There are other ways of bringing a tiger in than shooting him. You know that. You also know there are a

197

lot of other men more qualified to do it. Nobody's ever accused me of looking like Tarzan."

Statler took a crumpled piece of paper from his pocket and handed it to me. I unfolded it and recognized it as the front page of the local newspaper. TIGER ON THE LOOSE was splashed across the top. Below that was a picture of Sam's head, his eyes glowing with cat fire, his jaws gaping. His fangs glinted in the artificial light of the photographer's flash.

"Sam's never looked so good," I said. "That picture must be five years old."

"They got it off one of our publicity posters."

At the bottom of the page was a picture of a man who obviously enjoyed having his picture taken. Heavy-set, in his late thirties or early forties, he was the kind of man other men try not to prejudge, and always do. I studied the photo for a few moments and decided that Sam's eyes reflected far more character. Underneath the photo was the caption, GO GET HIM, REGGIE!

"Who's Reggie?" I said, handing back the paper.

"Reggie Hayes," Statler said, spitting into the snow. "He's the county sheriff, with headquarters down there in Ramsey. Sam's done a lot for him."

"I don't follow you."

"Seems Hayes is up for reelection. It also seems Hayes is not the model public servant. I don't know all the details, but up until a few days ago he'd have had trouble getting his mother to vote for him. All that's changed. People forget about corruption when they feel their lives are in danger, and Hayes is the man who's going to bag their tiger for them.

"People don't want their terrors drugged or carted away in a net; they want them killed. Hayes knows that, and he's been up in those woods every day for the past three days. Sooner or later he's gonna luck out. You read the local papers and you'll see how Sam's the best thing that ever happened to him."

"This is big gun country. I'd think Reggie'd have a lot of competition from the local sporting types."

"Sure. Must be hundreds of people around here who'd like to bag a tiger, but none of them want to tangle with a crooked sheriff who's out to win an election."

"I can see their point," I said evenly. I could. A county sheriff in an isolated area is the closest thing the United States has to an ancient feudal chieftain.

"I'd do it myself," Statler said, his eyes narrowing, "but I know I'm too old. I know I ain't got what it takes. I know you do. Besides," he continued after a pause, "you're the only one Sam ever really took to."

That took me back for a moment, then I realized it was true. I wondered if it was because both of us, in our way, lived life inside a cage—Sam's cage of steel, mine of stunted bone and flesh. I didn't dwell on it.

"I'll go after Sam because I want to," I said. "But there's no reason why I have to play Hayes' game. Seattle has a fine zoo. They should have the equipment I need."

Statler shook his head. "By now that cat's half-starved, and I think he's hurt. Pretty soon he'll be man-huntin', if he isn't already. I didn't bring you out here to get yourself killed, Mongo. You ain't goin' after a killer cat with a popgun. You take heavy artillery, or you're fired before you start. Sam ain't as sentimental as I am."

I shrugged. "Phil, I'll go after Sam with a tranquilizer gun whether I'm working for you or not. You knew that, or you wouldn't have asked me to come down here."

"All right," he said after a long pause. "But you'll take along something with stopping power too. With soft-nosed cartridges."

"Done," I said easily. I turned and looked back the way we had come. "One thing puzzles me. Seattle's fifty miles south, with at least a dozen towns between here and there. And there didn't seem to be that much cover. How do you suppose Sam made it all the way up here without being spotted?"

"He had help," Statler growled. "Some lousy bastards who don't know a thing—"

"Whoa, Phil. Take it from the top."

He flushed and spat again in the snow. "Somebody must have thought they were doing Sam a favor. We'd been getting letters for about a week attacking us for keeping animals in cages. I didn't pay much attention to them until this happened. But Sam didn't escape; he was let loose."

199

"You said he might be hurt."

"We were keeping the livestock in the back of the armory in the middle of town. John was the only man on night duty, and they must have got the jump on him. They slugged him over the head, then broke the lock on Sam's cage. The city police figure they backed a truck up and forced him in. They found tire tracks further up the road here, along with Sam's tracks in the snow. *Stupid!* That's a big forest, but it ain't India. The hell of it is that Sam didn't want to go. They found blood on the bottom of the cage, which means whoever took him probably had to prod him to get Sam into the truck. A hurt tiger ain't nothin' to mess with, Mongo." Suddenly Statler turned and slammed his fist against the fender of the Jeep. "Now I feel real stupid for askin' you to come here. It's . . . it's just that I can't stand the thought of Sam gettin' it from somebody like Hayes, and I didn't know who else but you to ask."

I took a deep breath of the cold, pine-scented air. "Phil," I said, "you know how much I appreciate that compliment, but I'm going to be damned angry with you if I should get myself killed."

•   •   •

I spent the rest of the day shopping with Phil Statler for provisions. The next morning I left him to pick up a few special items, and drove the Jeep into Seattle. It took most of the day and a lot of talking, but I left with a tranquilizer gun and a carton of darts.

The only items missing were a good horse and a modified saddle, and Statler was to meet me with these early the next morning. I was ready. I ate an early supper and headed up to my room. I'd have gone right to bed except for the fact that Reggie Hayes' feet were propped up on it.

Hayes' picture hadn't done him justice; in the flesh he was uglier. The skinny deputy leaning against the windowsill wore a uniform at least one size too large for him, and he had a bad tic in his right cheek. Taken together, they resembled something that you might expect to pop up in your room after a week of steady drinking.

"Why don't you make yourself comfortable?" I said, putting

the room key I hadn't had to use into my pocket. Both men stared. "What's the matter? You two never see a dwarf before?" I didn't wait for an answer. "Both of you are in my room uninvited," I said, looking directly at Hayes. "The least you can do is take your feet off my bed."

My manner must have taken him off guard; he took his feet off the bed. Immediately he flushed. "Look, now . . ."

"Hey!" the deputy sheriff said, trying and failing to snap his fingers. "I saw this guy hanging around the jail late yesterday afternoon."

Hayes' eyes narrowed. "You interested in jails, Frederickson?"

"You know my name?" The question was redundant, but I felt a strong urge to change the subject.

"Pete down at the desk told me," Hayes said, deliberately putting his feet back up on the bed. I said nothing. "This is a small town, Frederickson. We're all real friendly around here. That's how I know you and your friend been shopping for some real special items; a high-powered rifle, soft-nosed cartridges, and lots of raw meat. Today your friend ordered a special saddle with the stirrups shortened, so it looks as though that stuff may be for you. If you didn't look like you had so much sense, I'd think you were going tiger hunting."

"I hear the woods here are full of them."

The deputy started to say something, but Hayes cut him off with a wave of his hand. "Tell me," Hayes said, rising up out of the chair and hooking his fingers into his belt, "where does a dwarf get off thinking he can hunt a tiger?"

"I suffer delusions of grandeur."

Hayes' pock-marked face reddened. He was obviously a man who enjoyed making his own jokes.

"How come you ordered twenty pounds of dog biscuits, smart guy?"

"Sam has peculiar tastes."

"Sam . . . ?"

"The tiger you want to kill so badly."

The deputy could restrain himself no longer. He strode across the room and grabbed Hayes' sleeve. "That's what I wanted to tell you, Reggie; I just remembered who this guy is. I was

201

reading an article about him in one of those news magazines just the other day."

For a moment I was sure the man was going to ask me for my autograph.

"Mongo," the man continued. "Mongo the Magnificent. That's what they used to call him when he was with the circus."

"What the hell are you talking about?"

"The *circus*," the deputy said. "This guy used to be with the same circus that tiger came from. The article told how he quit eight, nine years ago to become a college professor. It said he teaches something called criminology. It said he's also a private detective."

The deputy sucked in his breath like a minister who had inadvertently mumbled a four-letter word in the middle of a sermon. Hayes eyed me coldly and touched his gun.

"We got elected officials in this county, Frederickson. We don't need no private law."

Hayes was starting to take me seriously, and I didn't like that at all.

"Those were exactly my thoughts," I said.

"What are you doing here, Frederickson?"

"Hunting."

"That's what you think," Hayes said. A thin smile wrinkled his lips, but did not touch his eyes. "You need a license to hunt in this county, and you ain't got no license."

"Mr. Statler mentioned something about that," I said evenly. "I think that's all been taken care of. Statler Brothers Circus has done a lot of benefits in this state, and I think you'll find a letter from the Governor on your desk in the morning."

"I want that cat, Frederickson," Hayes said tightly, making no effort to hide the menace in his voice. "You keep your nose out of this."

"You need Sam to keep you in office," I said, fighting the tide of anger I felt rising in me. "That tiger's running for your reelection, and it's a race that's going to cost him his life."

"I don't have to kill no tiger to get reelected," Hayes said defensively.

"That's not what I hear."

"You hear wrong!"

Hayes was breathing hard, his face livid. The deputy, taking his cue from his boss, was glowering at me. It was obvious that my attempt at suave diplomacy was getting me nowhere. Letter or no letter from the Governor, Hayes could be trouble. Bad trouble.

I took a deep breath and sat down in a straight-backed chair by the door.

"Sheriff," I said quietly, "I'd like you to explain something to me. You know, as a professional lawman instructing an amateur."

"What are you talking about?" Hayes said warily. His face had returned to its normal color, a reassuring sign that I did not think was going to last very long.

"I'm puzzled, Sheriff. I would think you'd be spending more time trying to catch the people who let that tiger loose."

"You are an amateur, Frederickson," Hayes said, his eyes glittering like black diamonds. "That happened in Seattle, and Seattle ain't in my jurisdiction."

"Right. But my guess—an amateur guess, of course—is that those men could live right here in this county. Consider: Ramsey County isn't exactly in a straight line from Seattle. In fact, you have to do a considerable amount of twisting and turning to get here. Now, why did they pick *this* particular spot to drop the tiger off? Why that particular stretch of woods? Maybe because it was the only area they knew of."

"Coincidence."

"I wonder. Second question: Why drop off a tiger in a section of forest so near a logging camp? Certainly, they must have realized an animal like that could be a threat to the men up there. I'm right, aren't I? Isn't there a logging camp up there? I thought I saw some smoke when I was out there yesterday."

Hayes said nothing. Now it was the deputy's face changing color, from its normal pasty shade to a light sea green.

"So, you see, it's just possible that whoever let that tiger loose does live somewhere around here. If so, it shouldn't take too much checking to narrow down the field of suspects."

"Impossible," Hayes said with a satisfied air of certainty. "They got away clean as a whistle."

"Yes, but you see it would take a special kind of truck to transport a cat that size. It would have to be completely enclosed,

203

and strong enough to hold Sam. Why, it might even look something like your paddy wagon."

Hayes' face read like a map. Or a sign warning of thin ice.

"There's another funny thing about this whole business," I continued. "Most of the people who go after circus owners know a lot about animals. They care about them. The last thing an animal lover would do is take a circus-trained cat and put him up in those woods in the dead of winter. It is kind of peculiar, isn't it?"

"I thought you weren't on a case, Frederickson."

"I'm not," I said evenly. "Like I said, all I'm after is a tiger. It's just that I can't help thinking aloud sometimes. It's an awful habit, and I'm trying hard to break it."

"Who hired you?" Hayes voice was clipped, brittle.

"You might say I'm here on a mission of mercy."

Hayes laughed, but there was no humor in the sound.

"C'mon, smart guy, tell me how you'd go about figuring who let that cat loose."

This surprised me. Hayes was calling my bluff, and I could feel the damp, cold sweat starting under my arms.

"Well, first I'd start looking around the county for a truck that would do that kind of job. Chances are it might have some wood in the interior. If it did, I'd take some chips."

"Why?" The deputy's voice was high-pitched and nervous.

"To check for signs of tiger blood or hair," I said, raising my eyebrows modestly. "Tigers are notorious pacers, as I'm sure you're aware. Sam probably left traces all over the inside of that truck."

"What if the truck had been washed?"

"Gee, I hadn't thought of that," I said with a straight face. "Like I said, I'm new in the business and the tough ones sometimes get away from me." I shot a glance in the direction of Hayes. His eyes were riveted to my face, wide and unblinking, like a cobra's. "Of course, there are blood tests. Blood can't be cleaned completely from wood. It soaks in. And you could always take some paint scrapings off the outside of the truck."

"What good would that do?" Hayes said quietly.

"Whoever backed that truck up left some paint on the cages." I didn't have the slightest idea whether or not that was true, but it would certainly be worth looking into. And I hoped it was enough to keep Hayes at bay.

"That's pretty good thinking, Frederickson," Hayes said evenly. "Of course, it's only guesswork. Things don't always work out that simple in real police work."

"Of course not."

"Uh, have you told anybody else about these ideas of yours?"

I smiled. "I'm sure I haven't come up with anything you haven't already thought of, Sheriff. I'm never one to interfere with another man doing his job." I paused to give my next words emphasis. "All I want is a shot at that tiger, then I'm on my way."

"That a fact?"

"That's a fact." I found it surprisingly easy to lie to Hayes. I'd repeat my scenario to the state police later; but Sam came first.

"That cat's dangerous, Frederickson."

"I'll take my chances. All I want is my chance. Without interference."

"I *need* that cat, Frederickson," Hayes hissed, leaning far forward in his chair. "You don't understand."

I tried to think of something to say, and couldn't. An iron gate had slammed shut over Hayes' eyes and I could no longer read them. There was a long, tense silence during which the deputy watched Hayes watching me. Finally Hayes rose and walked quickly out the door. The deputy followed. I went after them and closed the door.

• • •

I didn't sleep well, a fact that might have had something to do with the fact that I was supposed to get up in the morning and go after a Bengal tiger that outweighed me by nearly a quarter of a ton. And the fact that I hadn't won the love and admiration of the local law didn't help matters any.

I got up around four and fixed some coffee on a hotplate in the room. Then I sat down by the window and waited for the sun to come up.

Phil Statler was supposed to be waiting for me at the edge of town with a horse and the rest of my supplies. At dawn I dressed warmly, picked up the kit with the tranquilizer gun and went down into the morning.

They'd probably been waiting for me all night.

I had a rented car parked out in the back of the rooming house, and the first man went for me as I emerged from the mouth of the alley into the parking lot. He had an unlit cigarette in his hand and was going through the pretense of asking for a match, but I had already sensed the presence of a second man behind me, pressed flat against the weathered side of one of the alley garages.

Somewhere I had miscalculated; either Hayes was very stupid, or I had overplayed my hand and worried him too much.

On dry ground, unencumbered by a heavy woolen jacket, I wouldn't have been too concerned. My black belt in karate, combined with the tumbling skills honed and perfected over the long years of traveling with the circus, combined to make me a rather formidable opponent when aroused, an asp in a world that catered to boa constrictors.

But snow wasn't my proper milieu. That, along with the coat wrapped around my body, spelled trouble.

The second man lunged for me from behind. I sidestepped him and ducked under the first man's outstretched arms. At the same time I clipped him with the side of my hand on the jaw, just below the lower lip. He grunted, spat teeth and stared stupidly at me as I stripped off my coat.

By this time the second man had me around the head and was beginning the process of trying to separate it from the rest of me. I gave him a stiff thumb in the groin, then jumped up on his back and onto a drain pipe leading up to the top of a tool shack.

There I stripped to my tee shirt and kicked off my boots while the two men stood in the deep snow below me. I thrust my hands in my pockets and waited patiently while they recovered slowly from their initial shock.

"*Get him,*" the second man said to the first, indicating the pipe.

He got me, promptly and feet first. I caught him in the mouth with the heel of my shoe, hit the snow in a shoulder roll and came up on my feet on the plowed gravel of the driveway. The man I had hit was sitting in the snow, his eyes glazed, his hand to his ruined mouth. After a moment he keeled over and lay still.

The other man was now indecisive, standing spread-eagled in the snow, glancing back and forth between me and his fallen partner.

"If you're going to do something, I'd appreciate it if you'd hurry," I said, bouncing up and down and flapping my arms against my body. "I'm getting cold."

The man frowned, reached into his coat pocket and drew out a knife. The steel glinted in the morning sun. I suddenly felt very unfunny. I stopped dancing, spread my legs in a defensive crouch and spread out my hands.

The man approached slowly, and looked almost comical slogging toward me through the deep snow. I backed up in the driveway until the gravel under my feet was relatively dry and hard-packed. The man, waving the knife in the air before him, stepped out into the driveway and stopped.

His muddy eyes were filled with fear, and it suddenly occurred to me that this man was no professional; he was probably a crony of Hayes who had been recruited for the seemingly simple task of working over a dwarf. He'd gotten much more than he bargained for. For all I knew, he might be considering using the knife in self-defense. I straightened up and moved back against the building, leaving him plenty of room to get by me and out through the alley.

"You can go if you want to," I said evenly. "But if you come at me with that knife, I'll kill you. I assure you I can do it."

He hesitated. I circled around him carefully, stopped and let out what, for me, was a relatively blood-curdling yell. The man dropped the knife into the snow and sprinted out through the alley.

I put my clothes back on and went to my car. The first man was just beginning to stir as I backed out of the alley and into the street.

It still bothered me that Hayes would have made such an overt move after the conversation we had had earlier in the evening. Using that approach with some people would have spelled a death warrant, but Hayes wasn't big city crime; he was small fry, a corrupt, local sheriff.

It appeared that I had underestimated just how far he would go to insure his reelection. I wouldn't make the same mistake again.

I drove slowly down the main street on my way out of town,

past the police station. The paddy wagon was in its usual place, covered with a shining new coat of fresh, green paint.

Within twenty minutes, I stood with Statler and stared at the fresh horse tracks that veered off from the road to the east, disappearing far in the distance at the edge of the forest.

"Hayes came through here about an hour and a half ago," Statler said through clenched teeth. "Just as happy as you please. Wished me good hunting."

"He had reason to; he figured I was sitting in whatever passes for a hospital around here."

I sketched in some of the details of the incident in the parking lot while I made a final check of my gear.

"Damn, Mongo, I didn't think Hayes would go that far," Statler said quietly.

"He's running a little scared," I said hurriedly, before Statler could start worrying about me to the point where he'd take his horse back. "And he's got good reason. He's the boy who let your tiger loose. Or at least he's responsible."

"What . . . ?"

Hayes had a head start on me of at least an hour and a half; I didn't want to widen it by taking the time to explain everything to Statler. I tightened the cinch on the special saddle once more and swung up on the animal's back.

"I think they used the county paddy wagon," I said. "There just might be some paint scrapings on Sam's cage. I suggest you make it your first order of business to find out. Then get the state bulls in here. Hayes had the wagon painted, but that won't do him any good if he didn't take the time to scrape off the first coat. And I don't think he did.

"Now, I don't know how long I'm going to be up there. You just make sure you're looking for my signal. When you see it, I'll be looking for the cavalry. With nets."

Phil Statler grunted, stepped forward and grabbed the reins. He was chewing furiously on a dead cigar, and that was always a bad sign.

"You're fired," he said evenly. I pulled at the reins, but Statler held firm. "I don't mind asking you to go up after Sam, but paying you to share the hills with that crazy goddamn sheriff is something else again. I've decided to save my money."

"You paid for the horse and the supplies," I said quietly, measuring each word. "The tranquilizer gun I got on my own. You take the horse, I'll walk up there, Phil. I mean it."

He grunted and tried to glare, but the feigned anger failed to get past the tears in his eyes. "You screw this up, Mongo, and you get no more of my business."

"When you get my bill, you may not be able to afford any more business." I grinned, but Statler had already turned and was heading back toward my car. I dug my heels into the horse's side, pulling up my collar against the rising wind.

• • •

The air was clear and very cold, but it was a dry, sun-speckled cold, and the net result was that special kind of euphoria that comes when a man alone slips between Nature's thighs. I moved easily with the horse beneath me, taking deep gulps of the frigid air, trying to flush the accumulated filth of city living out of my lungs.

In the distance, smoke from the loggers' camp plumed, then drifted west with the wind currents. The hoofprints of Hayes' horse veered sharply to the east, running a straight parallel to the tree line. It was reasonable for Hayes to assume that Sam would get as far away from the camp, and the people in it, as possible. He wouldn't know any better.

I did. Sam was a circus animal, and had spent most of his life around people. He had come to depend upon them for food and shelter, and I was convinced he would be somewhere in the vicinity of the camp, waiting.

That was good, and that was bad. If worse came to worse, he would kill and eat a logger. If that happened, there was no way Sam was going to get out of this alive. And he would be getting close to the edge; bewildered, wounded, cold and hungry, Sam had spent more than three days in the forest.

Working in his favor was the fact that he had always been one of the best and most reliable cats in the show, a strong and stabilizing influence on the other animals. On the other hand, he was—above all else—a tiger, a killing machine in his prime.

The horse, with his collective, primeval memory, would know

209

that, too, and there would be hell to pay if he got a whiff of Sam's spoor. I thought I had that problem solved.

I headed the horse in a direct line toward the smoke, then opened one of the saddle bags that was draped over the saddle horn. I opened the plastic bag there, and immediately the air was filled with the strong, ripe odor of bloody meat. Mixed in with the meat was a large dose of red pepper.

The horse whinnied and shied, but steadied again under a tug at the reins. This particular bag of meat had a dual purpose; to overwhelm the horse's sense of smell and, hopefully, also act as a powerful magnet to a very hungry tiger. In the second bag, among other things, was a second batch of meat, unadulterated, a suitable tiger snack. I hoped Sam would prefer it to me.

I was past the tree line, on the lip of the forest. It was immensely serene and peaceful. The vast canopy of brown and green overhead had cut down on the snowfall, and the floor of the forest was carpeted with a thick bed of pine needles.

In a few minutes we emerged into an open glen. To my left, high up on a mountain, I caught the glint of sunlight off metal. It could have been a rifle. Or binoculars. I hoped it was a rifle; if it was binoculars, it probably meant Hayes had already spotted me.

I veered back into the protective gloom of the forest, heading the horse on a path that would, if my sense of direction was correct, take us in ever-shrinking concentric circles around the camp's perimeter.

I ran through an inventory of my equipment for what must have been the tenth time. But I felt it was justified; when something happened, it was likely to happen fast, and I didn't want to be groping around for some needed piece of equipment.

I had the tranquilizer gun in a sheath on the right side of the saddle, just in front of my leg. I had a large supply of extra darts in one of the bags, but the gun would only take one dart at a time. I would have to make the first shot count. If it didn't, there was the high-powered hunting rifle on my other side.

I broke the chamber and checked to make sure it was fully loaded, took off the safety and replaced it lightly in its oiled scabbard. I was as ready as I would ever be.

Finally, of course, there were the dog biscuits crammed into the pockets of my wool parka. The ultimate weapon.

That brought me a laugh, and I relaxed in the saddle, putting myself on automatic pilot and letting my senses guide me.

Curious: It had been years since I'd last seen Phil Statler, and yet all the old feelings had come back, a love-hate ambivalence that would live with me to the day I died, like an extra limb that could not be amputated.

The reaction was not to Phil himself, but to what he represented—the circus, where I'd constantly struggled to show the world that the performer with the stunted body was a man with unique skills and capabilities.

Phil Statler was the man who had given me his faith, his trust, the man who had spoken to my mind rather than my body.

And there had been Sam. Always I had loved the animals, and had used their company to while away the lonely hours between cities and performances. And Sam had been my favorite, my friend, and we had spent many hours together, staring at one another from behind the bars of our respective cages.

But that had been many years before, and I would have been a fool to suppose that our friendship represented anything more than a small paper boat adrift on the raging river of Sam's natural savagery.

And now I was hunting him with a dart gun, a situation that suddenly seemed even more ludicrous when you considered the fact that Sam was hurt. I leaned forward and spurred the horse, trying to push the rising fear out of my mind.

I completed the first circuit of the camp, then reined the horse in and began another, tighter circle. It was growing dark, and I knew that soon I would have to stop and camp.

I opened a quart container of chicken blood and began dripping it in the snow behind me. I didn't like the idea of Sam coming up from behind, but it couldn't be helped; I had to find a way to lure him to me before Hayes got him.

A half mile into the second circuit I found something that made the blood pound in my skull; two sets of prints, crisscrossing each other. One set belonged to Hayes' horse, and the other belonged to Sam.

That told me two things, neither of which gave me any great measure of comfort; Hayes had spotted me and was staying close. And Sam was near, somewhere out in the darkening forest.

Sam's tracks were heading northwest. I swung the horse in that direction and bent forward in the saddle, reaching down for the tranquilizer gun.

The boom of the gun's report shattered the stillness, and a shower of splinters ripped at my face as the slug tore into the tree directly behind me. It was followed by a second shot, but I was already huddled down over the horse's neck, urging him on at full speed through the brush. Suddenly the trees were gone and we were floundering in the deep snow at the edge of a clearing.

My head down, I had no warning save for an intense, electrical sensation along my spine a split second before the horse screamed and reared. The reins were jerked out of my hands and I made a grab at the horse's mane, but it was useless; I flew off his back, landing on my side in the snow, half stunned.

I was still gripping the tranquilizer gun, and the bag of bloody meat had fallen off with me, but the rest of my supplies, including the rifle, were still on the horse that was galloping off through the snow.

I sat up and let loose a selected string of obscenities, vowing that I would never again go to see another Western.

I felt his presence before I actually saw him. That presence was very real, yet somehow out of place, like a half-remembered nightmare from childhood. I turned my head slowly, straining to pierce the gathering dusk. Finally I saw him, about thirty yards away, his tawny shape almost hidden by the shadow of the forest.

"Sam," I whispered. *"Easy, Sam."*

He seemed bigger than I remembered, magnified rather than diminished by the vastness of his surroundings. Thousands of miles away from his native India, crouched in alien snow, he was still, in a very real sense, home, freed from the smells of men and popcorn.

Sam flowed, rather than moved; his belly slid across the snow, and his eyes glittered. I was being stalked.

The snow around me was spattered red from the contents of the broken bag; I was the *pièce de résistance*, sitting in the middle of a pool of beef and chicken blood.

I began to giggle. Whether it was from the shock of the fall, or out of sheer terror, or an appreciation of the ultimate absurdity of my position, I wasn't sure. It simply struck me as enormously funny that a dwarf should be sitting in the snow facing a hurt, hungry tiger, with nothing but a tranquilizer gun and pockets full of dog biscuits.

As a last line of defense, I had the flare gun and one flare in an inner pocket, but that would have to be removed and loaded. It was obvious that I wasn't going to have time, even if I chose to use it.

Still giggling, my hair standing on end, I slowly crawled away from the patches of blood. Sam, seeing me move, stopped and crouched still lower, his ears pointed and his lips curled back in a snarl.

I slowly cocked the tranquilizer gun and brought it around to a firing position. The muscles on Sam's flanks fluttered; the movement had made him nervous, and he was ready to charge.

Still I waited. There was only one cartridge in the gun. One shot. I would have to make it count, waiting until the last moment to make sure I didn't miss.

The muscles bunched in Sam's hind legs, and I brought my gun up to firing position. At the same time I caught a flash of movement out of the corner of my eye, to the left, behind Sam.

Hayes. Ignoring me, he had drawn a bead on Sam. My next action was pure reflex. It had nothing to do with conscious thought, but with some mad emotional need deep within my being. I wheeled on Hayes and pulled the trigger on my gun.

The dart caught him in the left side, slicing neatly through the layers of his clothing and piercing his flesh.

His gun discharged harmlessly in the air as he clawed at the dart in his side. But the effect of the drug was almost instantaneous; Hayes stiffened, then toppled over in the snow, out of my line of sight.

Now I was in a bit of a jam. Sam had already begun his charge, and about all I could do was throw my arms up in front of my face. But the report of the gun had startled Sam, frightened him and thrown him off his stride. By the time he reached me, he was already trying to brake his charge, looking back over his shoulder.

He veered to the side, ramming into me and knocking me over. I rolled, frantically clawing at the zipper on my parka. But rolling in the snow, fingers frozen with fear, is not the optimum condition under which to unzip a jacket. Besides, it was stuck.

I ended up on my knees, staring at Sam, who was squatting about fifteen yards away. I could see the wound on his leg now where Hayes or one of his men had jabbed him; it was raw and festering, enough to drive any animal wild with pain.

But Sam wasn't moving, and he had his head cocked to one side. He seemed almost uncertain. I was past my giggling stage, and it occurred to me that there was just a chance he might have gotten a good whiff of me as he went past, and that it might have stirred memories.

A romantic thought, indeed. But it was the only hope I had.

"Sam." My voice was so weak I could hardly hear myself. I cleared my throat. *"Sam! Hey, Sam! Hey, Sam!"*

Animals occasionally grunt. Sam grunted.

"Hi! Sam!" It was time to assert myself. Gripping the tranquilizer gun by the barrel, I rose and slowly began to walk forward. "Okay, Sam. Easy Sam. It's all right. I'm not going to—"

I'd made a mistake, gone too far too fast. Sam was going to charge; I could see that now. He reared back, the muscles in his hind legs forming great knots. His ears lay flat against his head, and his lips curled back in a snarl. Suddenly he let out a thunderous roar.

And rolled over.

Sam was somewhat hampered by the wound on his leg, but he still managed a pretty fine roll. He came up and squatted, tongue out, staring at me. Not getting any reaction from me save a frozen, open-mouthed mumble, Sam decided to try it again. He rolled back the other way, sat up and whined. One paw was raised a few inches off the snow.

It took me almost a full minute to realize that I was crying. Sam waited patiently.

"Sam," I murmured. "Oh damn, Sam. You damn animal."

From that point on, I never hesitated. I threw the gun into the snow, walked forward and wrapped my arms around Sam's neck. Sam purred contentedly while I groped in the snow for some of the meat, stuffing it into his mouth.

I was laughing again, loud and long.

I gathered the meat together in a pile and left Sam long

enough to check out Hayes. The sheriff was breathing fairly regularly. As far as I could tell, his only lingering problem from the drug would be a pronounced desire to want to sleep for the next few weeks. But he'd make it.

If I made it. There was still the problem of Sam, and the meat was gone. Sam was looking around for more. I walked slowly forward, holding a dog biscuit. Sam's tongue flicked out and it disappeared.

At that rate, they wouldn't last long. I gave him a handful, then sat down in the snow. I managed to loose the zipper and reach the flares. Still muttering words of encouragement that I hoped a tiger would find soothing, I fired one off into the sky.

The flare burst in the night with an eye-piercing flash of blues and yellows, and then it was once again dark. Sam started, but settled down when I gave him another biscuit.

I vaguely wondered what the reaction of Phil and the state troopers would be when they arrived and discovered one very wide awake tiger waiting for them.

"Roll over, Sam."

Sam rolled over. I figured the biscuits would last longer if I made Sam work for them.

Somewhere in the distance I thought I heard the sound of snowmobiles. Sam heard them too, and his ears snapped back.

"Roll over, Sam. Play it again, Sam." Sam rolled over, but this time I withheld the biscuit for just a moment. "Now, Sam, you must be a very good tiger or you are going to be shot. Boom. Do you understand?"

Sam rolled over.

I was hungry. I took one of the biscuits out of my pocket and stared at it. It had a greenish tint. I took a small bite out of it, then gave the rest to the waiting tiger. It tasted terrible.

Speaking of the cost of membership in some belief systems . . .
 Of all my "older children," this is the one I found the most difficult thematically, the most difficult to write, the story that until recently nobody wanted, and it is the short story I am most proud of.

Candala

1

Indiri Tamidian wafted into my downtown office like a gossamer breath of incense from some Hindu temple in her native India. Her young, lithe body rippled beneath the rustling silk folds of her sari; her coal black eyes, sheened by that enormous zest for life that was Indiri's very quintessence, smoldered in their sockets. Blue-black hair tumbled to her shoulders, perfectly complementing the translucent, light chocolate-colored flesh of her face. Indiri was stunningly beautiful. And troubled; the light from her eyes could not disguise the fact that she had been crying.

Self-pity, unexpected and unbidden, welled up within me like a poisonous cloud, a hated stench from a dark, secret place deep inside my soul. Some thoughts have teeth; just as it is dangerous for an artist to search too hard for the murky headwaters of his power, it is folly for a dwarf to entertain romantic thoughts of beautiful women. I fall into the second category.

I pushed the cloud back to its wet place and clamped the lid on. I stood and smiled as Indiri glanced around her.

"So this is where the famous criminologist spends his time

when he's not teaching," Indiri said with a forced gaiety that fell just short of its mark.

I grunted. "You could have seen the criminology professor anytime on campus, even if you are majoring in agriculture," I said easily. "You didn't have to come all the way down here."

"I didn't come to see the professor," Indiri said, leaning forward on my desk. "I came to see the detective. I would like to hire you."

"Now, what would a lovely, intelligent young woman like you want with a seedy private detective?" Immediately my smile faded. The girl's flesh had paled, isolating the painted ceremonial dot in the center of her forehead, lending it the appearance of an accusing third eye. It had been a stupid thing to say. Worse, it had sounded patronizing, and Indiri Tamidian was not a woman to be patronized. "How can I help you, Indiri?"

"I want you to find out what's bothering Pram."

"What makes you think anything is bothering him?"

"He hasn't called or come to see me for a week. Yesterday I went over to his room and he refused to see me."

I turned away before my first reaction could wander across my face. Pram Sakhuntala was one of my graduate students, and a friend of sorts. A good athlete, Pram often worked out with me in the gym as I struggled to retain and polish the skills that were a legacy of the nightmare years I had spent headlining with the circus as Mongo the Magnificent. Like Indiri, Pram was part of a U.N.-funded exchange program designed to train promising young Indians for eventual return to their own land, where their newly acquired skills could be put to optimum use. Pram was taking a degree in sociology, which explained his presence in one of my criminology sections. He was also Indiri's fiancé and lover. Or had been. Losing interest in a woman like Indiri might be an indication that Pram was losing his mind, but that was his business. It certainly did not seem the proper concern of a private detective, and that's what I told Indiri.

"No, Dr. Frederickson, you don't understand," Indiri said, shaking her head. "There would be no problem if it were simply a matter of Pram not loving me anymore. That I could understand and accept. But he *does* love me, as I love him. I know that because I see it in his eyes; I feel it. Perhaps that sounds silly, but it is true."

It did not sound silly; Indiri came from a people who had produced the *Kama Sutra*, a land where life is always a question of basics. "Still, you don't have any idea what could have caused him to stop seeing you?"

"I'm not sure," Indiri said hesitantly.

"But you do have a suspicion."

"Yes. Do you know Dr. Dev Reja?"

"Dev Reja. He's chairman of Far Eastern Studies." I knew him, and didn't like him. He strode about the campus with all the imperiousness of a reincarnated Gautama Buddha, with none of the Buddha's compensating humility.

"Yes," Indiri said softly. "He is also the adviser to the Indo-American Student Union, and coordinator of our exchange program. Last week Pram told me that Dr. Dev Reja had asked to speak with him. I don't know if there's any connection, but it was after that meeting that Pram changed toward me."

It suddenly occurred to me that I had not seen Pram for more than a week. He had missed my last class. This, in itself, was not significant. At least it hadn't seemed so at the time.

"What could Dev Reja have said to Pram that would cause him to change his attitude toward you?"

"That is what I would like you to find out for me, Dr. Frederickson."

I absently scratched my head. Indiri reached for her purse and I asked her what she was doing.

"I don't know how much you charge for your services," the girl said, looking straight into my eyes. "I don't have too much—"

"I only charge for cases," I said abruptly. "So far, this doesn't look like anything I could help you with." Tears welled in Indiri's eyes. "Not yet, it doesn't," I added quickly. "First I'll have to talk to Dr. Dev Reja before I can decide whether or not there's going to be any money in this for me. If I think there's anything I can do, we'll talk about fees later."

I was beginning to feel like the editor of an advice-to-the-lovelorn column, but the look Indiri gave me shook me right down to my rather modest dwarf toes and made it all worthwhile.

2

Famous. That was the word Indiri had used—half in jest, half seriously—to describe me. It was true that I'd generated some heat and some headlines with my last two cases, both of which I'd literally stumbled across. But *famous?* Perhaps. I never gave it much thought. I'd had enough of fame; Mongo the Magnificent had been famous, and that kind of freak fame had almost destroyed me. What Indiri—or anyone else, for that matter, with the possible exceptions of my parents and Garth, my six-foot-plus police detective brother—could not be expected to understand were the special needs and perspective of a dwarf with an I.Q. of 156 who had been forced to finance his way to a Ph.D. by working in a circus, *entertaining* people who saw nothing more than a freak who just happened to be a highly gifted tumbler and acrobat. Long ago I had developed the habit of not looking back, even to yesterday. There were just too many seemingly impossible obstacles I had already crossed, not to mention the ones coming up; the look of disbelief in the eyes of an unsuspecting client seeing me for the first time, choking back laughter at the idea of a *dwarf* trying to make it as a private detective.

I squeezed the genie of my past back into its psychic bottle as I neared the building housing the Center for Far Eastern Studies. Mahajar Dev Reja was in his office. I knocked and went in.

Dev Reja continued working at his desk a full minute before finally glancing up and acknowledging my presence. In the meantime I had glanced around his office; elephant tusks and other Indian trinkets cluttered the walls. I found the display rather gauche compared to the Indian presence Indiri carried *within* her. Finally Dev Reja stood up and nodded to me.

"I'm Frederickson," I said, extending my hand. "I don't think we've ever been formally introduced. I teach criminology."

Dev Reja considered my hand in such a way that he gave the impression he believed dwarfism might be catching. But I left it there and finally he took it.

"Frederickson," Dev Reja said. "You're the circus performer I've heard so much about."

"Ex-performer," I said quickly. "Actually, I'd like to speak to you about a mutual acquaintance. Pram Sakhuntala."

That raised Dev Reja's eyebrows a notch, and I thought I detected a slight flush high on his cheekbones.

"My time is limited, Mr.—Dr.—Frederickson. How does your business with Pram Sakhuntala concern me?"

I decided there was just no way to sneak up on it. "Pram has been having some difficulty in my class," I lied. "There's an indication his troubles may stem from a talk he had with you." It wasn't diplomatic, but Dev Reja didn't exactly bring out the rosy side of my personality. "I thought I would see if there was any way I could help."

"He *told* you of our conversation?" This time his reaction was much more obvious and recognizable; it was called anger. I said nothing. "*Candala!*" Dev Reja hissed. It sounded like a curse.

"How's that?"

"Pram asked you to come and see me?"

"*Is* Pram in some kind of trouble?"

Dev Reja's sudden calm was costing him. "It must have occurred to you before you came here that any discussion Pram and I may have had would be none of your business. You were right."

I didn't have to be told that the interview was at an end. I turned and walked to the door past a blown-up photograph of a tiger in an Indian jungle. It was night and the eyes of the startled beast glittered like fractured diamonds in the light of the enterprising photographer's flash. In the background the underbrush was impenetrably dark and tangled. I wondered what had happened to the man who took the shot.

•   •   •

Pram showed up at the gym that evening for our scheduled workout. His usually expressive mouth was set in a grim line and he looked shaky. I made small talk as we rolled out the mats and began our warm-up exercises. Soon Pram's finely sculpted body began to glisten, and he seemed to relax as his tension melted and merged with the sweat flowing from his pores.

220

"Pram, what's a 'candala'?"

His reaction was immediate and shocking. Pram blanched bone white, then jumped up and away as though I had grazed his stomach with a white-hot poker.

"Where did you hear that?" His words came at me like bullets from the smoking barrel of a machine gun.

"Oh, Dr. Dev Reja dropped it in conversation the other day and I didn't have time to ask him what it meant."

"He was talking about me, wasn't he?!"

Pram's face and voice were a torrent of emotions, a river of tortured human feeling I was not yet prepared to cross. I'd stuck my foot in the water and found it icy cold and dark. I backed out.

"As far as I know, it had nothing to do with you," I said lamely. Pram wasn't fooled.

"You don't usually lie, professor. Why are you lying now?"

"What's a 'candala,' Pram? Why don't you tell me what's bothering you?"

"What right do you have to ask me these questions?"

"None."

"Where did you get the idea of going to see Dr. Dev Reja?"

Like it or not, it seemed I'd just been pushed right into the middle of the water. This time I struck out for the other side. "Indiri's been hurt and confused by the way you've been acting," I said evenly. "Not hurt for herself, but for you. She thinks you may be in some kind of trouble, and she asked me to try to help if I can. She loves you very much, Pram. You must know that. If you are in trouble, I can't help you unless you tell me what it's all about."

Pram blinked rapidly. His skin had taken on a greenish pallor, and for a moment I thought he would be sick. The fire in his eyes was now banked back to a dull glow as he seemed to stare through and beyond me. Suddenly he turned and, still in his gym clothes, walked out of the gym and into the night. I let him go. I had already said too much for a man who was working blind.

I showered and dressed, then made my way over to the women's residence where Indiri was staying. I called her room and she immediately came down to meet me in the lobby. I wasted no time.

"Indiri, what's a 'candala'?"

The question obviously caught her by surprise. "It's a term used to refer to a person of very low caste," she said quietly, after a long hesitation. "A candala is what you in the West would call an 'untouchable.' But it is even worse—I'm sorry to have to tell you these things, Dr. Frederickson. I love my country, but I am so ashamed of the evil that is our caste system. Mahatma Gandhi taught us that it was evil, and every one of our leaders have followed his example. Still, it persists. I am afraid it is just too deeply ingrained in the souls of our people."

"Don't apologize, Indiri. India has no monopoly on prejudice."

"It's not the same, Dr. Frederickson. You cannot fully understand the meaning and implications of caste unless you are Indian."

I wondered. I had a few black friends who might give her an argument, but I didn't say anything.

"Actually," Indiri continued, "the most common name for an untouchable is 'sutra.' A candala is—or was—even lower."

"Was?"

"You rarely hear the word anymore, except as a curse. Once, a candala was considered absolutely apart from other men. Such a man could be killed on the spot if he so much as allowed his shadow to touch that of a man in a higher caste. However, over the centuries it was realized that this practice ran counter to the basic Indian philosophy that every man, no matter how 'low,' had *some* place in the social system. In Indian minds—and in day-to-day life—the concept of candala fell under the weight of its own illogic."

"Go on."

"Candalas were forced to wear wooden clappers around their necks to warn other people of their presence. They were allowed to work only as executioners and burial attendants. They were used to cremate corpses, then forced to wear the dead man's clothing."

I shuddered involuntarily. "Who decides who's who in this system?"

"It is usually a question of birth. A person normally belongs to the caste his parents belonged to, except in the case of illegitimate children, who are automatically considered sutras."

"What about Pram?" I said, watching Indiri carefully. "Could he be a sutra, or even a candala?"

I had expected some kind of reaction, but not laughter. It just didn't go with our conversation. "I'm sorry, Dr. Frederickson," Indiri said, reading my face. "That just struck me as being funny. Pram's family is Ksatriyana, the same as mine."

"Where does a Ksatriyana fit into the social scheme of things?"

"A Ksatriyana is very high," she said. I decided it was to her credit that she didn't blush. "Ksatriyana is almost interchangeable with Brahman, which is usually considered the highest caste. Buddha himself was a Ksatriyana. A member of such a family could never be considered a sutra, much less a candala."

"What about Dr. Dev Reja? What's his pedigree?"

"He is a Brahman."

I nodded. I had no time to answer Indiri's unspoken questions; I still had too many of my own. I thanked her and left. The subject of our conversation had left a dusty residue on the lining of my mind and I gulped thirstily at the cool night air.

. . .

I needed an excuse to speak to Pram, so I picked up his clothes from the common locker we shared in the gym and cut across the campus to his residence.

It was a small building, a cottage really, converted into apartments for those who preferred a certain kind of rickety individuality to the steel-and-glass anonymity of the high-rise student dorms. There was a light on in Pram's second-floor room. I went inside and up the creaking stairs. The rap of my knuckles on the door coincided with another sound that could have been a chair tipping over onto the floor. I raised my hand to knock again, and froze. There was a new sound, barely perceptible but real nonetheless; it was the strangling rasp of a man choking to death.

I grabbed the knob and twisted. The door was locked. I had about three feet of space on the landing, and I used every inch of it as I stepped back and leaped forward, kipping off the floor, kicking out with my heel at the door just above the lock. It gave. The door flew open and I hit the floor, slapping the wood with my hands to absorb the shock and immediately springing to my feet. The scene in the room branded its image on my mind even as I leaped to right the fallen chair.

Two factors were responsible for the fact that Pram was still alive: He had changed his mind at the last moment, and he was a lousy hangman to begin with. The knot in the plastic clothesline had not been tied properly, and there had not been enough slack to break his neck; he had sagged rather than fallen through the air. His fingers clawed at the thin line, then slipped off. His legs thrashed in the air a good two feet above the floor; his eyes bulged and his tongue, thick and black, protruded from his dry lips like an obscene worm. His face was blue. He had already lost control of his sphincter and the air was filled with a sour, fetid smell.

I quickly righted the chair and placed it beneath the flailing feet, one of which caught me in the side of the head, stunning me. I fought off the dizziness and grabbed his ankles, forcing his feet onto the chair. That wasn't going to be enough. A half-dead, panic-stricken man with a rope around his neck choking the life out of him doesn't just calmly stand up on a chair. I jumped up beside him, bracing and lifting him by his belt while, with the other hand, I stretched up and went to work on the knot in the clothesline. Finally it came loose and Pram suddenly went limp. I ducked and let Pram's body fall over my shoulder. I got down off the chair and carried him to the bed. I put my ear to his chest; he was still breathing, but just barely. I grabbed the phone and called for an ambulance. After that I called my brother.

3

Pram's larynx wasn't damaged and, with a little difficulty, he could manage to talk, but he wasn't doing any of it to Garth.

"What can I tell you, Mongo?" Garth said. He pointed to the closed door of Pram's hospital room, where we had just spent a fruitless half hour trying to get Pram to open up about what had prompted him to try to take his own life. "He says nobody's done anything to him. Actually, by attempting suicide, he's the one who's broken the law."

I muttered a carefully selected obscenity.

"I didn't say I was going to press charges against him," Garth grunted. "I'm just trying to tell you that I'm not going to press charges against anyone else either. I can't. Whatever bad blood there is between your friend and this Dev Reja, it obviously isn't a police matter. Not until and unless some complaint is made."

I was convinced that Pram's act was linked to Dev Reja, and I'd hoped that a talk with Pram would provide the basis for charges of harassment—or worse—against the other man. Pram had refused to even discuss the matter, just as he had refused to let Indiri even see him. I thanked my brother for his time and walked him to the elevator. Then I went back to Pram's room.

I paused at the side of the bed, staring down at the young man in it who would not meet my gaze. The fiery rope burns on his neck were concealed beneath bandages, but the medication assailed my nostrils. I lifted my hands in a helpless gesture and sat down in a chair beside the bed, just beyond Pram's field of vision.

"It does have something to do with Dev Reja, doesn't it, Pram?" I said after a long pause.

"What I did was a terrible act of cowardice," Pram croaked into the silence. "I must learn to accept. I *will* learn to accept and live my life as it is meant to be lived."

"Accept what?" I said very carefully, leaning forward.

Tears welled up in Pram's eyes, brimmed at the lids, then rolled down his cheeks. He made no move to wipe them away. "My birth," he said in a tortured whisper. "I must learn to accept the fact of my birth."

"What are you talking about? You are a Ksatriyana. Indiri told me."

Pram shook his head. "I am a . . . sutra." I tried to think of a way to frame my next question, but it wasn't necessary. Now Pram's words flowed out of him like pus from a ruptured boil. "You see, I am adopted," Pram continued. "That I knew. What I did not know is that I am illegitimate, and that my real mother was a sutra. Therefore, on *two* counts, I am a sutra. Dr. Dev Reja discovered this because he has access to the birth records of all the Indian exchange students. He had no reason to tell me until he found out that Indiri and I intended to marry. It was only then that he felt the need to warn me."

"*Warn* you?" The words stuck in my throat.

"A sutra cannot marry a Ksatriyana. It would not be right." I started to speak but Pram cut me off, closing his eyes and shaking his head as though in great pain. "I cannot explain," he said, squeezing the words out through lips that had suddenly become dry and cracked. "You must simply accept what I tell you and know that it is true. I know why Dr. Dev Reja called me a candala; he thought I had gone to you to discuss something which has nothing to do with someone who is not Indian. It does not matter that it was said in anger, or that he was mistaken in thinking it was me who had come to you; he was right about me being a candala. I have proved it by my actions. I have behaved like a coward. It is in my blood."

"If you want to call yourself a fool, I might agree with you," I said evenly. "Do you think Indiri gives a damn what caste you come from?" There was a rage building inside me and I had to struggle to keep it from tainting my words.

Pram suddenly looked up at me. Now, for the first time, life had returned to his eyes, but it was a perverted life, burning with all the intensity of a fuse on a time bomb. "Having Indiri know of my low station would only increase my humiliation. I have told you what you wanted to know, Dr. Frederickson. Now you must promise to leave me alone and to interfere no further."

"You haven't told me anything that makes any sense," I said, standing up and leaning on the side of the bed. "A few days ago you were a fairly good-looking young man, a better than average student deeply loved by the most beautiful girl on campus. Now you've refused to even see that girl and, a few hours ago, you tried to take your own life. You're falling apart, and all because some silly bastard called you a *name!* Explain *that* to me!"

I paused and took a deep breath. I realized that my bedside manner might leave something to be desired, but at the moment I felt Pram needed something stronger than sympathy—something like a kick in the ass. "*I'm* not going to tell Indiri," I said heatedly. "*You* are. And you're going to apologize to her for acting like such a . . . jerk. Then maybe the three of us can go out for a drink and discuss the curious vagaries of the human mind." I smiled to soften the blow of my words, but Pram continued to stare blankly, shaking his head.

"I am a candala," he said, his words strung together like a

chant. "What I did was an act of pride. Candalas are not allowed pride. I must learn to accept what my life has—"

I couldn't stand the monotonous tones, the corroding, poisonous mist that was creeping into his brain and shining out through his eyes; I struck at that sick light with my hand. Pram took the blow across his face without flinching, as if it were someone else I had hit. The nurse who had come into the room had no doubts as to whom I had hit and she didn't like it one bit. I shook off her hand and screamed into Pram's face.

"A name means nothing!" I shouted, my voice trembling with rage. "What the hell's the *matter* with you?! You can't allow yourself to be defined by someone else! You must define *yourself*! Only *you* can determine what you are. Now stop talking crazy and pull yourself together!"

But I was the one being pulled—out of the room by two very husky young interns. I continued to scream at the dull-faced youth in the bed even as they pulled me out through the door. I could not explain my own behavior, except in terms of blind rage and hatred in the presence of some great evil that I was unable to even see, much less fight.

Outside in the corridor I braced my heels against the tiles of the floor. "Get your goddamn hands off me," I said quietly. The two men released me and I hurried out of the hospital, anxious to get home and into a hot bath. Still, I suspected even then that the smell I carried with me out of that room was in my mind, and would not be so easily expunged.

•　　•　　•

"He's changed, Dr. Frederickson," Indiri sobbed. I pushed back from my desk and the Indian girl rushed into my arms. I held her until the violent shuddering of her shoulders began to subside.

"He's told you what the problem is?" Pram had been released from the hospital that morning, and it had been my suggestion that Indiri go to meet him.

Indiri nodded. "He's becoming what Dr. Dev Reja says he is."

I didn't need Indiri to tell me that. I knew the psychiatrist assigned to Pram and a little gentle prodding had elicited the opinion that Pram had, indeed, accepted Dev Reja's definition of

227

himself and was adjusting his personality, character, and behavior accordingly. It had all been couched in psychiatric mumbo jumbo, but I had read Jean-Paul Sartre's existential masterpiece *Saint Genet*, and that was all the explanation I needed.

"How do you feel about what he told you?" I said gently. Indiri's eyes were suddenly dry and flashing angrily. "Sorry," I added quickly. "I just had to be sure where we stood."

"What can we do, Dr. Frederickson?"

If she was surprised when I didn't answer she didn't show it. Perhaps she hadn't really expected a reply, or perhaps she already knew the answer. And I knew that I was afraid, afraid as I had not been since, as a child, I had first learned I was different from other children and had lain awake at night listening to strange sounds inside my mind.

4

I burst into the room and slammed the door behind me. My timing was perfect; Dev Reja was about halfway through his lecture.

"Ladies and gentlemen," I intoned, "class is dismissed. Professor Dev Reja and I have business to discuss."

Dev Reja and the students stared at me, uncomprehending. Dev Reja recovered first, drawing himself up to his full height and stalking across the room. I stepped around him and positioned myself behind his lectern. "Dismiss them now," I said, drumming my fingers on the wood, "or I deliver my own impromptu lecture on bigotry, Indian style."

That stopped him. Dev Reja glared at me, then waved his hand in the direction of the students. The students rose and filed quickly out of the room, embarrassed, eager to escape the suppressed anger that crackled in the air like heat lightning before a summer storm.

"What do you think you're doing, Frederickson?" Dev Reja's voice shook with outrage. "This behavior is an utter breach of professional ethics, not to mention common courtesy. I will have this brought up—"

"Shut up," I said easily. It caught him by surprise and stopped the flow of words. He stared at me, his mouth open. My own voice was calm, completely belying the anger and frustration behind the words. "If there's anyone who should be brought before the Ethics Committee, it's you. You're absolutely unfit to teach."

Dev Reja walked past me to the window, but not before I caught a flash of what looked like pain in his eyes. I found that incongruous in Dev Reja, and it slowed me. But not for long.

"Let me tell you exactly what you're going to do," I said to the broad back. "I don't pretend to understand all that's involved in this caste business, but I certainly can recognize rank prejudice when I see it. For some reason that's completely beyond me, Pram has accepted what you told him about himself, and it's destroying him. Do you know that he tried to kill himself?"

"Of course I know, you fool," Dev Reja said, wheeling on me. I was startled to see that the other man's eyes were glistening with tears. I was prepared for anything but that. I continued with what I had come to say, but the rage was largely dissipated; now I was close to pleading.

"You're the one who put this 'untouchable' crap into his head, Dev Reja, and you're the one who's going to have to take it out. I don't care how you do it; just do it. Tell him you were mistaken; tell him he's really the reincarnation of Buddha, or Gandhi. Anything. Just make it so that Pram can get back to the business of living. If you don't, you can be certain that I'm going to make your stay at this university—and in this country—very uncomfortable. I'll start with our Ethics Committee, then work my way up to your embassy. I don't think they'd like it if they knew you were airing India's dirty laundry on an American campus."

"There's nothing that can be done now," Dev Reja said in a tortured voice that grated on my senses precisely because it did not fit the script I had written for this confrontation. Dev Reja was not reacting the way I had expected him to.

"What kind of man are you, Dev Reja?"

"I am an Indian."

"Uh-huh. Like Hitler was a German."

The remark had no seeming effect on the other man, and I found that disappointing.

"Dr. Frederickson, may I speak to you for a few minutes without any interruption?"

"Be my guest."

"I detest the caste system, as any right-thinking man detests a system that traps and dehumanizes men. However, I can assure you that Pram's mentality and way of looking at things is much more representative of Indian thinking than is mine. The caste system is a stain upon our national character, just as your enslavement and discrimination against blacks is a stain upon yours. But it *does* exist, and must be dealt with. The ways of India are deeply ingrained in the human being that is Pram Sakhuntala. I can assure you this is true. I know Pram much better than you do, and his reaction to the information I gave him proves that I am correct."

"Then why did you give him that information? Why did you give him something you knew he probably couldn't handle?"

"Because it was inevitable," Dev Reja said quietly. "You see, Dr. Frederickson, you or I could have overcome this thing. Pram cannot, simply because he is not strong enough. Because he is weak, and because he would have found out anyway, for reasons which I think will become clear to you, he would have destroyed himself, and Indiri as well. This way, there is a great deal of pain for Pram, but the catastrophe that would otherwise be is prevented."

"I don't understand."

"Pram was going to marry a Ksatriyana. Don't you suppose Indiri's family would have checked the circumstances of Pram's birth before they allowed such a marriage to take place? I tell you they would, and then things would have been much worse for everyone involved."

"But he could have married her and lived here."

"Ah, Dr. Frederickson, he could *still* do that, couldn't he? But I think you will agree that that does not seem likely. You see, what you fail to understand is that Pram is an *Indian*, and his roots are in India. Pram's adoptive parents are extremely liberal and far-seeing people. Not at all like most people in India, in the United States or, for that matter, in the world. Pram himself failed to learn the great truth that was implicit in his adoption. I know that if Pram were to attempt to return to India and marry

Indiri—as he would most certainly have done if I had not told him what I did—he would have been ridiculed and derided by Indiri's family, perhaps even stoned for even presuming to do such a thing. In other words, Dr. Frederickson, Pram has the same options he had before: to marry Indiri or not; to live here or in India. I'm sure Indiri is as indifferent to Pram's origins as his own family is. He is not able to do this because, as you say, the knowledge that *he* could come from sutra origins is destroying him. You see, in effect, Pram is prejudiced against himself. I had hoped that telling him the truth as I did would give him time to adjust, to prepare himself."

I suddenly felt sick at the image of a young man doing battle with shadows. Pram had had a glittering treasure within his grasp and had ended with an empty pot at the end of a fake rainbow. And all because of a label he had swallowed and internalized but which, for him, was no more digestible than a stone.

"I didn't know you'd said those things to him," I said lamely. "But now he's obsessed with this candala thing."

"I'm afraid you'll have to take the responsibility for that, Dr. Frederickson."

"You said it."

"In anger, without thinking. You felt the need to repeat it."

I could feel a cloak of guilt settling over my shoulders. I made no attempt to shrug it off for the simple reason that Dev Reja was right.

"It doesn't really matter, Dr. Frederickson. Even without you the problem would still remain. However, now I am curious. What would you have done in my place?"

I wished I had an answer. I didn't. I was in over my head and knew it.

"All right," I said resignedly, "what do we do now?"

"What we have been doing," Dev Reja said. "Help Pram the best we can, each in our own way."

"He has a psychiatrist looking after him now. The university insisted."

"That's good as far as it goes," Dev Reja said, looking down at his hands. "Still, you and I and Indiri must continue to talk to him, to try to make him see what you wanted him to see: that a

231

man is not a label. If he is to marry Indiri and return to India, he must strengthen himself; he must prepare an inner defense against the people who will consider his love a crime."

"Yes," I said, "I think I see." It was all I said, and I could only hope Dev Reja could sense all of the other things I might have said. I turned and walked out of the classroom, closing the door quietly behind me.

•   •   •

Pram's soul was rotting before my eyes. He came to class, but it was merely a habitual response and did not reflect a desire to actually learn anything. Once I asked him how he could expect to be a successful sociologist if he failed his courses; he stared at me blankly, as though my words had no meaning.

He no longer bathed, and his body smelled. The wound on his throat had become infected and suppurating; Pram had wrapped it in a dirty rag, which he did not bother to change. His very presence had become anathema to the rest of his class, and it was only with the greatest difficulty that I managed to get through each lecture that Pram attended. Soon I wished he would no longer come, and this realization only added to my own growing sense of horror. He came to see me each day, but only because I asked him to. Each day I talked, and Pram sat and gave the semblance of attention. But that was all he gave, and it was not difficult to see that my words had no effect; I could not even be sure he heard them. After a while he would ask permission to leave and I would walk him to the door, fighting back the urge to scream at him, to beat him with my fists.

The infected wound landed him back in the hospital. Three days later I was awakened in the middle of the night by the insistent ring of the telephone. I picked it up and Indiri's voice cut through me like a knife.

"Dr. Frederickson! It's Pram! I think something terrible is going to happen!"

Her words were shrill, strung together like knots in a wire about to snap. "Easy, Indiri. Slow down and tell me exactly what's happened."

"Something woke me up a few minutes ago," she said, her heavy breathing punctuating each word. "I got up and went to the window. Pram was standing on the lawn, staring up at my window."

"Did he say anything, make any signal that he wanted to talk to you?"

"No. He ran when he saw me." Her voice broke off in a shudder, then resumed in the frightened croak of an old woman. "He was wearing two wooden blocks on a string around his neck."

"Wooden blocks?"

"Clappers," Indiri sobbed. "Like a candala might wear. Do you remember what I told you?"

I remembered. "In what direction was he running?"

"I'm not sure, but I think Dr. Dev Reja's house is in that direction."

I slammed down the phone and yanked on enough clothes to keep from being arrested. Then, still without knowing exactly why, I found myself running through the night.

My own apartment was a block and a half off campus, about a half mile from Dev Reja's on-campus residence. I hurdled a low brick wall on the east side of the campus and pumped my arms as I raced across the rolling green lawns.

I ran in a panic, pursued by thoughts of clappers and corpses. My lungs burned and my legs felt like slabs of dough; then a new surge of adrenaline flowed and I ran. And ran.

The door to Dev Reja's house was ajar, the light on in the living room. I took the porch steps three at a time, tripped over the door jamb and sprawled headlong on the living room floor. I rolled to my feet, and froze.

Pram might have been waiting for me, or simply lost in thought, groping for some last thread of sanity down in the black, ether depths where his mind had gone. My mouth opened, but no sound came out. Pram's eyes were like two dull marbles, too large for his face and totally unseeing.

Dev Reja's naked corpse lay on the floor. The handle of a kitchen knife protruded from between the shoulder blades. The clothes Dev Reja should have been wearing were loosely draped over Pram. The room reeked with the smell of gasoline.

Candala. Pram had made the final identification, embracing it completely.

I saw Pram's hand move and heard something that sounded like the scratching of a match; my yell was lost in the sudden explosion of fire. Pram and the corpse beside him blossomed into an obscene flower of flame; its petals seared my flesh as I stepped forward.

I backed up slowly, shielding my face with my hands. Deep inside the deadly pocket of fire Pram's charred body rocked back and forth, then fell across Dev Reja's corpse. I gagged on the smell of cooking flesh.

Somewhere, thousands of miles and years from what was happening in the room, I heard the scream of fire engines, their wailing moans blending with my own.